This book is a work of fiction. Names, characters, businesses, organizations, places, events and incidents are either a product of the author's imagination or are used fictitiously. Any resemblance to actual persons, living or dead, or locales is entirely coincidental.

Published by Griffyn Ink

www.griffynink.com

Copyright © 2022 Griffyn Ink

For ordering information or special discounts for bulk purchases, please contact Griffyn Ink at Mail@GriffynInk.com.

SAVANNAH KADE

WILDFIRE
HEARTS

DOWN
in Flames

WILDFIRE HEARTS #5

PROLOGUE

5 years ago

Tierney tried to juggle everything as she stood at the front door.

Usually, her new mom came to pick her up if something went wrong. Instead, Tierney had to wrestle a sick four-year-old into the back of a cab.

Today, she'd had to leave early because Sean had a fever. When he came home sick, she missed the rest of her day, too. With an irritated huff, she struggled to get the key into the lock with one hand while balancing a cranky, too-heavy-to-hold-like-this kid on her hip with the other. It was a skill she'd not expected to have at twenty-one.

Raising a child on her own sucked, but it beat the alternative.

Inside, the house was blessedly quiet. She set Sean down and he immediately beelined for his toys, suddenly happy. *Suddenly not sick?* she wondered. But his daycare was strict. His temperature had been above ninety-nine. So, she'd had to come get him right away.

With another sigh, she headed down the hall to get the medical supplies from the closet. She was pawing through the bottles of baby cough syrup and teething medications looking for the child's Tylenol drops when she heard the moan.

Jolted to action like any mom, she ran back to check on Sean. He'd found an old teething ring and was trying to put it over the head of a toy pony.

The moan came again.

Someone was in the house.

Grabbing one of the silver candlesticks off the mantle, Tierney headed toward the base of the stairs. She stopped at the bottom, the heavy piece choked up like a baseball bat, deciding whether to check it out or leave the house.

Was the sound even human?

It came again and she breathed out a disgusted sigh as the candlestick fell, swinging at her side in her now limp grasp.

Someone was upstairs having sex.

The house was supposed to be empty. Mr. and Mrs. Doyle— her "mom" and "dad"—were running errands or showing up to the bar to cover for the fact that she'd left early. Snafu was open far too much, Tierney thought, but she didn't complain. This was a better outcome for her and Sean than any other option she'd had.

Had the folks come home for a nooner?

Did they do that a lot? Maybe. She wasn't supposed to be here now either. When she called to see if they could pick her and Sean up at the daycare, they hadn't answered. Maybe this was why. *She had to get her own place.*

Listening to the sounds from upstairs only made her more determined to save up faster!

She went back to the medicine box she'd left on the counter —thank God she hadn't dropped it for Sean to play with the bottles. Being a mom was juggling a thousand moving pieces. Being a teen mom had meant doing it while everyone else went to parties and proms. Now, everyone else was in college, but that wasn't an option for her either, not with her shitty ID.

Tierney picked out a fever reducer and turned on the TV so she didn't have to listen. She told herself to act surprised when her parents came down.

Twenty minutes later, she heard steps on the staircase and turned around. She didn't have to *act* surprised.

"You head out, I'm just going to get in the shower. We shouldn't be seen together anyway."

That wasn't Mrs. Doyle.

Tierney felt her heart drop.

No.

No.

That was Siorse.

And that wasn't Ronan.

Tierney turned around in time for her sister to let out a bloodcurdling scream.

"Jesus, Tierney! You're *not* supposed to be home!"

Siorse didn't even still live here. Apparently, she just showed up sometimes to shag ... whoever. Tierney didn't even know him.

"Sean got a fever. They sent him home." She said it calmly, though her heart pounded. Her initial fear had turned to anger.

Siorse was fine most of the time, but ... there were things Tierney knew, things she didn't like. Things she couldn't tell— or *warn*—anyone about. Especially Siorse's husband Ronan.

This was the worst one yet.

Her older sister's eyes narrowed at her. Her perfectly manicured fingers clutched the silk robe shut, as if Siorse had suddenly become modest. "You don't say a word."

Tierney knew there was only one answer here. She was screwed.

Eyes at the ground, she shook her head *no*. She wouldn't say anything. She *couldn't*.

But her older sister stalked over close, she leaned down, putting her mouth close to Tierney's ear, but she wasn't quiet. "I've kept your secret. You'll keep mine."

Tierney still looked at the old nubby carpet that had been here when they all moved in. The Doyles weren't rich, they hadn't been able to upgrade the house much. Tierney knew she was part of the reason why. So, she nodded.

If there was one thing in her life that mattered most, it was Sean. The secret Siorse kept for her protected *him*. So, Tierney would keep this one, even if it ate her inside out.

CHAPTER ONE

P resent Day

Tierney laid the cash out on the bar, stacking and bank facing it, collecting it for the end-of-night drop.

"You done yet?" Carter asked her.

"Close, but stop interrupting me." She kept her head down, but she had to start over on the stack she had. Counting didn't require any great intellect, but it did require focus.

Carter, who was also being bartender tonight was the only other worker left this late. The kitchen had closed a while ago and he headed into the back, but Tierney didn't pay attention while she filled in the tallies on the tablet, glad it was all digitized.

She remembered when her dad was still using paper accounting. But when they collected paper money there was no way to digitize the bank drop. That part she still had to do by hand. It wasn't like a check where she could take a picture and the bank would acknowledge it.

With the counting done, she put it all into the drop bag, zipped it, and twisted the bolt at the end to lock it. There was no messing with it now, only the bank had the key to open it.

"Are you ready?" she called out to Carter.

"I've been ready!" He appeared at the end of the bar, right near the door, bag in hand. Together they headed out into the parking lot. It was standard protocol, the Doyles wouldn't have it any other way.

"You good?" Carter asked as she climbed into her car.

Tierney lied and said yes.

She was technically fine, but the hair prickled at the base of her neck.

What even was this?

It was long over. She was safe.

She told herself it was because the night was so dark with the new moon and everything.

Sean was at his grandparents' and Tierney was grateful for all of it. She had a job that paid well enough for her to afford her own small rental for her and her child. She had built-in grandparents/babysitters which left enough spare money to have at least a little of a life. Then, once Sean had started school, it became clear her schedule didn't mesh with her child's, so the Doyles had given her only one weekend night shift.

She was able to keep her head down. She'd finished high school and eventually registered her child at the local elementary with no issues. She couldn't complain.

Ignoring the prickle at the back of her neck, Tierney waved goodbye to Carter and pulled out of the lot. She aimed for the bank, which of course was exactly the opposite direction of her parents' house. But, again, a small price for all she had.

Redemption, Nebraska wasn't big. The fact that she zig-zagged back and forth across town one night a week was nothing. She waited at one of the few lights and made her turn.

There was virtually no traffic. Without that concerning sensation, it would have been peaceful.

There was no one in the car with her. No child demanding snacks, no customers demanding drinks. She could just … be.

The thought flitted through her head—as it often did when she was left alone with her thoughts—*Sean didn't know they weren't his real grandparents.* If things went according to plan, he never would.

The drop off at the bank loomed before she expected it, and she cut a too-late turn into the lot. Had there been other cars around, she would have been *that driver.* But the streets were empty and she was glad she never had to get out of her car. Tierney pulled up to the drop, hit the button, and slid the cash bag in. She zipped away before the chill in her bones could catch up to her.

That sensation had saved her life in the past. But, she reminded herself, it was useless now, just an artifact of another time. Still, her eyes darted side to side, sweeping the still night for threats even as her brain told her she was being ridiculous.

Elliot wasn't here. Everything she saw, every glow under every streetlight, every dark nook and cranny that she could find, told her that he wasn't.

Pulling a normally impossible left onto the main road, Tierney headed back across town toward her parents' house.

She knew every light and pothole by heart, so her thoughts floated away. How different would her life be with different choices? She'd made such bad ones. Even so, she'd been a kid and she'd long since forgiven herself. The problem was that it wasn't one bad choice. It had been a series of them.

She hated keeping secrets, but she liked staying alive, so she'd gotten good at keeping them.

She'd come here with a family and a sister and her own baby on the way. When Siorse had died, Tierney had become the Doyles' only child. Maybe it was fate.

Maybe it was—

Her thoughts were ripped away by the sound of sirens blasting past her. Just down the street, a cluster of strobing lights flashed blue, red, and white.

Sitting up straighter, she slowed the car, hoping to slip around the accident. In a small town like Redemption, she probably knew the person. But she wasn't prepared.

Tierney was skidding to a stop before she'd made a conscious decision. She flew from the car forgetting to turn off the engine or even shut the door.

One of the police officers strode over to her as she rushed to the flipped car. She knew that car.

"Tierney, you need to stay back," Officer Ramos held out a hand to stop her. But it didn't work.

"No, no, I can't!"

CHAPTER TWO

Ronan had the worst headache of his life. *Was he hungover?* He'd been at Snafu last night drinking with his friends.

The place always reminded him of Siorse working the bar, slipping him free drinks... and then everything else.

Had he had too many? He couldn't remember.

He hadn't drunk to forget since a year after Siorse had died. Then, he'd been three steps away from needing AA. He'd managed to dial himself back through sheer force of will. Only in the last few years had he allowed himself to drink again. Only once the pain had receded enough to control it.

Had something gone wrong last night?

He reached out to touch his head, but his arm didn't move.

A voice came to him, "No, Honey don't."

Tierney.

Siorse's little sister. That much he remembered, but why was she here?

"You were in a car accident," she told him. The words soft and simple, as if she were informing him that his shirt wasn't green but blue.

It didn't work. His body reacted immediately, sitting up, eyes opening. *Or trying to.*

Why didn't his eyes open?

Maybe because, with the first movement, everything twinged and shot fire straight up his side.

Hands touched his shoulders. Tierney tried to calm him. "Lay back. You're in no shape to be sitting up. Put your arms down. You'll yank your IVs."

IVs?

Why weren't his eyes opening?

Lying still, breathing shallowly through the pain that continued to throb along his side, he tried to wait until it dissipated. Patience wasn't his strong suit.

He slowly opened his eyes. Sure enough, Tierney was standing over him, her hands open and spread wide, ready to grab his shoulders and push him back down if he disobeyed orders. The room beyond her was white and glaring.

Only now did he notice the beeping.

"What?"

"It's five a.m." She told him quietly, still hovering, still ready to push him back. "You were in a car accident last night. A truck ran the light and T'd your car. The doctor says you're going to be okay."

Okay?

The memories flooded back. He remembered Siorse's accident instead. He remembered finding the car on the grass, it had been flung so far. The rear seat dented and crushed. Paddy had died instantly, the car seat not enough to save him from that.

Tierney wasn't going to let him wallow, though. "Do you remember getting hit?"

He did, just not his own accident.

Reaching out, he grabbed Tierney by the wrist. "Wait."

He got the distinct sense that she hadn't been going anywhere. "What did they mean by *Okay?*"

"He said back to yourself," she assured him.

"I can—" his job was all he had left. He couldn't imagine if he couldn't …

"Yes. It will take a little while, but you'll be able to go back to work."

Of course, Tierney already knew all of this. Of course, she was here at five a.m. He breathed a sigh of relief even as he wondered if she was lying to him. When he laid back and seemed to let go of the tension, he tried again to open his eyes.

She talked to him again. "You had a minor surgery in the middle of the night, hence the pain in your side. But they got you mostly put back together."

He didn't like "mostly" but she was still going.

"I left a message with your mom and dad, but they haven't responded. I said I'd stay with you. We didn't expect you to wake up for a while."

Slowly, he was starting to focus even though his eyes wanted to close, and his brain wanted to wander away. Tierney would be hard to hold onto mentally if she didn't keep talking.

"Did you get breakfast?" he asked, though he realized as he said it that it was stupid.

"I will," she assured him.

Why did she sound strange? His thoughts began floating.

She must have seen something on his face.

"You're on some serious painkillers."

Then why was he feeling pain?

"Your thoughts are probably going to be a little muddled. You may ask people the same things twice, but it's okay."

"Why are you here?" *Oh shit. Was that rude?* He hadn't meant to be. He liked Tierney. She was alternately quiet and brash and didn't seem to care for him much, even after all these years. They'd been family for a while.

"I was driving home from the bar, and I saw the accident."

"You saw it?" He tried to sit up again. But her hands were immediately on his shoulders, soft and gentle, calming him but not taking any shit. Also, she wasn't Siorse, but she was close ...

Why did he think she was close?

"I didn't see it happen. I saw afterward. The police were there. B-shift was pulling you out of the car. So I followed the ambulance here."

That was nice of her. She wasn't his family, but she wasn't *not* his family either. As his late wife's sister, he wasn't sure if she was still his sister-in-law or not. That thought was floating away as the doctor came in.

Ronan blinked and the woman who was fuzzy at first sharpened as he stared. Oh, good, his eyes were open.

Oh, shit, the drugs were making him dumb.

The doc had dark hair pulled back tight in a bun. She held a hand out to him and waited while he figured out how to operate his own. "I'm Dr. Alexandra Cotton. I'm just here to check on you."

Tierney piped up from the other side of him, "His blood pressure has remained relatively stable—130 over 82. His heart rate has been a solid 78. He's a firefighter so it's normally low. That's probably a little high for him." Then she added, "When he came to, he waved his arms around. He may have loosened the IV. You may want to have someone check that."

What was even happening?

At least now he could look at the doctor. He saw a nod of admiration. She checked all the machines and told Tierney, "Very good." Then she turned to Ronan. "Now we need to talk about your next surgery."

CHAPTER THREE

"Mom! It's gross!"

Tierney jumped at Sean's disgruntled squeal. Her phone had just dinged, she was trying to get her constantly moving child out of the house, and now he was complaining about something gross. She could not deal with anything gross right now.

It was Saturday morning, and she'd worked until the bar closed last night. She had planned this poorly, but it was too late to change now. And way too early to be organized.

At 6:30am on a Saturday in Nebraska the temperature was well below freezing. Maybe she should be grateful her child was at least passing the front door. That was progress toward the car, right?

"What is it, Seanie Bean?" Tierney called out still stuffing his things down into a bag. He had ball practice after they went to Ronan's and she was running on coffee and fumes.

"You have to come see this, Mom! ... Mom! Mom!"

"One minute," she called back. This new thing where he kept saying *mom* over and over and over again until she showed up was going to drive her absolutely batshit. The bag was finally packed. She hoped she'd done it well because she'd done it far too quickly. With her stomach growling, Tierney grabbed her purse and headed out the door.

With a quick look at her phone, she realized she was screwed.

— Ready for the film fest today?

Oh crap, no. She was not ready for the film fest today. That was today?

She wasn't even going to make it at all. She'd double booked the whole day like an idiot.

With a hefty serving of anger at herself, and a side dollop of guilt, Tierney wondered how she was going to tell Talia that she'd fucked up. Her friend should give her ticket away, Tierney thought as she stepped out the front door and almost ran into her son.

What was he doing?

"No, mom!" He yelled from where he was bent over examining something. He stood up abruptly, holding his hands out to her.

Tierney brought herself to a sharp stop. She'd almost stepped on the dead rat. "Gross!"

"That's what I said, Mom!"

Tierney felt her stomach turn as she looked at the bloody mess on the porch.

"I think Mr. Kittens left it for us," Sean told her in solemn words, his eyes never leaving the disgusting sight.

"Probably," Tierney said, though she wouldn't have guessed a cat could make such a precise cut. The rat was gutted stem to stern, the entrails pulled out across the porch.

"Why would Mr. Kittens leave us a rat?" Sean was still babbling even as Tierney took his hand and used it to pull him away.

There was no good answer except to get their asses to Ronan's, where they were already late getting to. She hoped he wasn't up and around because she wasn't there. As she pushed Sean toward the backseat and reminded him to buckle in, her bag fell from her shoulder.

"Crap!"

"That's a bad word, Mom."

"It is. I'm sorry." But she didn't look at her child. She looked down and was supremely grateful that the bag stayed zipped, and she wasn't having to dust the driveway dirt off everything and pack it all over again.

She knew how to do this, Tierney reminded herself. She'd been doing fine until the phone dinged and Sean found the dead rat on the porch ... No, actually, she hadn't. She was already late, and she'd been thinking about being at Ronan's and seeing him ...

No. She couldn't think about any of that.

Stopping and taking a deep breath—the only way she'd ever really found to handle anything as a single teenage mom—she took a moment. She checked that Sean clicked his seatbelt correctly, picked up the bag and brushed it off. Then stuffed the bag into the footwell that he clearly didn't need yet. Then she closed the door before aiming toward the mess.

Ducking back, she shoved the key in the ignition and turned the car on so it would warm up for Sean ... and her. Then she told him to stay put as she surveyed the crap on her front doorstep.

The little rental house was adorable, but if she'd had her way there would have been an attached garage. It was definitely a must in a place with cold weather like this. First things first, she pulled the thermal blanket from over the hood. She should stash it in the shed out back, but she'd never had the time for that. So she shoved it into a little outdoor box she'd bought for just this.

"Stay put, Sean, the car will get warm."

Then she headed around to the back, stomping her feet in the cold. She was dressed to move from the house to the car, not for doing the manual labor of front porch cleanup. Getting her only shovel, Tierney used it to scrape the dead rat off the front step. Her lips curled and her head pulled back. The guts hung downward off the flat of the shovel, still attached.

Gross. Sean was right. This was disgusting.

Then she stood there, nearly gagging and realized she had to find a place to put it. She was beyond out of time. Her stomach grumbled again as she balanced the rat, and she opened her mouth to gag. "Ew!"

She didn't have a trash bag, but she wasn't about to go back inside and get one. With her time well past short, she gave up and tossed the dead body into the bushes. Hopefully that would be far enough away.

As she looked back, she saw the front porch was smeared with rat blood and for a moment she thought she'd vomit into the nice little hedge her landlord kept. But with another deep breath—with closed eyes—she instead dug into the black mulch and tossed it across the porch, rubbing it in with the shovel before scraping it back off. At least it didn't look like a blood trail anymore. It would have to do.

Tierney left the shovel beside the house. She didn't want to leave Sean in the car any longer or be any later getting to Ronan's. Buckling herself in, she offered her son a smile in the rearview mirror and hoped he didn't read her disgust at the rat, her irritation at herself for running late, or the simmering feelings she had for Sean's uncle.

She only barely remembered not to start the engine again. Then she shoved into reverse and backed out of the driveway as she checked her phone again. Ronan was too nice to ask if she was still coming. She worked her way through a massive apology to Talia, and by the time she was done, the short drive was over and she was sitting in front of Ronan's house.

"Why did Mr. Kittens leave us a dead rat?" Sean asked again.

This time she had to answer. "Cats leave dead animals as a

thank you gift or sometimes because they think people are stupid and can't hunt for them themselves."

At least that made Sean giggle. "Mr. Kittens is getting fat."

A mild subject change, she thought. He was getting better at staying on topic. "I don't think Mr. Kittens is fat. I think Mr. Kittens is a *Miss* Kittens. And I think *Miss* Kittens is about to have her own kittens."

Not something she was looking forward to. It was enough being responsible for herself and her child.

Sean giggled, "I don't think so."

Good to know he'd become an authority on veterinary medicine at the tender age of nine.

Tierney stared up at the beautiful craftsman house that made her heart ache. Her house was a rental. The roof sagged a little on one side. The porch was concrete, but there was a growing crack where it was pulling away from the foundation.

She was grateful for the size of the place and that she didn't have to cover repairs. But she was also sad that it wasn't hers to fix. It wasn't loved. It was painted cream and an odd shade of blue that she was pretty certain the owner had gotten on discount.

Here though, this house was a point of pride. Ronan had bought it and begun fixing it up before Siorse got pregnant. His little family had lived here for just over five years before Siorse and Paddy died. Tierney took one more look at the house before turning the car off.

Siorse had never deserved this house or this man.

But, as usual, Tierney had to stuff that down. There were things she couldn't say. She'd kept Siorse's secrets for herself. Now she kept them for her mom and dad ... and for Ronan.

With her mind on her task, she reversed the process of getting in. Though Sean hopped out and ran to the front door, she had to grab her purse, his bag, and everything she was bringing for Ronan.

She unconsciously checked the front porch for dead animals and thankfully found it clear. Of course, no cat would dare grace such a pristine home with rat entrails. She stepped up, wishing it were her home, but not saying anything.

"Here, Sean, hold this for a minute."

He reached up and carefully balanced the dish. He was a good kid. The best. She fit her key into the lock and let herself in.

CHAPTER FOUR

Ronan tried to toss back the covers, but even that simple movement ignited a slash of fire in his side. It had been a week since he'd been let out of the hospital, and he really thought he should be doing better by now.

He guessed he wouldn't be swinging his legs jauntily over the side of the bed and heading out to the kitchen on his own either.

He'd been awake for a while, but Tierney was late, and he wasn't supposed to get out of bed without her here. He was on medical leave from work, and he hated it. He'd always assumed that any medical leave would at least be work related, and fully covered, but noooo.

So, he was running out his paid time off, and paying to keep the house a little warmer than usual and being taken care of by everyone else in his life.

His mother had flipped out and tried to end their cruise early. But since it was only by a day, and Ronan was awake enough to assure her he'd be fine and that Tierney had everything well under control, they'd finished the trip. Then she'd touched down like a reverse tornado, sweeping through chaos and organizing everything in her wake. She had herself and Tierney and a home nurse on rotation almost constantly. It had taken everything he had to be allowed to sleep by himself overnight. But she'd insisted on early morning visits and the warmer house and … and … and …

The heating bill wasn't going to feel good. Nor was the hospital bill. He was bored out of his skull and eating casseroles brought by the fine single ladies of Redemption—none of whom he was interested in, and he wished his mother would quit sending them over. To add insult to injury, his accident had been almost identical to the one that had killed his wife and young son. So why had he survived when they hadn't? Why had it happened so close to the anniversary of their accident, too?

Fate was a cruel bitch.

Slowly, he settled his feet down into the fuzzy rug by the side of the bed. It had been Siorse's and he'd considered getting rid of it and the other fuzzy rugs she'd put throughout the house. But a year after she died, when the weather had turned cold again, he'd cared for the first time that his feet were cold in the mornings. So he'd stolen it from her side of the bed.

It was better to use it than let it rot. Some days he thought everything in the house was rotting. Some days he didn't want to leave because it was the place it most felt like they were both still here. The world had moved on, but he hadn't.

This morning, Ronan decided to be grateful for the soft rug. He stepped carefully, slowly along the edge of the bed, holding on in case he tripped or fell. He was *not* going back to the hospital. His hand traced along the nightstand, and then up to the wall for balance. He wasn't quite good enough to walk on his own yet. Tierney liked to remind him that he should be grateful he walked on his own at all.

Mostly he was mad he'd been left in the middle.

He should have been killed or he should have survived cleanly. He was far too impatient to suffer an injury like this. To top it off, the doctors told him that if he pushed too quickly, he could make the injury permanent. It was probably the only thing that held him back.

As he slowly and painfully picked his way down the hall, he heard a noise from the front door. If it was an intruder, he was toast. But Sean was running down the hallway to him, greeting him with a smile and enthusiasm.

Ronan was grateful that his nephew was older than Paddy, though he'd always felt sorry for Tierney. Tierney and Siorse had arrived in town Ronan's senior year. He'd fallen for Siorse immediately and he'd realized quickly that her younger sister had arrived in town already pregnant.

At the time, Tierney had just been a pregnant teenager. But now, he was glad of how it played out. If Sean had been younger than Paddy, or even the same age, Ronan would have lost his shit. If he'd had to watch Sean pass Paddy, that would have been too much.

As it was, he managed to keep his annoyance at having a nine-year-old in the house under check. Normally he liked kids. Normally he liked Sean. He didn't know why everything was irritating him now. Or maybe it was just all too obvious why he was pissed at the world, but he couldn't seem to change it.

"Uncle Ronan! We found a dead rat on the porch this morning!"

Lovely. Ronan reached the end of the short hall and slowly turned the corner, his hand on the wall, leaning heavily against it. He looked into the kitchen, where Tierney was already starting to cook his breakfast and hers. "You're late."

It came out far too harsh. He'd meant it as just a comment, not a criticism.

She shrugged as if it was of no importance.

But it *was* important. In his line of work, tardiness killed people. At least in hers, it just left his stomach grumbling longer.

"There was a dead rat to remove from my porch," she said by way of excuse.

When he didn't respond, she added. "It was a complete surprise. I apologize for not having saved enough time to clean up entrails in the morning. Would you like your free breakfast?"

It wasn't completely free. Some of what she'd put into the egg scramble was from his fridge, but she'd brought the bread, and the melon. And he was in no shape to cook it himself. So, he slowly moved from the wall taking a few free steps until his hand hit the back of the sturdy dark wood dining chair. Then he shuffled his way around until he sat gingerly in it. By the time his ass was in the seat, Tierney had put a fully cooked plate of food in front of him.

She next brought a glass of juice and a small dish full of pills.

Jesus, he hated this. But the only way out was through. He dutifully swallowed the pills and tried to move his arm slowly to not aggravate his wounds any further as he ate the scrambled eggs, sausage, and toast. Luckily, Tierney was a great cook.

Tierney brought the rest over and sat at the table, calling her son in for breakfast. Sean sat down next to him, chattering about school and ballgames, and not needing Ronan to hold up his side of the conversation at all. Within minutes, he was getting up and asking if he could go play.

"Check the stuff in your bag for your game this afternoon then you can go play in the back room for a little bit."

"Okay!"

There were a few more back and forths determining what TV he could watch and what games of Ronan's he was allowed to play. But he'd been to Uncle Ronan's house enough times that at least Ronan wasn't worried. Siorse had loved their nephew and babysat often, even after Paddy had been born.

With Sean gone to the other room, Ronan reached out to snag Sean's plate and eat what the kid had left behind. It was their usual M.O. on the days his sister-in-law showed up.

But then an odd stillness settled over the table, and he looked up at Tierney as she set her fork down and leaned forward, a solemn look on her face. "Do cats usually gut their victims?"

"I don't know." He wasn't really a fan of cats. He continued to slowly but surely devour the food, though he wished she hadn't brought up that topic while he was eating.

Then, after a moment of continued silence, he looked up. She was worried. He'd known her too long for her to hide it from him. Something was eating at her. The rat? "Tierney, what is it?"

Even as he asked, he realized it was stupid. He wasn't in any shape to do anything even if she told him.

"It's nothing." But she looked down at her plate and the words came out clipped and far too fast for him to buy her answer.

It obviously wasn't nothing.

CHAPTER FIVE

Did he know? Tierney wondered as she stirred the soup in the crock pot and checked the temperature. She was slow heating one of the dishes brought by some woman who wanted to snag the single firefighter.

She didn't have Sean with her today, having come by after she'd dropped him off at school. These breakfasts without her child were sometimes quiet, sometimes full of passionate debates, and sometimes—like today—simple small talk.

She wondered if Ronan even had a clue that she'd had a crush on him from the day she'd arrived in town. Unfortunately, so had Siorse. Both girls were redheads, which had absolutely helped push the sister narrative—probably what had saved Tierney's life.

But where Siorse was willowy and tall, blue eyed and striking, Tierney was shorter. None of the rest of it mattered because she'd arrived in town pregnant. She was already starting to show by fall break. There was absolutely no way she would have caught the eye of a senior like Ronan Kelly. She'd put it aside then and wondered why the hell her feelings were flaring up again ten years later.

The fact was, they'd waxed and waned, but never left. And his accident—almost losing him—had to be the root cause of this latest need for a man she would never have. *Could* never have. She knew better.

So, she showed up and cared for him and had the only relationship she could with him. It had been another week. While he was nowhere near ready for work, Ronan was at least a lot more mobile now. She needed to stop coming over so much. She'd carried this crush for way too long. And even though Siorse was gone, and even though Tierney had her questions about what Siorse had been up to the night she died, nothing was ever going to happen for her. And that was probably why she'd nursed this crush on Ronan for so long.

In a way, it was safe. She could feel these things and not have to act on them.

But it wasn't just Ronan. She couldn't have anyone. Until certain key parts of her old life were dead, she couldn't afford a relationship. Anyone who loved her would be lied to.

Tierney was always grateful though that she had Sean. That she and Sean had a very solid life that would not have been possible without the Doyles. Sean would be ten next year, something she'd thought she'd not live to see, not safely at least.

"What's wrong, Tee?" Ronan asked.

She hadn't even seen him come into the kitchen, let alone make his way over to the lovely granite island and lean on it.

Tierney jerked, splashing a little bit of the soup from the ladle onto the countertop, where she quickly wiped it away. It was clear he wasn't taking her pat answer.

If that hadn't been clear, he put it into words. "I've known you since the first day you arrived in town. I know when you're nervous and when you're upset. I can tell, right now, something's got you worried."

"Yeah, I'm worried," she confessed. Then she evaded. "You're not supposed to be walking around so much."

"I'm fine and that's not it. Don't lie to me."

Tierney looked into those gorgeous blue eyes. The dark hair that had grown too long with him not getting it cut while he was recovering. The irony was that she had lied to him the entire time she'd known him.

He was smart, wily, and usually good on his feet. Then again, Siorse had fooled him for years and he still hadn't caught on to that. So maybe Tierney stood a chance with yet another lie. "You're antsy to get back to work. Now you're trying to find a problem so that you have something to do."

Putting the lid back on the crock pot, she turned away, hoping that if he couldn't see her face he couldn't or wouldn't push further. But she should have known better.

The man was persistent. It was a trait she'd admired in the past. He'd persisted in being a good friend to her, even though she and her sister had never had the best relationship. Honestly, Tierney couldn't fault Siorse for that.

She'd been shoved on her older sister, just before her senior year of high school in the middle of a family move that was probably occurring at the worst possible time for her. It had been Ronan who made sure that Tierney was watched out for. It had been Ronan that she'd called when she went into labor, petrified at age seventeen and more alone than he could ever know. And he was still here.

His hand touched her shoulder, turning her around. Once again, the touch startled her. Damn, the man was stealthy. Tierney knew better than to pull her shoulder away. Resisting only proved his point, and she liked the feel of his hands on her, however she could get them.

He wasn't going to let this go. "Something's been bothering you."

"It's nothing. I'm a single mom with a bar job and a nine-year-old." All of that was true. She realized, of course, as soon as the words were out of her mouth, that it made Ronan sound like an additional burden on an already burdened life.

"Well, you've been doing a lot here for me."

"That's not it." She waved him away, wishing that she hadn't created the problem herself and wanting him to know that she was more than happy to do this. "We're family. You've stepped up for me far more times than necessary. This is the least I can do."

She said the words with a kind look and a gentle smile she was confident he didn't quite believe. When Siorse had died, his ties to the Doyles had diminished as well but Tierney hadn't let him fade away from her life.

He was *Uncle Ronan* to her son, and he was her hero and protector, whether or not he knew it. But right now he was staring her down and demanding answers. So, she fed him partial truths. "I think someone hacked my email and Sean hasn't seen Mr. Kittens in about three days."

"You're not worried about Mr. Kittens." Ronan had always thought the name was stupid. But Sean had been relatively small when the stray first began coming to their home and Tierney had thought it was cute that he wanted to name and feed the cat. To this day, her son refused to admit that Mr. Kittens might actually not be a Mister.

"When Mr. Kittens is about to have kittens of his own—"

"Ohhh," Ronan said, looking away. Clearly, feral kittens were not his thing.

That was ridiculous for a firefighter. Didn't he have to look all hunky rescuing them from trees? "At least we know Mr. Kittens is alive and well, because he-she left me another dead rat this morning."

She shrugged as she told him, as if to say, *you can see why I'm a little uptight.* But the problem had not been that Mr. Kittens had left a dead rat. This was the third one she'd found right on her front step. The problem was she was beginning to suspect that none of the rats had actually been left by Mr. Kittens.

CHAPTER SIX

Tierney sat at the small dining room table, her eyes scanning the street through the large front window. The window had been one of the selling points on this rental. She liked being able to see the yard, to watch Sean and his friends when they played outside.

It was too cold for that now, but she had her eyes out for the bus. It would be by soon after dropping the kids at the corner. Just a minute or so after that she would see Sean walking into her field of view.

Tierney was grateful for the bus and that it came so close to the house—another point in this rental's favor. It was too cold to walk too far these days, especially for a little kid.

Flipping open her laptop, she looked again. No bus. Checking her email and weeding out the spam should be something easy she could do while she waited. She didn't have the energy for much more.

She'd already put in a shift at the bar hauling in the deliveries, prepping burgers, chilling the beer, and then she'd waited tables for the lunch crowd. Luckily, she'd pulled a good set of tips today and she hadn't had to go to Ronan's this week. He was getting around better.

That didn't make her day job any easier though. Mom and Dad Doyle insisted every worker be able work every station possible. At first, Tierney had thought it was ridiculous. But later, as people called in sick or left the job, she'd seen it was a sound business plan.

It didn't change the fact that she'd covered a missing prep shift and was one shy on servers today. She'd run the place until her dad showed up at one. She was beyond exhausted. She'd worked almost without any break at all from the moment the bus had picked Sean up this morning until five minutes ago when she'd been grateful to beat him home.

He had a key, but she hated when he had to use it. So, she'd rushed back and just made it. *But where was the bus?*

A moment later, she'd checked the time and decided the bus was running late. The old laptop shuffled through several screens, finally bringing up her email and the pink sunset theme that she'd chosen. The colors would have soothed her had her heart and fingers not frozen at the sight.

Not another one.

She'd dismissed the first one as a random error, an email simply sent to the wrong person. Even though her email was a very basic Tierney.Doyle, she'd had things mixed up in the past. She'd gotten emails for Linda and McKayla and even Bob Pastor. Once, she'd been invited to someone's Napa Valley college reunion train ride and wine tasting tour.

So, when the first email showed up from a random T-shirt shop and said "Hello, Emily," her heart had tripped. But she told herself it was just an error. It had to be. Lots of people were named Emily. It meant nothing.

But this new one was from an underwear company thanking her for subscribing. She'd been about to hit the delete button when she saw the greeting. "Hi Emmie, Thank you for joining us!"

The overly cute name froze her blood in her veins.

She began to hyperventilate. Emmie. It said *Emmie.*

It didn't have to mean anything though.

It was mis-sent. She looked out the window again and tried to calm herself down, taking deep breaths. They should have been breaths, they were heavy gulps. Her eyes blinked as the bus pulled by in front of the house, yellow and black blurring in front of her vision.

Sean would be here any minute!

Should she hit delete?

She frantically scrambled to unsubscribe, but the screen took forever to load, so she smacked the delete button and pushed the laptop closed, as if the screen being out of her view could make the threat go away.

But was it a threat?

Did she need to pack everything and leave?

She'd had a good run. Maybe ten years was the limit. She'd gotten complacent, thinking she was safe—thinking she was safer the longer she lasted. Maybe the opposite was true, maybe he'd just needed time and hers had just run out.

She should pack everything and go. The Doyles would figure it out. She almost cried then—they would lose another daughter when they'd already lost the first so suddenly and harshly. They'd lose their only grandchild. What would it do to Sean?

And where was he???

Had something happened already?

But it wasn't Sean walking with his cold hands stuffed into his pockets because he'd forgotten or lost his gloves again. What came into her view was a car. Low, sleek, and sporty, it made her heart kick again. Where was her son?

The windows on the car were tinted; it was hard to see who was inside. But Tierney jumped to her feet and ran to the couch, bracing her hands on the window as she leaned forward, peering down the street for her son. The street was empty.

She'd suffered this level of worry several times before in her life. Once when Sean was small and she and Mom Doyle had rushed him to the ER. And before the Doyles, when she'd fled the first time.

Tierney stared at the car as if she could will the person to get out. She was petrified they had Sean. She hoped it wasn't him.

But no one got out of the car.

Why wasn't anyone getting out of the car?

Was he sitting there staring at her? Should she back away? Had she already screwed up everything, letting him know that she was afraid?

And she was afraid.

But, as she stepped back and failed to forcibly calm her racing heart and pounding nerves, she saw the passenger door open and out stepped Sean.

Her heart slowed even as the anger surged. Who the hell had he caught a ride with? He knew better! But she told herself he was upright, he was fine, and his breaking the rules hadn't cost them anything. *Today.*

She started to take a deep breath, the first one in which she could really relax. Then, the driver's side door opened, and Tierney braced herself. She watched as a man she'd not expected to see stepped out of the car.

CHAPTER SEVEN

Ronan climbed from the low slung car, his good mood solidifying in his chest as Tierney raced down her front steps and whacked him on the arm.

"You scared the shit out of me!"

"What?" Man, she'd gotten him right on one of his last fading bruises from the accident. "What did I do?"

"You showed up on my doorstep with my child in a strange car. And you didn't warn me!"

Oh, that part hadn't occurred to him. "I'm sorry."

What more could he say? He could explain, and he was sorry. But whatever damage Tierney had suffered to her nerves, it was fading. Sean was fine—the kid loved the new car.

"Mom drove me to the doctor this morning and I got cleared to drive."

"That's good." Tierney was looking away. Obviously, she still hadn't fully come down from whatever crazy high his driving her child in a strange car had elicited.

"My car was totaled. So, I got a new one."

"It's so cool!" Sean ran up and tugged on her shirt. The move hit Ronan square in the chest like many things did. He'd not get to see his own child get big enough to tell him about cars and video games, but now wasn't the time for melancholy.

He looked Tierney over as she crossed her arms against the cold.

She wasn't dressed well enough to be out here, but she was still looking at him again like he was a little crazy. She was still breathing a little too quickly.

He told himself her nerves should have faded faster. How much had he upset her? Was it really that big of a deal?

"It's got bucket seats!" Sean was still going on. "And inside the car, the speakers have lights that blink with the music."

"That sounds distracting." Tierney was now looking everywhere but at Sean or Ronan. Her eyes darted around behind him and over to the other side. *What was she looking for?*

Seeming to realize what she was doing, she met Ronan's gaze finally. "And cool," she added. "It sounds cool."

"You know me. I don't do distracted driving." He'd helped cut too many people out of totaled cars to text or even call people while he was driving. Blinking speaker lights would not pull his attention from the street.

Hell, he was barely-walking proof that you could drive completely undistracted and still wind up nearly dead.

The three of them stood on the front lawn, staring at each other for a moment. Tierney's distress dampened the mood. She tried not to look like she was scanning the street, but she was still doing it. And though their feet were planted in dry, frosty grass, she didn't have a coat on.

That wasn't like her. She was such a mom, the idea that she would stand out here in just her shirtsleeves seemed odd. She was only half following the conversation, while Sean still babbled at her about all the cool features of Ronan's new car.

"I came to say thank you." Ronan tried again to catch her attention but failed.

She uncrossed her arms for a moment to wave one hand at him as if to brush the thanks away.

"No, really, you went above and beyond. And I wanted to take you two out to dinner." As if one dinner out would make up for all the times she'd shown up at his home. That she'd gotten her kid out the door before school and made breakfast for the three of them at his house. He had company, and a doublecheck that he hadn't injured himself overnight. He got hot food each morning, and something in the crock pot to feed himself until his mother checked in later.

With a nine-year-old in tow, it was a lot. And she'd simply made a habit out of it, until the doctor cleared him down to his mother just peppering him with text checkins all day.

He knew Tierney had adjusted to his early mornings. He was just an early riser—firefighters often were—and she knew he'd be up and wasn't supposed to be walking around on his own. He knew she'd showed up more than once before seven a.m. after having worked into the wee hours at the bar the night before. She'd never complained and never asked for anything.

"Come on." He tried again to grab her attention.

Sean helped. "He'll take us to Delmonico's!"

It was Tierney's favorite place just on the Redemption side of Lincoln. He also knew she couldn't afford it. He couldn't really either right now, but it seemed the least he could do. Because when the chips were down, it ultimately wasn't about what was in his bank account, but who was willing to show up at 6am repeatedly to make him eggs.

"That sounds nice," Tierney said, but she didn't sound excited. The words trailed off and her eyes followed a white car that passed through the intersection at the end of her block. It didn't turn on to their street, so she turned and looked the other way.

"Tee?" He leaned down to get into her line of sight. Ronan

wanted to ask *what is going on?* but Sean was still jumping up and down.

"Come on, Mom, this is great. You know you want to go!"

Ronan had introduced the child to steak two years earlier. And he knew the nine-year-old was going to spend a good chunk of money on the best cut in the restaurant. The good news was Ronan didn't care. What concerned him right now was the woman standing in front of him.

She crossed her arms again, bumping her breasts upward. One curved hip stuck out, but she shivered a little in the cold. He couldn't help noticing all of it.

Tierney was more than worried, she looked almost angry. He'd known her since the day she arrived, and he could read her like an open book.

"Hey, Sean." He pushed the kid lightly on the back, "head inside. Check over your homework. We have to make sure we get that done before we go."

"Do I?" The whine was real. Something else Ronan wouldn't hear from his own child.

"Do you want steak?" Ronan realized as he asked that he was playing the parent, and it wasn't his job.

Still. Tierney had always told him she was grateful that he had a good male role model in his life.

"Okay, okay." Sean conceded quickly, practically bouncing up the stairs, stepping on a stain of color that made Ronan frown. He could only guess that it was left over from the dead rats she'd been finding.

He wanted to tell her to get inside too. She had to be freezing, but he didn't want to ask her in front of Sean. If there was one thing he knew about Tierney, it was that she guarded that child with everything she had. If something was really wrong, she wouldn't say so if Sean was in sight.

"Tierney, what's going on?"

"It's nothing." She started to turn away to follow Sean, but

Ronan reached out, grabbed her elbow and gently tugged her back around.

She could have pulled away, but he was grateful that she didn't.

"I know it's something. Tell me what it is."

She looked left, then scanned right, as if making sure no one was coming up behind him with a gun or a baseball bat or something equally concerning. The move made her concern turn into his.

Tierney, at last, looked him in the eye. "I got a weird email."

What email could make her act this strangely?

"You know, one of those where they said they've hacked your account." But her eyes darted down to the dead grass at her feet. "They actually put my password—the right one—in the email."

"Those don't mean anything. I've gotten those. Do change the password, but don't worry." He tried to soothe her and then realized it had to be something more. "What? Did they demand money or something?"

"No." She looked away again. "They said ... they said—"

She looked down the street, pausing her words as a car turned onto the road. But she must have recognized it or something because she shook her head as if to shake it off. "They said they had video of me ... masturbating in front of my computer. You know, one of those threats."

Damn. Why did that flare the heat in him? Suddenly his coat was too hot.

"Could they?"

"Jesus! No!" Her reaction was swift, the pink in her cheeks the only thing making him think she wouldn't freeze.

He swallowed down the heat that suffused his system. "So, change your password. They can't extort you. It's not a real threat if they can't have the thing they are threatening with. I've gotten those ones, too."

He should not be thinking about jerking off to internet videos right here with his sister-in-law.

She nodded. "You're right."

It seemed in that moment both of them realized his fingers were still wrapped, warm and firm, around her elbow. She gave him an odd look that let him know he needed to let go.

But he didn't want to.

Still, he forced his fingers to open, and he watched as she turned to walk inside, her movements still stiff. All Ronan could do was stand there and wonder why he was feeling this heat and why she was lying to him.

CHAPTER EIGHT

"Honey." There was a pause as Mom set the rag down on the bar top. Stopping her perpetual motion was almost a threat. Aileen Doyle always seemed to be moving, and this meant it was serious. "What's going on?"

"It's nothing, Mom."

The rag didn't start moving again. "It's something. It's something enough that Ronan asked me about it."

Interesting. How often did Ronan talk to his ex mother-in-law?

Tierney had to stop now, too. Clipboard in hand, she turned to face her mom after making the last mark. They'd enter all the numbers into the system later. Hashmarks were still the easiest way to record stock. She couldn't hit a four instead of five when she was writing it herself. "What did Ronan say?"

"He said that you seemed jumpy and nervous."

Did he now?

"He thought you were worried. I don't like when you're worried." That was fair. Mom knew what had happened—at least the basics of it—before they all moved here. And that there could be real reason to worry. "So, what's going on?"

"It's nothing." But even as the words came out of her mouth, Tierney watched her mother's face pull into a disbelieving scold. Aileen didn't even have to say the words, Tierney knew she'd have to tell her mother more. "It's stupid. You know? Just the kind of thing that makes me paranoid."

"Okay." It wasn't a full concession but at least her mom's hands started moving again.

They'd be opening in just ten minutes. A car had already pulled into the lot and was waiting with the engine running. Tierney had learned long ago not to take pity on the people waiting outside and open the doors early. As much as it seemed a nice thing to do, it only made everyone upset when they weren't ready.

Normally, she'd be snacking now, shoving much needed food in her face to fuel her through the lunch rush. But she was still full from that amazing steak dinner last night. A small smile graced her lips. They'd felt like a family. But they weren't. And they couldn't be.

She looked at the clock again. Nine minutes. She couldn't be daydreaming.

At least there was a nine-minute limit on this interrogation —she could feel that there was more coming even though Aileen was waiting patiently for her daughter to cough up information. Tierney didn't like lying—even though she'd spent a very large portion of her life doing it—certainly not to this woman who had risked so much for her and Sean.

Unlike the lie she told to Ronan, she could tell her mom more. "I got an email addressed to *Emily*."

That made Mom Doyle's head snap up and her hands freeze in place. "What?"

"It was just a subscription to something ... A sale announcement from an online t-shirt shop." Tierney waved her hand around trying to dismiss it. She should be counting stock. But, while mom could clean the bar while she talked,

Tierney couldn't count and talk at the same time, not without errors.

So, she picked up cleaning supplies and headed out to wipe down the tables. She could count later when she wasn't being questioned.

Mom was still mulling over the meaning of it. "So not written to *you* as *Emily* specifically?"

"No, they were trying to sell me shirts."

"Oh." The relief in her mom's voice ricocheted throughout the bar and Tierney decided not to add that she'd gotten a second email addressed to Emmie. With an I E, not a Y, the same way *he* used to spell it.

"Is that all?" Her mother wasn't quite placated yet.

Tierney wasn't willing to put everyone who mattered into panic mode over what was likely a casual mix-up. It had to happen sooner or later, right? *Emmie* wasn't that uncommon a name. She tried to downplay her own concerns. "I wish that was it. I'm twenty-six. I'm a mom. I'm *completely* single." *And that couldn't change.* "The feral cat that we feed isn't a male. I'm pretty sure Mr. Kittens is expecting a litter of her own kittens any day now."

She paused. Then added, "And she must be feeling maternal because she's left several dead rats on the doorstep for me."

"That's gross."

Despite her mom's relief, Tierney's didn't come quite as easily.

It was much easier to placate someone else than herself. The loud slam of a car door from the parking lot turned both their heads. The subsequent soft churn of gears signaled that Talia had arrived.

Sure enough, a minute later, a knock came at the door, but no shadow was visible through the classic yellow diamond-cut glass. That was Talia—she wasn't tall enough to peer through given the wheelchair.

"She's here!" Cheering, Tierney set her cleaning supplies on the table and headed over to the door.

Undoing the bolt, she pulled the door wide for Talia's souped-up chair to roll through. It left little traces of snow on the floor from the rugged tires. But it was no different than shoes would be doing in just a few minutes when they officially opened.

"I come bearing gifts!" Talia announced, pointing to the full plastic bin she had balanced on her lap.

She held it up and Tierney took it from her, setting the whole thing onto the bar. "We've been waiting for these!"

There would be a town business crawl for Valentine's Day in two weeks. Tierney was looking forward to their annual event. But this year Ivy Dean, the town librarian, had taken over and she was going full steam ahead.

Talia had rolled in and opened a much-needed cupcake shop and bakery. She'd bought a shop front down main street and had it outfitted for herself with special counter heights and more. The only bakery in town was owned by an elderly couple, and Talia had promised to start making bread when they finally went out of business. But so far, she was doing gangbuster business with cupcakes, special occasion cakes, muffins, and a solid coffee selection.

Standing slowly from the chair, she made her way to the bar. "We've added the fire station, the wood shop, and the new game place to the crawl."

Tierney raised her eyebrows. "Of course, you added the fire station!"

They had expected Ivy to be one of the singles on the Valentine's crawl with them, but a recent turn of events had left Ivy no longer single. With her new boyfriend being a firefighter, it was a no-brainer that the firehouse would be on the crawl.

"Yes, but now they will not just have the doors open, they'll have their new fire dog and they'll be serving cookies from my bakery." Talia grinned. She was smart, getting her food featured at two stops on the crawl.

"The new vet is in, too?" Tierney continued to pull pieces out of the packed bin.

"Zadie says she'll have the shelter at least up and running by then. She's hoping to adopt out some dogs and cats on the crawl."

"Is the florist in?" Mom Doyle asked.

"They've been in from the start. Flowers, Valentine's Day, that's a no brainer." Talia reached down into the basket and pulled out a handful of laminated signs. "These go with each item on the display. Everyone is advertising everyone else."

"Perfect!" Tierney said, but she was looking through the cards, checking the discounts.

Talia leaned on the counter and sorted some of the items she'd brought. Walking in the parking lot in the inches deep snow would have been too much, but inside she could move around easier. Tierney also suspected Talia didn't want to walk outside. She'd been around enough when Talia stood up that she'd heard people ask why she needed a wheelchair at all.

It was frustrating at best trying to explain over and over. Luckily, it was a small town and Talia would educate them all soon enough. Tierney hoped.

"Okay, all three shirts have to go up to show the assortment the town is selling for The Crawl. Ivy talked them into men's and women's sizing and three colors. The sign has the code for ordering them." Talia plucked one of the laminated signs from Tierney's hand.

It should be big enough for phones to link to the website just by leaning over the bar, Tierney thought. But she set them down and rummaged through more stuff. There was a vase and several wrapped flowers. She handed them off to her mom.

"These need water!" Aileen declared and ran off.

There were library books on loan, a beautiful wood cutting

board, and more. Everything came with a matching tag for the store hosting another spot on the crawl. Redemption wasn't big enough to have a pub crawl. It would simply be two places—Snafu in the center of town and Addison's, a run-down bar that served watered whiskey on the cheap just beyond the edge of the city limits.

Besides, Tierney thought, this was always much more interesting. It was unusual enough to bring people in from surrounding towns, even Lincoln and a few from Omaha.

"Are you coming?" Talia asked her. She was perched on a stool, arms crossed on the bar as she helped sort through all the pieces.

Tierney began to put them up on the empty shelf in front of the mirror where she'd been saving space. "You know I am. I'm your date."

"Always." Talia grinned.

"What is this?" Tierney asked as she reached down into the bin again and found a foil covered pan heavy and full of food.

"Lasagna." Talia nodded with a grin on her face. "It's for Ronan. I heard he's up to his ears in casseroles."

Tierney laughed. "If he gets another turkey tetrazzini or chicken enchilada bake, he's going to smile a polite thank you and dump it right out."

"I know he likes lasagna. You'll deliver it?"

"Of course, I will."

Was Talia making a move on Ronan?

CHAPTER NINE

Ronan turned a hard right, pulling into Tierney's driveway. She'd offered to make the delivery to him, but he'd refused.

He'd been stuck in his damn house for so long convalescing that any chance to get out on his own was welcome. He still wasn't fit for work, and he was bored out of his head.

Opening the wide car door, he planted his feet on the ground, and honestly looked a little like an idiot. Soon, he'd be in good enough shape to look good getting out of his sports car, but today was not that day. Right now, Sean was the only one who was low enough to the ground to look cool.

Ronan had to twist himself and baby his side while pushing up with his arms like an old man. Once he was upright, though, he slammed the door shut and hoped if any of Tierney's neighbors were watching him, he could at least pull off a slightly better swagger up the walkway.

He managed it up the short path to the porch, but then stopped dead. A flare of heat shot through his side at the sudden movement, but he ignored it.

Holy shit.

The rat lay sideways, its mouth open, tiny paws up in the air. It was filleted from its throat to tail, the entrails yanked out and draped across the steps as if making sure someone would see them.

Ronan looked around for something to clean it up with, but he didn't see anything. Also, something about it bothered him. He couldn't put his finger on what, though. He didn't want to show Tierney, yet knew he should.

Gingerly, he stepped around the mess and pulled the screen door open, but only wide enough to wedge his body inside the space and knock. He tried to step back, but with the entrails looped along the front step he couldn't. The landing was barely large enough to sweep the door open anyway. He was simply going to have to scare the crap out of her when she opened the door.

Standing in the cold air, he watched his breath and figured he looked like a stalker. But she didn't come.

He tried checking for anything that would tell him why she wasn't answering. Instead, he almost lost his balance and stepped back into gooey, bloody, dead rat.

He'd parked behind her car. Since she was the only driver, she had to be here. Right? Maybe she'd walked somewhere? But it was really cold—he watched his breath form in the air in front of him—and she'd called and told him she was home.

He knocked again and waited. When he got no response, he tried the knob. The door swung open far too easily. His nerves began to twist. Something about the dead rat didn't look right and now Tierney wasn't answering the door.

He would have called out, but a soft shuffling noise from the back of the house drew his attention.

Was she in trouble?

Should he not alert someone that he was here? Two steps inside and he was standing in the middle of the small living room. It was painted a bright sunshine yellow, which continued to the other side where the living room connected to the eat-in dining area which was really part of the kitchen. To his left a hallway cut the space, leading from her bedroom at the front of the house. Past the bathroom and around to the back was Sean's room, next to a small laundry area. That space connected the loop back to the kitchen.

The rooms were tiny. The kitchen was tiny. The house was tiny. But Tierney did okay for herself. He didn't know why she'd never gone on to college, she was plenty bright. She'd graduated at the top of her high school class despite having to leave periodically to take her sick child home.

The noises and shuffling from the back sounded low to the ground and not quite human. So, he stepped cautiously down the hall. Her bedroom door was closed, and he paused when he didn't hear anything. The bathroom door was open, and noise there caught his attention.

As he peered in, he saw her perfect ass in the air, her head and hands shuffling through whatever was under the sink. Looking away, he scanned the hallway and didn't see or hear anyone else. Whatever had been in the back was likely just the house settling.

With a frown he leaned over and the floorboards beneath his feet squeaked ominously.

Squealing loudly, Tierney flung herself backwards, banging her head on the underside of the sink cabinet. She dropped whatever she'd grabbed and sat back on her butt.

"Tierney!" He leapt forward to help, but she probably didn't need him. What had he done? She simply hadn't heard him knock because she'd been doing something under the sink.

One hand reached up to the back of her head, as the other reached out and slammed the sink cabinet shut, making sure he didn't see whatever she'd held. "Ronan? What are you doing here?"

Was she bleeding?

He leaned over but saw her shoulders sink as her free hand reached out and pushed the cabinet until it clicked closed. It clearly wasn't okay for him to see.

"I'm so sorry." He felt like an idiot. She was probably just getting tampons or whatever out from under the sink. But he'd seen tampon boxes before, and whatever he'd glimpsed didn't look like that. He didn't imagine Tierney being the kind who would be embarrassed about a perfectly normal box of tampons.

What was she hiding?

But he didn't ask. Sitting on her butt, she swiveled around to face him, her hand still holding the back of her head. "Hi. Sorry about that."

"Why are you sorry? Come here." He grabbed her by the hand and lifted her. The bathroom was so small that, when she stood, she was almost pressed full-body against him. Ronan quickly dropped her hand as though it burned.

He hadn't felt anything for some time and now all his feelings returned in sharp relief for the one person he probably shouldn't feel anything for. She was his sister-in-law. She looked like Siorse. No matter what happened, Tierney would think she was a replacement for his dead wife. And, if anything did happen, he told himself the morning after would be too awkward to even contemplate.

He shouldn't be thinking any of this.

"Turn around. Let me see your head." There, that was appropriately brother-in-law-ly.

Reluctantly, she did so. He pushed his fingers through her soft hair telling himself he was just looking to see if she was cut, not touching a woman in any meaningful way for the first time in years.

Her hair was as red as Siorse's but slightly darker. Where her older sister had a riot of bright curls, Tierney had slightly darker waves. He focused on the task at hand. "I don't see anything."

"Good. It's really hard to bandage the back of your head." She turned around to leave, but he'd stupidly not moved, and she bumped right into him.

Shit. The flare that scorched through him made him feel stupid and reminded him he wasn't just her brother-in-law.

He stepped backwards to let her go. Of course, she brushed against him getting out of the small space. Three years! For three years, he'd felt nothing. One year, he'd drunk himself silly, and for two he'd been sober. All the local women were bending over backwards, showing up on his doorstep to bring him casseroles and he felt *nothing*.

Instead, everything he felt was for the one woman he couldn't take advantage of.

"It's in the kitchen," she told him.

"What is?" His brain was in the gutter, and he was really confused.

"Not a casserole!" she laughed. "It's lasagna."

"You made me lasagna?"

"Talia made you lasagna."

"Oh, yum. Why didn't she drop it by herself?" As soon as he asked it, he saw the flare in Tierney's eyes.

"You wanted Talia to drop it off?"

Was she hurt by that? No, that would be stupid. She was probably trying to set him up with her best friend.

"Talia is the only one that I actually *want* to stop by with her food." Again, he saw the shift as Tierney's shoulders stiffened. Whether it was jealousy or a scheme to set him up, he decided to put a stop to it. "Talia is the only one *not* trying to get into my pants. She's smart, she makes good conversation that's not about how big her bathtub is or that she was at the lingerie store the other day. And she makes a damn mean lasagna." He paused.

"I think she just does it because she's nice. Like, she knows what it is to be in the hospital for an unexpected stay."

"That's true." Tierney said as if maybe she hadn't considered it that way before. "Here, let me grab it for you."

She opened the fridge and leaned down, her jeans molding around her backside.

Shit, he thought, *shit, shit, shit.* Maybe he should have let her set him up with Talia. It would be the safer move.

"I've got it." He reached out and took the foil covered pan as soon as she stood up. He needed something to do with his hands. Leading her toward the front door, he realized that was a dumb move. He was full of them today.

As he reached the front door, he stepped back. "Stop."

With his hands full, he had no way to stop her other than to bump right into her. Her soft breasts pressed into him, and he held his breath before blurting out, "You've got another dead rat on your porch. And there's something not right about it."

Just then he heard a low hiss behind him. He almost dropped the lasagna as he whipped around to face whatever was threatening Tierney.

CHAPTER TEN

He was right. *Shit,* Tierney thought.

She was glad Ronan hadn't seen what she was doing under the sink, but she'd been right to check her stash. Every two years she bought a new batch so it didn't expire.

But she had been interrupted before she could see the date. She needed it, expired or not, if she was going to pull the trigger now. Looking at this rat she was right to be thinking about enacting her escape plan.

But Ronan was looking at her oddly, and her escape didn't work if anyone knew what she'd done. She would simply have to disappear.

"Look how pale it is, Tierney. It's practically white. You said the cat's been inside since last night?"

She nodded, agreeing with him.

She and Sean had let Mr. Kittens in when he—she—wailed and pawed at the back door, right around Sean's bedtime, of course. Her son was happy to stay up late to help. Normally Mr. Kittens wanted food and, though they had refilled the little food dish, the cat had ducked inside when they opened the door and disappeared behind the washing machine.

"Did you see that cat?" Tierney asked. Ronan had agreed when she showed him the blanket and cardboard box that she and Sean had set up in the laundry room. "I don't think she could waddle fast enough to catch anything."

Tierney was glad she'd thought this might happen. There was no way Sean was going to let feral kittens stay outside, so she could either bring them in, or find them later. She'd put one of the on-the-skin flea meds on the cat when she was eating earlier in the week. For that, at least, she felt smart. The rest of this, not so much.

"I agree the cat's too fat to have done this. The rat would have gotten away from her." He gestured.

That wasn't the real problem. Tierney took a deep breath. "I got home about an hour ago. It wasn't here then."

She'd brought Talia's lasagna from the bar when Ronan said he'd pick it up. She'd worked a little late today because Sean was at a friend's house after school. She was supposed to go get him in an hour.

Tierney figured she needed to have some things decided by then. But Ronan was still on the rat.

"So it happened within the last hour or so?"

"Mister kittens couldn't have gotten out. We don't have a pet door or anything. Do you think it could be another cat?" She didn't think so, but she wanted to be wrong.

"That's not a wild rat. Nothing that color would survive outside. It has to be a pet store rat. And look at that cut …"

She hated that she agreed. "That's what I thought about the first ones."

"You didn't get any pictures?"

She tipped her head and stared at him as if he were an idiot. "One of them happened when I was already late out the door on the way to your house." *Shit.* She'd told him that day that she was late *because* of the rat. Hopefully he didn't notice her slip. "I only find them when I'm coming or going. It makes me late to have to stop and clean it up. I didn't think to photo document it."

He paused and looked her dead in the eye. "How many have you found, Tierney?"

"This is the fourth."

"Since?"

"The first one was the day Sean and I told you about it at your house." Four in a few weeks. She definitely had a predator. She only hoped it was the four-footed kind.

"That's too many."

She bit her lip to keep from retorting "No, shit Sherlock!" All she managed was a curt nod.

"Let's get pictures of this one though." Ronan pulled out his own phone and began snapping shots from different angles. "I think a person did this. But who?"

Tierney lied and said she didn't know, but she was afraid that she did. Though she turned and looked down the street, she didn't see anyone. It had been ten years. What would he even look like now? If he saw Sean, would he figure out that Sean was his?

Had he found her, or was this just some stupid kids playing a gross prank? Maybe she was overreacting because she had a bad past.

"Do you think it's professional?" she asked, wondering if someone had been hired to torment her. She could believe that one, it sounded right up *his* alley.

Ronan only frowned at her. "Like a rat hitman?"

Okay, that was a dumb question. One she couldn't explain any better than to say she had a case of the stupids. She tried again. "Do you think it's kids?"

"I hope not. It's kind of sick. I can't stomach the idea of kids torturing an animal. That's some serial killer behavior right there."

Lovely. In case she hadn't thought her past was dangerous enough.

Ronan was still going. "I don't like the idea of you being here with this going on."

Well, she didn't either. But ... "I don't have a lot of other options."

She'd done her best to save money. Tierney had always known that one day everything could change, and she might have to flee. So, she'd scraped and saved for it. The bar did well enough that her income covered some savings.

Snafu had been on the brink of death when the Doyles bought it and took over. They knew what they were doing. Despite the fact that the town was small, they turned it into a thriving business. They made it family friendly during the day and *the* place in town to be at night. The firefighters all came in on their off days. The police hung out, too.

The town wasn't big enough for the city workers to have their own bar. Not unless they wanted it to be Addison's and only the hardcore drinkers left Snafu in favor of Addison's.

Her thoughts ran wild. She tried to mentally count how much she'd saved. She thought through what to do with Sean. Again, Ronan wasn't paying attention to her existential crisis.

"Did anything happen at work? Did you date somebody, and they're pissed off?"

She let out a bitter laugh. He had no idea how close to the truth he was, but she turned and once again, gave him the *as if* face. "When have you ever seen me date?"

"Never. But I figured you were probably able to do it even though I hadn't seen it."

"No." She shook her head. "I have a kid and rent to pay." Then she waved her hand around as if to say, *and dead rats to clean off my doorstep.*

"Well, this one's photographed," he announced. "Let's get it disposed of. Do you want me to take it to the vet or anything?"

"I don't think she's open yet and for what? It's a rat and it's dead. It's not like she can save it. Do they do rat autopsies?"

"Probably not." Ronan helped her clean the front step off. This time they put it in a trash bag and he tossed it into the can before climbing into his car with his Talia-made lasagna.

Then he drove away with every hope she'd ever had.

Her heart heavy, Tierney headed back inside, closing the door behind her and hopefully stopping anyone who was watching. In the laundry room, Mr. Kittens meowed pitifully. But Tierney crawled back under the bathroom sink to finish the task that had been interrupted earlier.

Pulling out the box, she flipped it over. *Thank God! Not expired.*

Tapping it against her leg, she tried to decide if she should pull the trigger or not.

CHAPTER ELEVEN

Tierney clutched the steering wheel, her knuckles white with tension. Fighting with her subconscious, she tried to loosen her fingers and hoped that Sean wouldn't notice. But her eyes glanced into the rearview mirror far too often. The road was mostly deserted, still she slowed down and let most every car pass so she couldn't be followed. She was strung far too tight, and Sean was a bright child, he had to have figured out at least part of it.

So far, she thought they weren't being followed. One point in her favor.

The problem was the more she told him, the more dangerous it was for him. And everyone else.

"Are you going to be okay, Mom?"

What a shitty question for a kid to have to ask. He was being far too quiet. His usually boisterous personality had been completely squashed with the tension. Tierney saw no other options, but she wished it hadn't scared him so much. She couldn't just say *yes*, not without lying. She'd promised herself she'd not lie to her child. The last time she'd been in this position, she'd barely survived. She couldn't just toss out a pat "don't worry!"

After Ronan had left her house, she'd checked out her stash, grabbed her bag, and gotten everything ready just in case. Sean wouldn't be pleased if she cut his afternoon with his friend short, so she'd burned some time.

She'd rolled around social media, started dinner prep, then logged in and checked her email again. Though she told herself she was being paranoid checking so often, it also relieved her stress. When nothing new popped up, she could breathe easier for the next several hours.

Not this time.

Another email taunted her from her inbox. Her heart leapt upward, clogging her throat as she wished she hadn't checked. The anxiety was better than this feeling. She could see in the preview that it was from a medical supplement company promising to make her sex life better. It would have been funny except that, when she clicked on it, there was no denying that it was addressed to *Emmie Baby.*

The first *Emily*, and even the *Emmie* email, could have been coincidence. But they'd come so close together—that had been the first sign. She hadn't gotten any mislabeled emails in so long. Not to Jana or Tucker or even for Sean. So, she'd told herself that it was coincidence. Now she told herself, she lived a life that didn't allow for coincidence.

No one would have done that. No one but *him.*

He'd found her.

She grabbed the bag and pulled the burner phone from the bottom drawer of her dresser. Using the number she'd long ago memorized, Tierney made the call she'd always feared making.

The voice on the other end of the line had answered after the third ring, bless her. "Hey, are you checking in?"

"No." That one word was enough to cut deeply. She'd never

wanted to have to do this, but Tierney reminded herself that she was grateful she'd been smart and set this up years ago.

"Oh shit. Are you safe?"

"So far."

She and Raven had met in the maternity ward when she'd had Sean. Raven had given birth to Jacob and asked Tierney about her baby's father. At sixteen, Tierney hadn't been great at evasion. Raven, at twenty, had been through it herself and figured it out really quick. They'd agreed to be each other's backups.

The two young mothers had met face to face only once more, when the babies were two weeks old. They exchanged numbers, and the burner phones they were still using today. They maintained no contact in any way other than random check-ins several times a year to say they were safe and be sure the other was too.

That they didn't have any contact in any traceable capacity was important. It made it much, much harder to be traced if either of them needed a place to stash their child. Their lack of any obvious connection might be Tierney's only saving grace right now.

She breathed deeply and checked the time. She'd picked up Sean and headed straight out of town. At the two-hour mark, she pulled over and ordered a pizza. It was the least she could do given how she was pulling her child up by the roots. She next paid for the motel room in cash, and then they picked up their order.

But they hadn't stayed. All she had done was take the box of hair dye she'd stashed—so there would be no recent record of her purchase—and colored Sean's hair. He'd not dyed it since he'd made it bright blue one summer. That had been for fun, and she tried to make it fun now though she knew in every organ that it was anything but. Tierney changed her child from a towheaded blonde, like his birth father, to a brown-haired imp. It changed the shape of his face and made him look older. She felt like shit that the changes made her relieved.

When the pizza and soda was decimated, and his hair was dry and his clothing changed, they climbed back in the car. There was one more hour to go and way too much to explain.

Tierney glanced over at him, her heart breaking.

Sean rolled his eyes. "Just tell me, Mom."

"Okay. Before you were born, I knew someone who was terrible. He almost killed me, and I think he's back."

What a horribly awful thing to have to say to her child.

"Is he trying to kill you?" Sean didn't seem like he was losing it. Good kid. It just sucked that he had to be.

"He hasn't tried yet." She had to say *yet*. She always promised herself she'd never lie to him. Her parents had lied to her. They said they were trying to protect her—she no longer believed that—but based on what they told her, she'd thought one way and made shitty decisions. She couldn't do that to him.

Sean might only be nine, but if he got stuck somewhere, he needed to know who he could trust and who he couldn't. He would need to make better choices than she had.

"Is this why we had dead rats on our porch? It wasn't Mr. Kittens?"

"I think it wasn't Mr. Kittens," Tierney answered, her grip too tight and her nerves stretched too far.

"Like a warning?"

"I think so." She took a deep breath and told him. "And more. Someone emailed me under my real name."

"What do you mean your real name?" Sean was looking at her now, more with curiosity than fear. That was the only thing keeping her sane.

It was time to come clean. "The email used the name I used to go by before I had you. So, I'm taking you to go live with my friend Raven until it's safe again. Safe for you to come back."

At least, that was Tierney's dream. Raven could take Sean forever if she needed to. That had always been the agreement.

"How long will I be there?"

"I hope not more than a couple of weeks. But it might be several months. And I need you to know that your name is John now."

"John?"

"It's your real name." Tierney saw a sign and switched to a smaller state road. The vice around her heart ratcheted down. This was real. But so was his birth certificate: legally he was John Seamus. She'd always called him Sean, just in case this ever happened. John was a close enough name that he should learn to answer to it very quickly.

She hated this with all her heart. She was tempted to take a different turn and just disappear. She had the paperwork to become someone else. She could find someone to forge documents ... and she could stay with Sean. But how long before she was found again? How long could she live always looking over her shoulder?

She had to tell Sean so much and there were even more things she couldn't tell him. Some because he wouldn't understand. Despite his anxious acceptance of getting torn out of his life, he was still just a kid. Some of it she couldn't tell him because it would make him a target. Because he might inadvertently turn around and make the Doyles a target if he knew and said certain things.

Lights shone heavy in her rearview. The state road wasn't well lit and was now just one lane each way. Was the car behind her trying to blind her? *Shit shit shit.*

Had she made it this far and been so stupid she'd led them almost to Raven? If anyone had followed them this far, they'd done it perfectly invisibly. Using her blinker like a sane person, she turned off at the next small exit and made a loop in the gas station there. The car with the brights on passed above her on the road and went on its way.

It shouldn't be this hard.

It was her only hope that she'd gotten away with this. For Sean's sake, she had to.

Before she knew it, Tierney was pulling into the back parking lot of a restaurant that had closed hours ago. This was where they decided to meet, so even Tierney wouldn't know where Raven lived, where Sean now lived. That way no one could get the information out of her. The deal had always been to pick a meeting point, but have no idea which direction the other had come from. Tierney turned off the engine, making the moment real in a way it hadn't been before.

Another car was sitting in the lot, dark paint concealing it in the shadows.

Holding her breath, Tierney put her hand out and stopped Sean from moving. When the car door opened and Raven stepped out, Tierney breathed again. Then she took in the long camel colored coat that shielded her from the wind. Raven's hair was in thin braids, long and down her back, a touch of color reminded her of the young, about to be single mom in the hospital bed next to her all those years ago.

Tears leaked out of Tierney's eyes as she opened the door and threw herself into her friend's arms. "Thank you! Thank you!"

Taller and willowy and not under her own threat, Raven returned the fierce hug. "I've got you baby girl. And don't thank me. This was always a mutual deal. We've got this."

Raven's car and her clothing spoke of how she'd elevated herself since they'd last talked. Raven seemed to notice. "I'm married, we have three kids now. He adopted Jacob. Sean will be safe with us. He'll be John with us."

Tierney had thought being sixteen and pregnant was

difficult. She thought escaping the first time was difficult. But at 2:13 on a Saturday morning, she handed over her child to a woman she trusted with all of her heart.

Then Tierney drove away.

CHAPTER TWELVE

Ronan sat in his car, wishing for the first time he'd bought a minivan or anything bigger than this little sport car. It was not designed for PI work.

He rubbed his hands together still inside his gloves as though that might work. Looking up the street and then down, he waited through a beat of cold clear silence then started the engine again. He was blessedly relieved as the heat slowly seeped through his clothing and into his feet. It was difficult to be stealthy in the middle of the night in a Nebraska winter. He was simply grateful the snow wasn't piling up as it fell gently all around him.

Still it made his worries much clearer.

The snow was part of what concerned him. Hell, everything concerned him. He'd driven by around nine that night to convince Tierney to get out of the house. There were too many dead rats for his comfort, and she was as twitchy as an addict needing a fix. He'd figured he'd invite her and Sean to stay with him.

There was something about the idea that settled warm and inviting in the pit of his gut. He ignored that part and reminded himself that she was family. Despite the fact that he'd distanced himself from the Doyles after Siorse's death, they'd always been good to him. They'd grieved as hard as he had and yet they'd managed not to drink themselves into a stupor or alienate everyone they should have stayed in touch with. He would be forever grateful.

He told himself that was why he showed up at Tierney's with the intent to invite her and her child to come live with him—at least temporarily.

She wasn't here.

Thinking little of it and reminding himself that it was absolutely fine that she had a life, Ronan hadn't even gotten out of the car. He'd simply circled the block and headed back home. Still, the whole drive back, he thought through every possible reason she wasn't there, or more accurately he overthought it.

Hadn't she said she was picking Sean up at a friend's? Maybe they'd gone out to dinner, but would she really have her nine-year-old out to dinner past nine p.m.? Maybe they'd gone to a movie, or ... Or ...

All the "or"s helped calm him down. Telling himself everything was fine, he'd swung back by at eleven. But she still hadn't been here. Her car was gone, too.

This time, he'd gone up and knocked on the door. Maybe they'd been out and the car had broken down. They would have gotten a tow and a ride home. She hadn't called him, but he reminded himself that she'd spent the last month helping him. She wouldn't necessarily look at him as her help. He needed to change that.

Again, he told himself a lie that made it more palatable. *He owed her.* She'd helped him and he was returning the favor. He didn't try to consider that it wasn't working, and that he'd come back again and again, pulled by some invisible need to take care of her.

He had no job right now. It would be two more weeks before

his next check-up and his first possible chance to be back on duty. He could at least be useful. She hadn't answered the door though. And this time—though he'd reluctantly driven himself back home—he'd been more worried.

So worried, in fact, that he'd turned around and come back in an hour.

If anyone was watching him, they'd know he was a bona fide nutcase, driving back and forth the short distance, checking on the same house each time then leaving.

By then, the snow had begun falling. The driveway showed no evidence of tire tracks, letting him know she hadn't been here at all. This time, he'd not gone back. Now he was sitting and waiting. Maybe he'd find her. Maybe he'd find whoever was leaving the dead rats and he could bring this nonsense to an end.

That thought alone compelled him to stay where he was, even though it wasn't a bright decision.

He hadn't been smart. If he'd prepared for this, he would have a thermos of coffee and a blanket. He dressed warmly enough, he thought, but now he was barely keeping from freezing as he sat here with his eyes on her front door.

One of his concerns was that he wasn't the only one keeping an eye on Tierney. The rats were evidence enough. So he'd parked several houses down under an overhanging tree. Turning off all the running lights, he hoped he wouldn't be seen, but there was nothing he could do about the engine running except freeze to death, and that would serve no one.

Now, the time hung close to five a.m. He looked up into the dark sky. Whatever the answers were, they couldn't be good. Should he call the police? And tell them what? That he was her second stalker?

Movement caught his eye and his gaze snapped to a house about five down from hers. The soft light made the man easy to see against the pitch black night. Between the clouds dropping soft flakes around him and the disturbingly late sunrise of winter down the street, movement was easy to spot.

Ronan watched as the man stepped out his front door. He reached over and flipped on the porch light, illuminating his tracks in the snow as he headed to the car. Peeling the thermal blanket from the engine, he ducked into the driver's seat, started the car and stomped his way back inside. A few moments later, the man retraced his steps, got into the car, and probably headed to some early job, maybe into Lincoln.

Rubbing his hands together again, Ronan stomped his feet as best he could under the low dash. This car was not made for stealth or comfort. He sighed and considered turning the car off again now that people were out and maybe looking, but the cold was getting to him.

After sitting for a few more minutes, and watching the time tick over, he put the car into drive and pulled away. It was 5:07. The drive thru at the nearest fast food would be open and he could get a hot coffee. He needed it.

A short while later he was back. On the short drive, he'd drunk half the coffee and eaten one of the breakfast sandwiches. As he pulled back into the same spot—if only to cover the empty space he'd left in the snow—Ronan reached into the bag to grab the second one.

As his cold fingers closed around the hot food, he saw her car pull into her driveway.

Stunned, he watched as Tierney climbed out.

The clock on his dash read 5:27am.

Where had she been all night? What was she even doing?

She headed to the front door, but then turned around, obviously changing her mind. At the side of the house, he watched as she pulled something out of the bushes, but it made more sense when she opened it up and tossed the thermal blanket over the hood of the car. This time when she hit the front door, she jammed the key angrily into the lock and opened it.

Ronan was starting to open his own door before he even realized he was following her.

Tierney was here. She was awake. *But where was Sean?*

Ronan pulled his own car door shut against the snow and jammed the car into drive. He slid into her driveway in his normal spot right behind her car. He meant to block her in. He needed answers.

He was up the front steps, his hand on the knob, twisting before he realized that he was angrily forcing his way into someone else's home. The knob was locked and, from the rattle the door gave, she'd slid the bolt, too. He didn't know if she normally did that. Why didn't he know that?

Instead, he knocked and called out a little too angrily, "Tierney!"

Only then did he realize her neighbors on either side might not be awake yet, and him causing a scene probably wasn't what she needed. He was pulling out his phone to call her to tell her to come open the door when she did.

There'd been no dead rat on the doorstep this time.

He was opening his mouth to … what? Yell at her? But he saw Tierney's eyes flick to something over his shoulder. She grabbed his coat and yanked him inside. He was still stumbling to get his feet under him as she slammed the door shut behind her. She cranked the locks with a harsh move and threw both the bolts before turning back to face him.

She stood arms down at her side, feet shoulder width apart, but there was nothing casual or relaxed about her stance. "What are you doing here?"

He asked the opposite question. "Where were you all night?"

"Why were you watching me?"

That one, at least he had an answer for. "I told you I didn't think it was safe to stay here. So when you wouldn't come stay with me, I came to check on you."

"All night long?"

He wanted to answer "Obviously!" but it seemed a little too stalkerish right now.

"Where's Sean?" He changed the subject, his eyes darting toward the back of the house, wondering if Sean had been here, asleep in his room the whole time.

He didn't think Tierney was that kind of mother, but her next words shocked him.

"He's somewhere safe. Somewhere you'll never find him."

CHAPTER THIRTEEN

Tierney sniffled. She had to look like shit. She needed a tissue or twelve.

She'd cried most of the three hour drive back. Covering the distance without stopping had been the only thing keeping her half sane, though it had been tempting to lay over at the motel she'd already rented. If she stopped, she could catch some sleep. But Tierney knew she would never sleep in a strange place, with Sean now gone. She still needed to get up and be at the bar at eleven.

It wasn't safe for her to not show up, for her to step out of routine. Maybe it was safer to disappear herself. But there was "safer for Sean," "safer for her," and "safer for everyone around them." All three were radically different choices, and she couldn't make it all happen at the same time. That's what had her worried.

If she disappeared, what would happen to mom and dad Doyle? What would happen to Ronan? Ronan, who was standing there, looking at her like she was the worst mother ever. Like she was a liar and a thief. When the fact was, she was only one of them.

"I have to get to sleep. I have to be at work at eleven."

"What?" Ronan was clearly confused, and she wasn't helping. But he asked, "You put Sean where I'll never find him?"

Tierney shook her head. "I meant that he's somewhere safe. No one will find him."

She was struggling to stay awake, to stay sane, to be so near to this man and not fall into his arms and tell him everything. But then he'd be at risk, too. She needed to get rid of him, and fast.

Ronan was looking beyond her, toward the back of the house, then into the living room. He saw the laptop she'd left on the table in the scramble to get her child somewhere where he couldn't be touched.

Leaving it out had been stupid. Then again, there were no good choices right now. When he looked back at her, the concern on his face had doubled down.

"There's more to this than just the dead rat, isn't there?"

She couldn't help it. She snorted at him. His underestimation of the situation was hysterical. If only he knew. "Of course, there is. I'm not going batshit about a dead rat."

Hopefully, she'd made it clear she wasn't going to tell him everything. Then again, her head was spinning and she wanted to curl up and cry herself to sleep ... with her largest knife tucked under her pillow.

"So you moved Sean, but you're going to show up for work?"

She sniffled again. It was hard to breathe. Her eyes were still watering. She wasn't making any sense but she didn't have the energy to do better. It was five thirty in the morning and she hadn't slept but she had given her child away.

Tierney threw her hands up in the air and shook her head, as if to say she didn't know anything. So that's what she told him. "I think it's the safest option."

He took a visible deep breath. "It concerns me that you're

talking about things in terms of who's safe and not being able to be found."

"Well, it concerns me, too!" Her sarcasm dripped though she didn't mean to. He needed to leave so she didn't say anything mean. With one hand Tierney motioned him away. "Please. I need to get some sleep. I'm going to show up at work today."

Ronan didn't say anything, but he didn't move either. He just stood there staring at her until she figured maybe she would be the one who would have to move. Maybe she should just go and climb into her bed and then he'd leave. But that wouldn't work. She needed to check all the window locks again—make sure no one had been here while she was gone. Maybe the snow would help her see tracks? She could only hope. She'd also have to bolt the door behind him when he disappeared.

When he finally got the hint, or just stared at her long enough to figure out she was truly incoherent, he asked, "How well are you going to sleep here?"

This time she practically guffawed. Obviously, she wasn't going to sleep much at all. Everything was chaos. She'd just enacted an endgame plan she'd hoped she'd never have to use. But today she was going to go prep burgers and serve tea and rum and pretend everything was just peachy fine.

She wanted to say this was not the life she'd chosen. However, in a twisted way, it was exactly the life she'd chosen. She'd been young and stupid and honestly, there was a path that had been much much worse. She'd seen it.

"Ronan, I can't right now. Please, just leave this for later." She was breaking down. She could feel it.

"Come stay at my place."

She almost couldn't process the words.

"You'll be able to sleep better. Someone else will be in the house I'll stay awake and keep an eye out."

His words melted over her like butter. The thought of someone watching out for her even for just a few hours was so, so tempting. But she'd been tempted before and look where it had gotten her.

"More importantly, you won't be here." He pointed at the floor, still building his case. "Whoever left those dead rats expects you to be here. Maybe it'll be better if you aren't."

She'd passed running on fumes hours ago. As much as she wanted to take him up on his glorious offer, Tierney shook her head. "It would make you a target, too."

The problem with her mistakes was that she hadn't just brought this upon herself, she'd brought it to everyone who'd done the wonderful work of keeping her and Sean safe and happy for so long.

He launched into an immediate rebuttal "I can handle being a target, Tierney—"

Slashing the air with her hand, she cut him off. "You're not even fit enough to go back to work! How can you defend me from—" she didn't say what it was.

She didn't need to. She saw his face. He would have looked less stunned and less hurt if she'd actually hauled back and slapped him across the cheek.

"I'm sorry," she whispered. This time the tears did come.

His lips pressed together, his broad shoulders stiffening at the insult she'd heaped on the man who'd watched her at five in the morning to be sure she was safe. "You're right. I'm not quite up to speed to go back to my very physically demanding job. But I'm sure as fuck better than you staying here alone, Tee!"

His voice was demanding, his shoulders taking up her entire field of vision. He was leaning in, towering over her, mad. Whether he was mad that she'd insulted him or refused him, she wasn't sure. But she was in no shape to deal with an angry Ronan right now.

Swallowing back the sob that forced its way up, she only managed to get out a small, weak protest. "I can't."

She meant I can't accept your help. Or maybe I can't put you in danger. Even I can't explain. But Ronan didn't read it that way.

"Then let me," he said gently, "because I can."

It was too much. Sparkles and darkness closed in at the edge of her vision. She felt as if she developed a fever in the last few seconds and the world started to sway. The last thing she felt as she passed out was his arms closing around her.

CHAPTER FOURTEEN

"Tierney?" Ronan moved forward, slowly lifting his still sleeping body from the large armchair in the corner of the bedroom. He moved toward where Tierney was nearly strangled by the covers but had finally stopped tossing and turning.

He'd expected to sleep in his own bed, instead he'd spent the better part of a long morning in the chair Siorse had put here. Not that she sat in it ever. She'd simply decided the room needed it for decor, though mostly she'd thrown her clothes over it.

Ronan, whom she teased for being a firefighter both on the job and off, was absolutely a "place for everything and everything in its place" guy. With Siorse gone, nothing had graced the chair in quite some time. Only now was he grateful that he hadn't moved the ridiculous thing out of the way. It had given him a place to sleep close enough to Tierney that she didn't cry out.

Not that she'd said anything useful. No, she just woke him periodically with her incoherent babbling. He'd needed the sleep as much as Tierney had. But it was ten a.m. So he said her name again. "Tierney."

"What?" She sounded as though everything from the night before had simply disappeared from her memory.

"You said you needed to go to work."

Work must have been the magic word. It was clearly difficult to untangle herself from the covers, but she slung her legs over the side of the bed and stood up. Though she almost toppled over, her sock-covered feet landed on the boots he'd unlaced and left bedside for her last night.

When she'd passed out in his arms, he'd gone directly into EMT mode. In a few moments though, it became clear it wasn't a medical emergency but just fear and exhaustion, and probably running on adrenaline for too long.

Sure enough, she'd come around enough that he'd felt more comfortable not rushing her to the ER, but not comfortable enough to tuck her in and leave her alone. It seemed to be enough to convince her of the same and she'd finally agreed to stay with him.

She hadn't been in any shape to pack up or make plans. So he'd walked her out to the car and helped her in, cursing the stitch in his side from having scooped her up when she fell. He didn't need her to remind him that he wasn't immortal.

So here he was, with his sister-in-law stomping around the room as the sheet tried to follow her away from the bed. She brushed her hand at it frantically, trying to release herself for good. She'd wound it fifteen different directions around her the night before.

With the covers finally banished, one hand went into her hair while her feet were shoved into her boots. "I—"

She looked around quickly, and Ronan could tell the sleep had done her good. She was here. She was sharp now.

"I—" at last she looked up at him and he could almost see all her memories from the night before flooding her. Tierney looked up at him and shook her head. "I don't know. Maybe I pulled the trigger too soon."

"But he's safe? From whatever this is?" Ronan asked

Tierney nodded once, sharp and clear.

"Are you going to tell me what's going on?"

"I don't know."

That was at least better than he'd gotten last time, so he let it stand. Whatever this was, it had to be bad. Though there was nothing he could think of in Tierney's life that would even begin to warrant anything like this. The Doyles had shown up in Redemption when Tierney was a sophomore, and Siorse a senior. Ronan had been a senior and more than ready to get out of town. But, one look at the Doyle girls, and he knew that was going to be the end of him.

Siorse had made a play for him. Tierney had kept to herself. It became apparent relatively quickly that Tierney was about to become a mother.

For him, everything had proceeded naturally onward. He'd dated Siorse and they left for school together. Tierney—who could have gone on to college on a scholarship—had decided to simply stay in Redemption. She helped at the family bar. She ran Sean's life. She eventually rented a small house and probably lived relatively close to hand to mouth.

She could have gone further and done much more. Though she'd often expressed a desire to go to medical school, and he knew she occasionally took online courses in biology and chemistry, this was the life she'd chosen. And somehow, he'd missed something huge.

Standing in front of him now, Tierney looked up, her green eyes meeting his. "Did I drive here?"

"I brought you."

"But I have to—"

He waved his hand to cut her off. Maybe he shouldn't have done it. Maybe it was egotistical or simply stupid to think he knew what she wanted. Still he tried. "We need to get you home so you can shower and change."

She nodded.

"And then I need to get you to work."

"Well, I'll—"

"Please." He stopped her again. "Whatever this is, it's big. Let me at least drive you in."

She took a moment to let the words and the offer soak in. He had to admit he appreciated that. She gave him only a slow nod, but then waved her hand toward the bedroom door. "I'm ready to go now."

Of course, she was. He needed a few minutes. "I'll be quick."

He shooed her out of his own room so he could change clothing then brushed his teeth faster than should have been possible. He skipped at least three steps but took a moment to wash down the antibiotic he despised. He was so close to finished, but he'd missed last night.

In a few minutes, they were both in the sports car heading back across town toward Tierney's house. The one that didn't have Sean in it.

They pulled into the driveway behind Tierney's car, now covered in an extra inch of snow. The snow had stopped falling hours ago, he'd noticed. It wasn't heavy enough to keep anyone off of the roads or out of work, but it was enough that as Tierney came around the car he put his arm out to stop her.

His hand, gloved and warm, lay flat against the front of her puffy coat, and for a moment, he thought even that padded contact was too much for him.

"Tierney, look!" There were fresh footprints in the snow leading up to her front door.

"Someone just came and knocked," she said.

Ronan turned and gave her a look that told her either she shouldn't be stupid or she shouldn't think that he was going to be. "They don't even go up the bottom step. The person didn't get to your door to knock. And your car is here. Someone would have thought you were home."

"Shit." She whispered it on an exhausted sigh, making him wonder what else was going on that having someone sneak around her home didn't seem to elicit anything else.

Tierney turned a full one-eighty, scanning the street and looking for ... something.

"Should we go around back?" he asked.

She shook her head. "Just take some pictures, I guess. I don't think there's anything we can do. It's not a crime scene."

Not that they thought ... not yet anyway.

She let him snap a few shots with his phone and, in her haste, she walked right up the steps, messing up the footprints. As though, by walking over them, she could actually make the whole offense disappear. Putting her key in the lock, she headed inside, and Ronan stuck close behind her. But he didn't see anything out of place.

If Tierney did, she didn't let on.

She disappeared and emerged a few moments later in a long-sleeved thermal shirt, layered by the polo with the Snafu bar logo on it. Her jeans hugged her like a second skin. She held her hands out at her sides, as if for inspection. "I'm ready."

Ronan didn't move. He just asked again. "Are you going to tell me what's going on?"

CHAPTER FIFTEEN

"Hi Mom!" Tierney pushed through the back door, trying to sound cheerful as she called out. She wanted Mom Doyle to know it wasn't just her.

"Hey, baby," her mother called back, her voice coming from the front of the restaurant. She sounded like she was in motion.

Aileen didn't know what was coming, but Tierney was about to ruin her day.

"Ronan is with me," she called again as she hung her coat on the dark wood stand by the back door.

Ronan did the same, including calling out, "Hi mom!"

"Hey!"

Tierney could hear the change in her voice. The woman had stopped whatever she was doing and her new action was coming to greet her former son-in-law. One who usually didn't show up at the bar unannounced or come in through the back door.

When Siorse had graduated high school, she'd gone to the University of Nebraska and gotten herself an economics degree. She'd helped with the budget for the bar and more, but she hadn't really worked here since she'd been eighteen. Ronan had been only a casual visitor to the place all along. That didn't matter to her mom, though.

The woman stepped forward, looping her arms around Ronan's neck, and giving him a sincere hug. She'd missed him. It flashed into Tierney's mind right then, just how far away her desire for Ronan had to be stashed. If anything were to happen between them—and she knew it couldn't—what would that do to mom and dad Doyle? How would they feel having Tierney usurp their real daughter's husband?

"What are you doing here?" Mom looked up at Ronan, not suspecting anything.

"I brought Tierney in," he answered it with the kind of tone that didn't alert anyone, but Tierney could read that he was aiming to get more information.

His sudden interest in being chauffeur elicited some glances as Mom Doyle tried to figure out what was going on. The easiest thing was to simply rip off the band aid.

"Mom." Tierney stood still, her hands at her side. "I pulled the trigger."

Mom Doyle's eyes flew wide. "What?" She took a moment to get herself together. Then she sucked in a breath and asked, "It was more than what you told me?"

Her mom's eyes flicked quickly to Ronan as if to ask, *what does he know?*

Tierney realized then that she hadn't told either of them the whole story. No matter what she wanted, everything was about to come out. The only question was, to whom?

Her mother quickly got herself together and looked at Tierney. "So, he's safe?"

Tierney knew her mom was putting all the pieces together. She knew what it meant that Tierney had "pulled the trigger." "He is but I don't know what to do about the rest of you."

Mom Doyle surprised the shit out of her. Stepping forward, she wrapped Tierney in a fierce hug. "Sean is safe. That's what matters right now. It's just me and your dad and you don't worry about us."

Aileen always referred to them that way—just Mom and Dad. No hesitancy. No casual reduction of their relationship. Now, she doubled down. "We knew this might happen. We knew what we were signing up for."

She put her hands on Tierney's shoulders and held her tight, her stare fierce.

Tierney's own parents hadn't been willing to sign up for that and the tears sprang into her eyes. She'd not really expected this and maybe she'd been stupid not to.

Mom shook her slightly, "We're ready. Tell me everything. Wait, no— Let's get your father , too."

Tierney shook her head no. Ronan was still here.

She made a motion backward toward him. "Everyone who knows will be in danger. I came into work to keep up the appearance of normal, because I didn't want to alert anyone to what I did in the middle of the night last night." She took a deep breath. Even though she was relieved to have Sean safe, it hurt so much to have him so far away. "We just say that Sean got an offer to travel with a friend. So he took it. It came up suddenly."

"Smart," mom said, "Believable." But she grabbed Tierney's hand and pulled her toward the bar. Ronan trailed behind. Pushing Tierney onto a stool, she quickly walked around behind the bar and served her up a lemonade.

That's what she'd served Tierney when she was sixteen and pregnant. Somehow, it had always stuck as her solution when something came up.

Tierney took a sip. It tasted like trouble and support and family. Not for the first time, she understood that the Doyles had been a better family to her than her own.

"How were you and my mom such good friends?" she asked. But only after she asked it, did she realize that Ronan had settled himself into the seat beside her, and she'd just tipped her hand and revealed one of her major cards.

His head had snapped back with surprise. *Nope, it hadn't casually sailed by him.*

Mom Doyle stayed planted on the other side of the bar, and asked him, "What do you want to drink?"

"Whatever it is, it needs rum in it."

He'd not been ready for that one, had he?

Mom stayed in motion, mixing him a rum and a lot of coke. It was, after all, 10:45 in the morning. She set it in front of Ronan and continued talking while her hands kept moving.

It took a moment for Tierney to realize the woman was making herself a Seven and Seven. She pushed her own glass forward and it didn't take long for her mom to catch the hint. She pulled their best vodka off the shelf and topped up Tierney's lemonade.

"I think," Aileen said as she went back to mixing her own drink, "I think you tell everybody. I think you gather everyone you trust, and you tell them everything. If you don't have secrets, there isn't much leverage." She took a long drink from the glass as if to fortify herself.

Tierney did the same. "Someone will spill the beans though. We made it this far by telling no one anything."

She could see Ronan following the conversation like a tennis match. He had no say in it but he wasn't going to lose sight of the ball. When he wasn't getting answers, he chugged the glass, and set it on the counter before too-casually sliding it over to her mom.

With only a glance, he convinced Aileen to refill it.

Her hands worked quickly, then she pushed the glass back toward him, brimming with another rum and coke. But she looked pointedly at Tierney. "Then tell him. He's about to figure it out, anyway."

Tierney hadn't even agreed, and Mom was off on another

tangent. The woman could organize anything. "I'm calling your dad and we're going to have ourselves a family meeting and figure this out."

Ronan gulped the second glass down then smacked the glass onto the bar top.

Tierney wasn't ready to agree. "We have to get the bar ready. We have to open."

"Well, shit." Mom looked out the front, somehow seeming to have forgotten everything that was normal swirling around her right now. "Well then, I'm calling your dad. He'll be here in fifteen minutes. You two help me get the bar ready and then you —" she stared hard at Tierney, "—You go tell Ronan everything. Once we get the regulars in to cover the shift, then we'll have our family meeting."

"I might just leave. I don't like you being in danger." Tierney reached out lacing her fingers into the warm grip of the woman who'd loved her maybe more than anyone else ever had.

"It doesn't matter." Mom squeezed her hand back but then let go to finish lowering the chairs to the freshly mopped floor. She rubbed down the table surfaces she'd exposed, but she spoke backwards over her shoulder. "If you had enough information to do what you did then the danger is already here. They already know about your dad and me. They already know about Ronan."

Tierney gulped. Mom was right. It was too late. She'd put everyone in danger just by being here. Her only consolation was that she was the one he wanted.

Mom Doyle didn't have time for Tierney's guilt. "There was never any way you could have protected us. And it isn't your fault."

But it was, Tierney thought. *It was all her fault.*

Ronan was looking at her. Like he'd figured that out, too.

CHAPTER SIXTEEN

"**M**y real name is Emily Gallagher."

Tierney sat in front of him and delivered the shock of his life with all sincerity. Her fingers laced together, her eyes were cast down but then she looked up at him quickly. "You can't repeat any of this to anyone."

He nodded, as though he were agreeing, but not having heard the whole story there was no way to know what he was agreeing to. What he did know was that there was a fierce, sharp knot in the middle of his chest telling him that he'd almost definitely be keeping her secret because he would do anything to protect Tierney Doyle.

But the woman sitting in front of him apparently wasn't Tierney Doyle.

She swallowed audibly and started again. "My mother—my birth mother—and Aileen Doyle met back in college. They'd been roommates their freshman year, and they mildly stayed in touch through social media."

So, Tierney had come to stay with the Doyles when she'd gotten pregnant, as if it were some kind of family secret. But what family worried about a pregnant teenager these days? He wanted to ask all the questions swirling in his head, but so far, the name change didn't make any sense. He knew he wasn't holding all the cards ... yet. It was difficult to keep his mouth shut and wait for her to get the story out. But he tried.

"My mom came from a nice middle-class family but then she married my dad, Adam Gallagher, and dad started his own company and made a mint. Mom began to work the charity circuit. By the time I was five ... it was a lonely only child."

Ronan was still trying to wrap his head around it. If he was following correctly, then she and Siorse weren't actually sisters. Maybe they were of no relation at all. He was struggling to hold all the pieces to keep the balls juggling and moving smoothly in the air. But Tierney wasn't done throwing little bombs at his feet.

"By the time I was fourteen, I was already treated as my mother's showpiece. And expected to play assistant to her charity work, despite being in a difficult private school and prepping for college. Elliot Vander clef took a shine to me."

Interesting term, Ronan thought.

"Elliot was twenty."

Oh, hell no. His mouth did not stay shut this time. "That's not dating. You know that, right?"

She tipped her head one way or another. "Yeah, I see that now. But at the time, I was fourteen. I thought I was an adult. I was treated like one in a lot of ways, and I was lonely. This very, very wealthy, very well-connected man told me that I was beautiful and that I was mature for my age."

"You are beautiful." The words were out before he thought about what he was admitting, and that he'd left the insult hanging.

Ouch.

Ronan had seen that situation more than once just doing

house calls. Girls needed to understand that there was basically no such thing as dating up. Girls—actual minor females—couldn't consent to these things. He knew the stats on teen pregnancy, that well over half of pregnancies in girls under seventeen were fathered by men over twenty. It wasn't love.

Tierney—*Emily* he corrected himself in his thoughts—seemed to realize that now at least.

"He swept me off my feet. Dressed me up and took me to lavish parties. He introduced me to everyone as his beautiful and amazing girlfriend—"

"And no one noticed you were a kid?" He was stunned when she shook her head no.

"No one asked. Then he started saying he was going to marry me."

Ronan tried not to let the internal cringe show in his expression. His insides were knotted. Tierney—*Emily!*—had arrived in Redemption at sixteen, already pregnant, and he believed he was starting to put the story together.

"What people didn't know, and what I didn't acknowledge, was that Elliot very quickly became very abusive."

So, he wasn't just dating an underage girl, he was abusive to her too? It did seem to make the final pieces snap into place. The hasty exit, the name change, all of it.

Tierney was still talking. "At first, it was little things. He'd berate me, tell me I didn't remember correctly. Then he threatened to hit me. He didn't hit me ... not at first."

"That's verbal abuse and gaslighting," Ronan told her. The station did training on this. The police weren't the only ones who wound up dealing with domestic violence calls.

"I didn't even know at the time those things had names, or that they were things. I thought they were just Elliot. And I didn't think it was anything other than me just being stupid. I mean, I was young. Everything he said made sense. He was much older, he knew more, and was very clearly in charge. I was along for the ride. At first, much of the ride was amazing and beautiful. He told me wonderful things and he shone this intense attention on me."

She'd needed it, Ronan thought. The story had started with her parents neglecting her. No wonder she'd fallen for it.

"I did try to leave." She looked up at him when she said that. It was important to her that he understand that she figured it out on her own and she'd done her best. Then her breathing grew ragged and her eyes darted away. "He didn't want me to leave. That's when he became physically abusive. I got bruises where no one would see. I had to change a gala dress at the last moment to hide the handprints he left on my arm."

Even now, she didn't say that this Elliot asshole had *done* it to her. She said it as though it was a thing that happened.

"The other problem was his father—Alder Vander clef."

Why did Ronan think he knew that name?

"Alder is richer than God and thinks his son is perfect. Elliot can do no wrong. So when I left him, both Alder and Elliot *persuaded* me to come back." She'd used air quotes around persuaded.

Ronan had thought his stomach couldn't sink more with the telling of this story. But there it went.

"I left more than once. They would hire PIs to trail me. Men threatened me if I tried to date anyone else. My date would get harassed—"

"For one date? Not a new boyfriend?" Some of the puzzle pieces were fitting together, but others virtually unimaginable.

"He was possessive. So yes, one date, and this guy would get a brick through his window. One guy was shot at in a seemingly random drive by. One guy was in a car accident that he didn't think was coincidental." She paused as though there were something else she wasn't telling, then she sucked in a breath. "It was made very clear to me that, for my safety and the safety of those around me, I needed to be with Elliot."

"What did you do?" The words came out in a whisper, and Ronan knew he didn't want to know.

CHAPTER SEVENTEEN

Tierney hated this part worst of all. It was bad enough that the story detailed just how stupid and naive she had been. She'd forgiven herself years ago, because she was young and ultimately all she'd been through had brought her Sean. She loved Sean with everything she had, but it had cost her everything else.

There was no medical school like she'd always dreamed, because Tierney Doyle's records weren't legal. It was part of the reason she continued to work at the pub, where she could be charted as a family member and no one would worry that her social security number didn't quite match up with her story.

She didn't tell that to Ronan. It would just incriminate the Doyles and she couldn't stand to do that. But this part, this part was worse. There was no excuse like she was young or dumb. It simply made it clear that she hadn't been of any value to her own family and that was still a hard thing to bear.

"The fifth time I left—"

"Wait, you dated him and left him multiple times? During which you dated other people? Before you were sixteen?" Ronan was scrambling. She let him get all his questions out. "Wait. Were you actually sixteen when you arrived here?"

At last, he paused and she shook her head *no* in response. "But ..." she didn't want to tell him about her stolen and forged paperwork. "I had been in a private school. I was supposed to be a freshman, but my entry test here moved me into tenth grade. We took it because it would help hide me better."

"It helped hide you," he repeated his eyes looking into the distance. She could tell he was starting to get a full picture. If he was going to have it, because surely Elliot was here, or at least someone connected with Elliot was sending information back, that meant Ronan needed the full picture to stay safe.

There was no way around confessing the thing that made her most ashamed. She took a deep breath and tried again. "So, the fifth time I left him, he threatened my mom. My Dad brought me into his office and sat me down ..."

The tickle started at the back of her throat, the pressure pushed at the back of her eyes. All her stupid fantasies about Ronan—imagining that she was the sister who wasn't the refugee from upstate New York, that she was the sister who wasn't pregnant, that she was the one that Ronan had loved and wanted from the very start—fled like dandelion tufts on the wind. There was no way to sustain a fantasy like that once he knew the truth.

"They sat me down and told me to go back to Elliot."

"What?" Ronan almost flew out of his chair. The small back office at the bar couldn't contain his reaction.

"Be quiet!" she motioned. She couldn't blame him for being stunned. How awful was she that her parents didn't trust her or even listen. That they thought so little of her as to send her back to some other man just because he wanted her. Siorse had been awful sometimes. She'd lied to her parents, cheated on her tests, cheated on ...

Tierney couldn't even bear to think it.

But the Doyles had always treated Siorse with more respect than her own parents had treated her.

"At the time it was the easier option."

"To throw their child to a monster?"

Why did she defend them? But she did. "They didn't think he was, and Dad didn't want my mom threatened. Honestly, if I was making most of it up—"

"You had bruises!"

"Yes, but hadn't I just gotten them being klutzy or—?"

"Are you shitting me?"

It felt good that he was outraged on her behalf, but it didn't erase the shame that her own family thought so little of her as to barter her away so easily. She shook her head—she'd lived through all of it.

With a deep breath in, he tried to put her back on her story. "How did you get away?"

"I didn't. I gave up and went back. I did what I was told but ... I got pregnant. That's when I tried to go back and explain again to my parents what was happening. They didn't want to have anything to do with it. But I'd brought a gun I took from one of Elliot's friends, and when they said I had to go back, I pulled it out and threatened them."

She'd probably waved it around the room like a madman. She'd been so distraught. It wasn't her steely resolve that had convinced her parents to do the right thing, it had been fear that she'd just randomly pull the trigger and kill one of them. Either way, it had worked at the time.

"I held them at gunpoint." Not her finest moment, she knew. "I told them I was leaving, and they could help me fake my death or I could kill them and use it as cover to fake it myself."

Even as she said it, she felt her eyes dart to the floor. She couldn't look up and see what he thought of her. The whole scene would have been comical if it weren't so terrifying that she'd actually done it.

"I said that I would kill them and make it look like I was kidnapped. I kind of hoped the world would blame Elliot for it. But the problem is: No one blames Elliot for anything. His father buys his way out of everything he does. He gets pulled over for DUIs all the time. He shot his friend while they were hunting, but that got brushed off, too. He doesn't have a single mark on his record. Alder cleans all of it up for him."

Ronan's eyes grew wider as she spoke. She whispered, "They have enough money to make it all disappear."

"So, *you* disappeared."

Tierney only nodded. "My mom did not like me pointing a gun at her, certainly not while she was wearing a Dior from the charity event she'd been at that night."

Ronan's eyebrows climbed further. But there wasn't much she could do about where she had come from. It had taken her parents several hours of her holding them at gunpoint, several hours of debating and planning to get rid of her safely. Tierney had done it because there'd been a baby to think about, a baby who absolutely could not ever be exposed to Elliot. She'd had to get away before she showed or he figured it out. He had to never know about Sean.

"My mom checked her social media for friends she trusted but didn't contact. And she called Aileen. The link between the two of them was tenuous. I made her use a burner phone— Elliot or Alder would have tracked my family's phone records. The women worked together and set up this drop in the middle of the night. Looking back, I'll bet Aileen figured out most of it."

Ronan was leaning forward, but this time he had no outbursts. He was waiting. So she told him.

"They gave the maid a bin of laundry with me inside of it. I had only the clothes I was wearing. If I took anything, phone, ID, identifying jacket even, it might be recognized as mine. The maid wheeled me out to the van for the 'new' laundry service. Honestly, she had to suspect something. That had to have been the heaviest laundry she'd ever dealt with. My mom had hired a driver, too, so no one ever saw her and Aileen together. The driver drove me twenty minutes out of town, at which point he traded the laundry basket to Aileen and left."

It had been a harrowing night. She'd been certain that Elliot would show up at any moment and kill her or, worse, force her to go back with him.

She paused then, thinking through it. Ronan knew everything now. No, not everything, but everything important.

"So the Doyles settled you in as their younger daughter?"

"They were amazing." She smiled as she said it. Disappearing had been a last-ditch effort, but it had changed everything. The Doyles had not only given her a safe home, they'd loved her in a way she'd been needing all her life. "They were moving anyway. It was the perfect timing. We all came here as a family and they've been wonderful to me and to Sean."

Her voice cracked on the last sentence. Mom Doyle had said to her more than once in the past several years that taking in Tierney had been the best thing they'd ever done. If they hadn't, when Siorse had died, they would have had no daughters and no grandchildren left to love. Having seen all the devastation when Siorse died, Tierney had been glad to be here for them. She'd missed her sister, too, despite all the secrets between them.

She didn't say any of that now, not to the man who'd married Siorse. Not to the man she still wanted. Not to the man who still didn't know everything.

"I'm sorry," she said, and sniffled. She needed to stop whining over her own shitty circumstances, ones that she herself was responsible for. And Ronan wasn't. "I have all of you messed up in this, too, now. Elliot's found me. I don't know if he's here or if he's hired someone to do this and report back. But he obviously knows where I am. Which means he knows about you."

She was crying as she said the last part, hating that she'd done this to him. He'd been so kind to her for a decade, in fact, that she'd harbored fantasies about him the whole time.

"I'll be fine." He said it with a hard stop, as if trying to reassure her.

As he shook his head to ward off any concern she had, his hand moved up to his side, grabbing at his torso. Maybe he didn't even realize he'd done it. But she guessed he'd been sitting too still, too tense, and he'd twitched something from his healing injury from his accident.

If Elliot found Ronan, he wasn't going to be fine.

CHAPTER EIGHTEEN

Ronan fidgeted like it was going out of style. With everything Tierney had told him, he'd not been surprised by the fierce and overwhelming need to defend her.

He'd been ready to pick up arms or, hell, maybe a good high-pressure firehose. People didn't know the damage those could do. Keeping her and Sean safe was the only thing that mattered to him right now. Though Tierney being Tierney, she'd already taken care of Sean. She'd done the same thing her family had done for her: ported her child off with a loose connection that should be untraceable.

Still, despite his zeal, there was nothing he could do.

Tierney had set him free for the afternoon. She'd caught him up to speed and there wasn't much more to say until her parents were able to get away and they could make a game plan. They had to keep the bar appearing normal. Ronan wasn't sure what normal was anymore. He hadn't had a good normal in years, and whatever had been twisting or changing over the past few weeks, it had culminated today in blowing *normal* out of the water.

"You should go. It's unusual for you to be here." She looked at him as she stood up and headed out the door of the tiny back office.

She was right, it wasn't *normal* for him to be here. "What are you going to do?"

"Help with lunch." Then she'd been gone, leaving him with thoughts and fears and anger for her swirling through his head.

He'd headed out the back door, trying to do "normal," but it would take several hours for the lunch rush to die down.

Not wanting to bother them any more than he already had, he'd climbed into his increasingly uncomfortable sports car and headed to the fire station, supposedly just to say hi. At least he was always welcome there ... *if* they were in. But everyone had noticed he was off kilter and they immediately crowded to ask if he was okay.

So he did what Tierney had done for a decade and lied straight to their faces. "Yeah, man, I'm fine."

He'd slapped Jordan on the back in a hearty way, as if he always did that. As if the lie needed physical punctuation.

"You sure?" His brother Aidan looked up from the recliner, a disbelieving look across his face. It didn't help that Aidan knew him better than anyone, and that he'd been subbing for Ronan during his time off. Aidan subtly gave him the stink eye, silently calling him on his bullshit.

"Okay, fine!" Ronan threw his hands up. "I'm not fine. I haven't been to work in weeks. I'm going stir crazy!"

At least that worked, but not in the way he wanted.

"You can clean the kitchen for us, bro." Aidan grinned at him, tipping his head to the cabinets, sink, and cooktop that lined the far wall.

"I've not gone that crazy yet. Clean your own damn kitchen."

They'd watched a show together until the phone rang in the Chief's office. Aidan stood up first, typical. It was clear right away the alarm was about to ring and his time was up. He could hang out at the station, but it wasn't quite legal to be the only one there when he was on medical leave. And what would he do besides clean the damned kitchen?

A few minutes later, the engines were gone. Ronan left the empty building, heading into the back lot to his car. At least the visit had burned some time.

Ronan drove through the sub shop and took the food to a park. The parking lot where he'd sat faced a playground area, volleyball courts, and a small pond that was now frozen over. Had it been warmer weather he would have looked like a stalker himself. But with no one there, it was just a safe place to hang out and enjoy the scenery. Or *look like* he was enjoying it. His brain was going twenty different directions.

He'd eaten the footlong sub in the car, thinking once again, that it looked amazing from the outside but it was definitely built for looks and not comfort. Then he went through the series of concerns that he was eating a footlong sub and not burning it off. He wasn't doing his daily workouts or rushing headlong into burning buildings with everyone else. And he couldn't do either of those things, the doctors had forbade it.

He wasn't just in bad shape, he had to be getting worse— right when Tierney needed him at his best. He'd left the last part of the sandwich and chips, wadded up the trash, thrown it away, and pulled out his phone. Within a few minutes he'd learned that Elliot and Alder Vander clef had way too much money. Anything Tierney did to retaliate, no matter how justified, would likely land her in jail and not Elliot.

Angry at what he'd found, Ronan peeled out of the lot and had taken the long way back across town, but he hadn't gotten any messages from Tierney or the Doyles. Not that Mom or Dad Doyle messaged him much, but they had his number. He arrived at Snafu and headed in the back door again, but still waited another half an hour before everyone was able to leave.

"We'll go to our house." Ewan Doyle announced, as he finally grabbed his coat from the back hook. Ronan had barely taken his off, but he followed suit and grabbed his, too.

"Probably not a good idea, Pop," Tierney told him.

Whatever had happened ten years ago, Emily Gallagher had become real family with the Doyles. At least that much was good, and they loved Sean with everything they had. Thinking back, Ronan realized suddenly that none of that had changed when Paddy came along, even though he now knew that Paddy was their only biological grandchild.

"We need to go somewhere else," Tierney added. Then her tone turned somber. "Elliot's here. He's going to know my place and your place. He probably has someone watching. They'll definitely see us having a meeting."

"Lincoln," Ronan offered. "I know a place with a back room. We get something to eat and a private space."

He didn't mention that he'd already eaten and that the last thing he needed was more food. The other three looked at each other and agreed. Before he knew what he was doing, he found Tierney in the car beside him. The drive wasn't long, but it wasn't short either.

At first, she didn't speak. Then she said softly, "Thank you. You don't deserve any of this. And neither do they."

Ronan shook his head at her, his hand automatically reaching out, his fingers lacing through hers. Despite the fact that probably every other human emotion had rocketed through his system that day, he was surprised by the rightness of the feeling.

She squeezed back and he wondered if she knew what she was doing to him. Before he could ask anything, or even formulate the words if he wanted to, she turned in her seat to face him. He tried to keep his eyes on the road.

"Did you do a search on Elliot?" she asked, but immediately added, "Don't search him."

"Why?" Ronan asked.

He'd found all of it. Alder Vander clef and Clef Industries, too. These guys made Midas look like a third-class citizen.

"You did it?"

He nodded and asked again. "Why shouldn't I have looked him up?"

What was it about Elliot that she didn't want him to know?

"All that money? They've got the best people on this. I wouldn't be surprised if they're monitoring who's searching him, especially from this area."

Ronan hadn't thought of that. For a moment he looked at his phone sitting on the little magnet on his dash and stared at it as if it might bite him. Hell, it might have already bitten him.

Every time he talked to Tierney, things got more complicated.

He'd heard about what had happened to the men in her past: bricks thrown through windows, car accidents ... Was his own accident coincidental? Ronan was suddenly wondering ...

Still, he thought, he ran into burning buildings for a living. He would run headlong into this, too. The only other option was Tierney leaving ... or worse.

So he squeezed her hand where it had stayed tucked in his, the warm heat of it radiating up his arm and through his system, all the way down to his toes. The thick, rich feeling warned him there was more here than he'd even admitted to himself.

Maybe it was better now that he knew she wasn't actually Siorse's sister. But what was he thinking about that her being Siorse's sister was bad? Was he really ...?

"Don't worry about me," he told her. "I'm not in any danger here. I'll be fine."

But when Tierney didn't respond and just looked out the window, he had to wonder what else she hadn't told him ...

CHAPTER NINETEEN

"I'll be fine," Tierney protested despite Ronan looking at her sideways. She knew she deserved that look. "I've got Mr. Kittens." She waved her hand toward the back of the house.

Upon arriving to a series of small squeaky noises, she and Ronan had scoped the place out and arrived together in the laundry room where Mr. Kittens was hunkered down in the cardboard box. Beside him snuggled five of the tiniest mewling little kittens she'd ever seen.

"Mr. Kittens is of no help," Ronan protested, seeming to hear his own voice as he said it. "Can we please stop calling him Mr. Kittens?"

Just the question brought tears to Tierney's eyes. Sean had named the cat, and though she'd had the exact same thought, right now she couldn't deal with it. Ronan must have noticed because he simply let the question pass unanswered.

"All right. Besides a very distracted new mother cat, what other weapons do you have?"

She'd been thinking about it, though she wasn't fully ready for show and tell. Ronan was right, she had to be ready, and a second pair of eyes around her home would reveal things she didn't see. Heading first into the kitchen, she pulled her heftiest knife out of the block. Using one of Sean's chunky magnets from the fridge, she stuck it to the side. With one grab, she could yank it and wield it.

"Handy."

Ronan's praise meant too much and she tried to brush it off. Hopefully he didn't know the stupid thoughts running through her head. "That's the idea."

Putting the knife back, she moved around him and headed toward the front door. The living room was tiny. She'd set up the couches and the chair to form a little walkway. Now she reached behind the couch and pulled out the Louisville Slugger.

Ronan frowned at her. "You just got back from taking Sean when I found you and I've been with you ever since. When did you ...?"

"It's always been there." She looked away. "I always knew he might find me one day. I'm trying to be grateful that I had ten good years."

Then she motioned him out of the way again, letting him trail along into her bedroom where she crawled under the bed and pulled out the lockbox she stashed there. Quickly, she entered the push button code and opened the lid.

"Nine millimeter," she told him as she held the box up for inspection.

Ronan reached in and hefted the weapon. "Loaded?"

"It has to be."

"Tell me the code isn't Sean's birthday."

"It's the random combo sent with my first credit card." At least that she could smile at. It had no relation to any number in her life.

Nodding, Ronan took a deep breath, and his smile washed over her. She shouldn't let him have this kind of power over her emotions. But she couldn't control it and it was better than letting Elliot control her.

"The lockbox is smart," Ronan told her as he handed the gun back to her, "especially with Sean in the house."

She understood then where he was going. Sean was no longer in the house.

"It might be better to keep it handy."

She nodded. "Hold on."

It took a few moments to rummage through the back of the closet where she put things she wasn't sure she'd use. But it wasn't there.

She tried the top shelf of the closet. It was completely useless for someone of her size, except as storage for things she never needed. Reaching up as high as she could on tiptoe, her fingertips brushed the edge of an old printed cardboard box, but she couldn't grab it. This might be where she'd put it.

She hadn't wanted it to look interesting to Sean at all. The green bean box had done it. As far as she knew, her son had no idea she had a gun in the house. But she pushed up a little higher and tipped a little as she lost her balance. Tierney felt Ronan's body right behind her. Her breath sucked in at his heat radiating into the cold that seemed to have seeped into her bones since last night.

Without thinking anything of it—at least he didn't seem to think the same things she did—he reached up over her head, grabbed the box, and lowered it just enough for her to grab it. Then he stepped back. Air washed between them, bringing a shift of cold and a reminder that he wasn't hers at all. Even if she'd pretended so for half a moment.

He was just being helpful. It shouldn't set her off like this. Maybe it was just the trauma of it all. That had to be it, she told herself.

With the box now in her hands, Tierney turned around and set it on the bed as though the moment hadn't happened. Rummaging through, she pulled out a holster. "Good!"

She handed it to him and closed the box as he looked it over.

It had a slide clip to go into the waistband of jeans or some equally sturdy kind of pants. Maybe a pocket. And it had a holder specifically formed to her gun.

"How are you with it?"

She tipped her head and almost laughed. "Look at it."

He turned it over but stared at her as though he had no idea what he was looking for.

"It's basically brand new. I've practiced with the gun, but not the holster. Hence why I had to look two places for it."

He handed it back. "Depending on how twitchy you are, put the loop over it or not?"

She pushed the little bar up and then down. It was rectangular, shaped to flip up and over the edge of her gun, so she couldn't just grab it and yank it from the holster and wave it around willy nilly. But it was a good question: *Just how twitchy was she?*

She pushed the gun down into the holster, adding pressure until she felt the little shift that let her know it had clicked into place. Then she lifted the edge of her shirt and slid the whole thing onto the waistband of her jeans. She tried lifting the shirt over it, but it was blazingly obvious she was carrying.

That didn't seem to matter to Ronan though. He grabbed her shoulders and turned her toward him.

"I want to stay."

"It's not normal." she protested.

"None of this is normal." *What was he getting at?* "Sean being gone isn't normal. You've already alerted whoever is watching you that you're onto it."

Had she?

Tierney felt that Sean being gone for a few days was perfectly normal. It was long enough to say he'd gotten a chance to go to a winter lodge with friends for a month. She thought it was perfectly believable. Though Ronan was right—believable or not, it wasn't *normal.*

Ronan was still staring into her eyes, making his case. "If something happens, I want to be here."

"If something happens, Alder Vander clef is going to try to make it disappear. And whoever acts out against Elliot is going to prison. You can't be that person. You have no case for it. I might. You *can't* stay here," she protested.

It sank in then for the first time that it was entirely possible her son was going to spend the rest of his life with Raven and her family. Whether or not Elliot killed her, if he'd found out he had a child, he wouldn't stop looking. Everything was a possession to Elliot, and Sean would have no right to a life away from him.

"I don't like this," Ronan told her.

"Well, neither do I!" she snapped back, but she didn't really feel that she had other choices.

At least he didn't seem offended by her awful response. "Okay. I can't promise you I'm going to stay away. But for now—"

"For now, it's just dead rats on the doorstep and some emails. There's absolutely no evidence that anyone has gotten into my home. Honestly, he's more the kind for overarching emotional threats than doing anything physically to me."

Ronan nodded again. "But if he does get in, and if he does threaten you—" he pointed to the gun bulging under her shirt at her hip, "—are you willing to use it?"

CHAPTER TWENTY

An uneasy feeling settled in Ronan's stomach as he headed home. Was it because of everything Tierney had told him? Everything he learned about Emily Gallagher? Was it because of the picture of Elliot Vander clef that he now had parked on his phone?

Ronan had looked through a handful online and even shown them to Mom and Dad Doyle. It had been a relief when dad had pushed the phone away as if he didn't need it.

"I know what the asshole looks like. And I always stay up to date when he gets a new haircut or something stupid like that. He's not walking into this bar without me knowing it."

Ewan Doyle had said it low enough to keep the words away from Tierney and Ronan got the feeling he'd never told his daughter that he was checking up. Hell, Tierney hadn't even wanted Ronan doing a basic search on the man.

As Ronan opened the door from the garage and headed through the laundry room, it hit him that the place felt stale and unused, even though they'd been here just a number of hours ago. Why did it feel that way? It felt like when he and Siorse would go on vacation and no one had been here for a week. But that wasn't it now.

It was because Tierney wasn't here. He wanted her here.

He wasn't going to sleep without knowing she was safe. Thank God he wasn't working shifts right now, because a firefighter running on no sleep was a menace. Heading into the back of the house, he aimed for his little-used office.

It was one of the few rooms he'd changed since Siorse and Paddy had died. It had just hit him one day: the room was Siorse's "office" and she was never coming back. She was never going to need the pretty envelopes or crinkle cut scissors things. He didn't even know if he should worry if tissue paper could go moldy? Not to mention it was all a fire hazard.

He'd been using his laptop on the kitchen table or a tv tray at night while he watched something. There was no need. There was no one to be offended by his taking the room apart. Besides, he hadn't touched their bedroom other than to buy new sheets, and he hadn't touched Paddy's room at all. Three years later, it was still set up for a toddler. Ronan glanced at it as he passed by, for the first time thinking he would have to dismantle it ... soon.

His office was the smallest of the three bedrooms and now he used it for records and a place to keep a desktop model—a computer that was surely growing more out of date by the moment. Sitting down, he pulled out the small slip of paper and logged into Tierney's email. She'd given him her password, brushing him aside about interfering with her privacy.

"You'll see what I got Mom and Dad Doyle for Christmas. And something I ordered for Sean. I don't think there's anything in there incriminating. It's the email I use when I sign up for book clubs or things like that."

So he'd logged in as if he were her and started looking through her saved and deleted emails. It didn't take him long to find the first email sent to *Emily* three and a half weeks ago. The next one had come to *Emmie*. She'd said that was her spelling with an IE, at least that was the way Elliot had done it. The most recent had come to *Emmie Baby* just the day before, but he wasn't finding more than what she'd already told him. All this did was allow him now to monitor the system and see that she had gotten a really great deal on the game she'd gotten for Sean.

The kid had come in here waving it around like it was gold. Ronan had even played with him for a good bit. Sean had been a great distraction from long empty hours while he was healing up.

But there wasn't anything else in the emails, and it all felt useless. He stood up, stretching. The skin no longer pulled where he had had his surgery and everything seemed to be functioning. He took the last of his antibiotics, grateful to have that finished and he chucked the container into the recycling with a satisfying thud. With nothing else to do, he got in some steps, pacing the small house twice before figuring out something else that might be useful.

Sitting down, he searched *how to get a login record* on Tierney's email.

He'd logged in from his home and Tierney had logged in from her home, maybe several times from her phone, maybe in different spots around town, but Ronan wondered if there might be anything useful there.

It took a while, he was no hacker. Luckily, her email provider was older than Sean and Ronan was pretty sure it was the same one she'd had since high school. So there were numerous websites and helpful tip lists walking him through what he wanted. Unfortunately, many of the explanations involved buttons that seemed to have gone out of date.

It took an hour of sheer determination. He'd given up, frustrated, and headed into the kitchen where he opened a beer and took a long swig. That was all it took to realize he couldn't afford to not be functioning at his best should something happen. He poured the remainder down the sink and grabbed himself a soda. Back at the computer, he'd drunk the whole thing before, at last, the log popped up on the screen. He'd gotten there mostly by getting frustrated enough to click several buttons that look like they might be right.

Holy shit. Six weeks ago, there had been a login from upstate New York.

Ronan knew he shouldn't search the Vander clefs, but didn't he remember their location as upstate New York?

He'd been smart enough to get screen grabs on a few of the articles he pulled. If anyone got his phone, it would be clear that he'd been researching Elliot Vander clef. Right now, he didn't care. Quickly, Ronan pulled up the article and scanned what he had saved.

His memory was right. The Vander clefs absolutely did have a home in that area.

Back in Tierney's login records, he checked further back. Another login had occurred from the same physical location about two months before that. Before the dead rats had started.

As he'd suspected, Elliot—or someone associated with him— was checking her email from the inside. It was one thing to use her email to subscribe her to things, but Elliot seemed like the kind who would either be obsessed enough or rich enough to pay someone to be sure he had it right.

He would have needed to be sure that the email *Tierney.Doyle* belonged to his *Emily Gallagher*.

Finding the password and logging in would certainly help verify he had the right person and as long as his tracks were covered, or if Tierney hadn't set up any alerts for logins from different locations, she would never know.

Ronan looked around the small room, wondering if she'd gotten some kind of pop up that he had logged in from across town. Everything else he scanned through looked like it was her

—checking her email from her phone somewhere in town, from her laptop at home. But ...?

He scrolled back further and found a login from a city several hours away to the west. Hadn't she rented a cabin with Sean and hiked the waterfalls? So that would have been her, too.

With the phone still in one hand and the other clacking away at the keyboard, he dialed her. "Tierney."

"What?"

It felt far too good to hear her voice, to know she was still safe. But Ronan didn't think she would appreciate him telling her that now.

"He's been logging into your email."

"What?" She'd clearly had no idea.

"That's how he knew it was you. That's how he knew to sign you up. He may have even had to verify the email to sign you up for those things."

He heard her take a deep breath, and then she talked herself down from what might be absolute terror. "Well, I don't think there's anything damning there."

"No, but it's definitely interesting. Like you said they have enough money to check places other people wouldn't think to look." Even as he talked, Ronan continued to scroll back, checking the login dates and locations and looking for anything suspicious.

"Holy shit!" he said as the screen popped up a date from a year earlier.

CHAPTER TWENTY-ONE

Tierney woke up with a sick knot in her stomach.

She had heard nothing about Sean, which meant he was safe. That small comfort was the only thing that let her keep going.

Ronan had found where her email had been hacked a year earlier. So Elliot had known about her for that long but hadn't swept in and grabbed her. Maybe he hadn't been certain she was Emily. Maybe Elliot just wanted to play a waiting game.

Whatever Elliot's intentions or whatever game he was playing, he'd known about her long enough that she had to assume that he knew Sean existed. If he did the math, he would know more than that.

Still, nothing had happened. Nothing except her going to the bar, getting up in the morning, and locking the doors and windows like a madman. She and Ronan had put bars in all the windows and added another bolt at each of the front and back doors near the top where they probably wouldn't be suspected. Of course, not so high that she couldn't reach them.

She wasn't sleeping well. Mr. Kittens was up every few hours with her kittens. The tiny mews should have been obnoxious, but they were cute. The cats weren't why she wasn't sleeping, they were simply company when she was awake.

She'd hauled the whole family into the living room wanting to watch over them. Maybe she was just missing her own child. The kittens were round jellybeans, their legs tiny, skinny sticks with little pink toes on the end. Not even good for walking yet, just for waving around.

Sometime in the wee hours each night she'd fall asleep on the couch, Mr. Kittens purring contentedly in the box at her fingertips. The gun waited quietly under the throw pillow, the bat near the end of the couch. On this, the third morning, she started to wonder how long it could go on.

She called Zadie Sosa, the new vet in town, and asked how she should be caring for her newborn kittens. The good news was that she just needed to watch them. Until she saw a problem, she mostly wasn't to interfere.

"You'll need to bring them in for a wellness check sometime in about five days or so if you can." Zadie gave her the rundown on what she was to look for, in case a kitten needed milk supplement or needed to get in sooner.

Tierney didn't know how she was going to afford all of this, but it was apparent that was the least of her worries. She wasn't going to let Mr. Kittens or the litter suffer; she needed them to all be here and healthy when Sean returned. Tierney was glad though, that Mr. Kittens wasn't venturing outside. Whoever had left those rats wasn't trustworthy around animals at all.

Her phone pinged, startling her.

She'd managed to get up and head toward her bed for a few hours last night. She'd even managed to sleep three reasonable chunks of time, though she'd woken up in a cold sweat between each of them.

— Are you up?

Ronan texted.

— Yes. All good.

He didn't ask about Sean. She'd promised to let him know any news and if anyone was monitoring her communication, Tierney didn't want to flag them. There were already enough changes.

Dad came into the bar more often. He'd set up a knife and shotgun under the bar within easy reach. He'd showed Elliot's picture to all of the employees and though he never told anyone who Emily Gallagher was, he did tell them that Elliot had stalked his daughter and that they were to report if they saw him. But so far no one had.

Tierney had pulled out her minimal computer skills and tried to see what Elliot would look like with longer hair. She tried him with a better tan, darker hair, glasses, a beard. She needed to recognize him even if he tried to look different. Then again, she was confident if Elliot was within fifty yards of her she would feel his presence.

Had she? Over the last year, she thought she was feeling more paranoid, more concerned, she looked over her shoulder more often. There was the occasional feeling she was being watched. *Maybe she'd been right.*

— On my way, she told Ronan.

A little while later, when she'd gotten her teeth brushed and her clothing on and her hair pulled up, she headed out the door. They'd agreed to meet for breakfast today. He was in her life constantly now. Though she insisted on staying at her own home and maintaining some level of normal, he insisted on horning in. Tierney both loved and hated it.

It was wonderful that he felt so protective of her. It was awful that she was falling harder for him than she ever had before.

It sucked even more that it was happening right when she needed to be getting over him. It was wonderful to be near him and sometimes have him hold her, and it was petrifying to know that she'd made him a target. She couldn't just ask an old friend to take him away out of town for a month. Ronan wouldn't stand for it either. It didn't help that he didn't even have a job to go to.

The poor guy was bored out of his gourd without work. That was probably the main reason he was watching her so closely. She turned the key in the car, braced for an explosion that didn't come and told herself that Ronan couldn't really feel anything more than familial protection for her. She was a project, nothing more.

Her hand dipped to her side to check the holster clipped to the waistband of her jeans. The weight of it now felt normal as did the way her eyes scanned the street behind her as she pulled out. She looked for anything out of the ordinary but didn't see it. With nothing pinging her senses except that it was too easy, she headed into town to a local diner.

Sliding into one of the red vinyl booths, she waited for Ronan to show up.

He was there in a few minutes, and less than twenty seconds after that, Diana, the waitress, sidled up to the table with coffee. "Well, don't you two look cute?"

Ronan only grinned at Tierney and then up at Diana as if he had a secret. *He did, but it wasn't that!*

Jesus, the things he was going to let people think. But she tried to let it pass as they both flipped their mugs upright. Ronan outright flirted with Diana, while Tierney searched the tabletop for the right kinds of sugars and the little creamer pot.

It was only Wednesday, and it was going to be rough. Lack of sleep could only be replaced by caffeine for so long.

As Diana headed away with their orders, Ronan turned back to her, now solemn. "I pulled another email this morning."

"I didn't see anything," she paused as she'd been starting to take a sip of her coffee.

"I archived it as soon as I saw it."

Trying to protect her again. "What was it?"

"Another subscription for Emmie Baby."

She tried to fight the shudder but couldn't. "What was it for? Socks? Leftover vegetables from the harvest?"

"It was for a relatively pornographic calendar."

She leaned back in the booth, trying to absorb news that she did not like. Elliot was stepping up.

"Are you sure you want to go through with this?" Ronan asked.

"I think I have to," she said. "Because I don't think tonight's going to be safe."

CHAPTER TWENTY-TWO

Ronan walked through the large, open bay doors at the Redemption fire station. It felt bizarre to be coming in this way, not dressed for work, not at the right time for shift change.

His fellow A-shift firefighters walked forward, hugging him tightly and clapping him on the back.

Jordan hugged him. "How much longer, man?"

"Just under two weeks."

Jordan looked at him sideways, squinting at him. "Is that best case scenario or worst?"

"Best," Ronan admitted. But he was the guy who always aimed for best case scenario, so he tried to ignore the worst case option.

Two long tables had been set up along the front of the empty bay for the Crawl tonight. This was one of the earlier stations for those who started on this side of town, which most people did, especially this early in the day. While it was still daylight, the station would have an engine out for the kids to play on, provided the crew wasn't called to a scene.

Aidan was setting out Fire station cookies. "Come help me, bro."

He was trying to make neat lines of little cellophane-wrapped goodies that Talia's bakery had provided them.

Ronan shook his head. "I've got to go see the chief."

"Whatever." Aidan waved him away and went back to making a remarkably crooked display.

Taggart must have heard Ronan coming because he was already hopping up from his chair as Ronan pushed the door open. He stepped through and tried to be cordial. "Hi, Chief!"

"How are you doing? I heard two weeks."

It wasn't a surprise that he'd already heard. "That's my goal."

"We'll be glad to have you back. Been hard pressed to fill an empty space this long." The chief held up his hand though as if to ward him off. "But it's not a problem. You take what time you need. We've got the manpower to do it and the guys do like the overtime."

Ronan grinned. He would like anything, even just regular time. Medical leave sucked on many fronts but, instead of continuing the banter, he pulled out a chair. "I need to catch you up on something, Chief."

"Oh?" Sure enough, the older man looked plenty worried and honestly with what Ronan was about to say, it made sense.

"I've been helping Tierney Doyle."

The chief tipped his head. "Your wife's sister, right?"

Ronan nodded, though he hadn't really thought of Siorse as "his wife" in a while and he sure didn't think of Tierney that way anymore.

He explained to the chief what he'd been doing, and that he'd been handing over files to Detective Gomez at the police department.

"Gomez has been keeping it pretty hush," Taggart mused.

"I don't know what he's planning to do, but he's monitoring the case. He did say with stalker cases there wasn't much you could do until after a crime was committed. Tierney doesn't even have enough evidence now for a restraining order."

"That's how these things often go." The chief looked disheartened. The fire department saw more domestic disputes than people realized, not just with fires but with medical calls and more.

"I'm trying not to be public about it," Ronan started, "But the more people who know what they're looking for the better we can keep Tierney safe."

The chief only raised one eyebrow, as if to question Ronan's dedication to the cause, but he wasn't going to be swayed.

Ronan went on to explain about the emails and the dead rats, watching his chief's face contort with disgust. Then he showed the photos he had.

"This is the guy you're certain is responsible?"

"We don't have hard evidence and that's the problem. But it really couldn't be anybody else. He's the one who called her by the nicknames used on the emails. Apparently, he's sick enough to leave dead rats on her doorstep." Ronan held his phone up to show off the man's picture and watched the Chief's eyes scan the small screen. He saw the moment the older man read the name.

"Are you fucking serious?"

"Unfortunately, yes." Ronan hated this—that Vander clef's money bought him a measure of protection even from this far away. At least, Ronan hoped he was far away.

"Hell," the chief looked away. "I'm out here in the middle of Nebraska and I've heard of the Vander clefs."

Ronan could only nod.

Then the chief warned him. "If you misstep on this, the Vander clef family is going to bury your butt so deep you'll never find it again."

"I know." There was nothing else he could say. But he wouldn't back off when Tierney needed him.

The conversation stalled. He didn't quite know how to tell the chief that he'd thought it all through and he still believed it was worth it. He couldn't fathom walking away from Tierney and he tried not to imagine why he couldn't fathom it.

With nothing more he could add, he tried another angle. "I want to show this around to the guys. I want more eyes on The Crawl tonight."

"Shit," Taggart said, tapping his pen sideways on the desk. "Yeah, there are going to be a lot of people in town. I don't know how we'd keep track of them or even find him if we knew he was here."

"That's exactly the problem. Look," Ronan pulled up more pictures. "Tierney also gave me these."

He held up the altered photographs of Vander clef and the Chief nodded. "Do it. Show the guys. We'll be on this. I just don't know how to make any guarantees."

That was the best they could do, Ronan knew.

Fifteen minutes later, he'd gone to the guys one by one, interrupting their tasks and explaining the story. He didn't want to make a big announcement in case anyone was listening in. Some of the local families were starting to trickle in, the earlybirds on the Crawl. They'd go hit the bakery next, probably skip the bar, and check out the new animal shelter that was opening where Zadie was hoping to adopt out a handful of dogs and cats tonight. The diner was serving ice cream and more.

Avoiding local ears, he made the circuit. Leslie was the last one he got to and he pulled her aside, telling he the same story.

"Oh shit," she said. "I had a stalker a long time ago and I thought he was bad. Looks like he was just a regular hometown variety though." She looked at the pictures again and checked out the name. "I have to admit Tierney went for it! How did she even meet him?"

Ronan could only shrug in response. Tierney Doyle would never have had the opportunity to cross paths with Elliot

Vander clef. For Emily Gallagher though, it had been a different story.

"I've got my eyes out." Leslie never questioned that the wealthy, good-looking charmer could be a stalker. "Should I call you if I see anything?"

Ronan nodded as he sent her copies of the photos. He'd sent photos then to each of them as soon as they agreed. The whole shift was on the lookout now. "Thanks, Leslie."

"Heads up!" she told him as he turned around to see Tierney walking through the open bay doors, her long coat on, but open.

Ronan looked her up and down, glad she seemed safe. She walked with confidence. The cold weather had forced her into a fluffy, fuzzy, fitted coat that he wanted to get his hands into. It didn't quite conceal the bump of a gun at her hip. He wondered if it was as noticeable as he thought it was.

Heading toward her, he passed a few odd looks from the guys as he made his way. She didn't see him yet, and he liked checking her out. Were the guys thinking he was a lovesick fool? Was he?

As he sidled around the table, he took her hand in his, tugging her away from prying eyes. "Shall we start at the next place?"

"No," she replied, tugging her hand back with a sly grin. "I have Fire station dogs to pet and a cookie to pick up!"

"You sure you don't need a fire safety pamphlet, too?" Aidan held it out to her, silently razzing his brother with his interruption.

"That is an excellent idea!" She grinned again and took the pamphlet even as she made sure to grab one of the cookies.

She was chatting with the guys like the old friend she was. So he stepped back and let her hang out for a few more minutes. Even in that timeframe the crowds began to pick up. His eyes scanned everyone and he hoped he didn't look like he was doing it. He'd never been as subtle as he wanted to think he was.

The sun would go down early, so the families were all coming out now while they could. They crowded the table and the kids' questions stole the firefighters' time and attention away from Tierney. Ronan tried not to be happy about it.

With her hand finally tucked in his again, he walked down the block while she ate the cookie. Red frosting dusted the edges of her lips and for a moment he had thoughts he shouldn't have about his late wife's sister.

He asked one more time. "Are you sure you want to do this?"

Tierney just looked at him like he was crazy. "I think I have to. We don't know where he is. I can't let him control my life if he's not even here!"

"And if he is?" Ronan pushed.

"Well, I've been his bait before. I can handle it again."

He didn't like the idea of Tierney as bait or the determination in her voice.

CHAPTER TWENTY-THREE

Tierney and Ronan stepped into the diner and looked around. The place was already filling up with people enjoying the Crawl.

Later though, the children would disappear and the small dishes of ice cream would trade out for pies with whiskey sauce. Even as Ronan picked up one of the small scoops of ice cream with chocolate sauce, Tierney turned to Diana, "Peach, please."

The owner was serving up dishes herself in line with her staff all gathered behind the counter. Reaching behind the counter, she pulled out one of the pies for Tierney. Though the serving was smaller than normal, Tierney was grateful. There was no way she'd make it all the way down the street with businesses serving up their usual portions. Her second fire station cookie was still in her pocket.

So she'd happily eaten from a kid's ice cream dish with the silver fork and licked every last bit of it off.

Diana and Tony, her husband, had decided the Crawl was an opportunity to try out new pies.

"Peach pecan is good," Tierney said as she set her dish in the bin they'd left out.

Ronan had polished off the small ice cream already and wound up in a conversation with someone else. At which point Diana scanned the room and held up one finger. "You got a minute, hon?"

"Sure." That was odd.

Tierney followed her through the swinging doors and down the back hallway. Diana leaned back against the wall and looked to be sure they were alone. Her arms crossed as though she was unsure about what she was going to say.

"I heard the firefighters saying that you were concerned about an old stalker?"

Oh God, where had she heard that? Were they simply going to tell the whole town? But the information wasn't wrong, and Tierney wouldn't lie.

"It's true," she said. If the firefighters were talking, everyone would believe it. Though she knew Ronan wouldn't have given away her real name or any of that pertinent information, she wondered what everyone now knew.

"Well, I'm sorry, hon," Diana looked disappointed. "I'd have told you before if I'd known, but this guy came in looking for you—"

"*What?*" Blood froze in her veins. Tierney knew the answer, but she waited. She tried to calm down and ask pertinent questions. "Who?"

"He didn't say. Just asked if I knew how to find you."

"How to find Tierney Doyle?"

Diana nodded, a small frown settled between her brows as if to say 'who else?' But that was a relief.

Diana went on. "I didn't recognize him. So, I said yes."

Tierney nodded slowly. She had to work to school her expression in such a way to not make Diana feel bad for what she'd said. She couldn't get mad and lose information. She now needed to wring out every last drop of detail.

"Then he asked if I knew where you lived. So, I just gave him a funny face and said, I don't give that information to people I don't know."

"Thank you!" Tierney felt the words come out in a gush. "That was the right thing to do."

Diana tipped her head back and forth as if she wasn't sure she agreed. "I told him I'd be glad to tell you he stopped by, but he didn't want to leave his name. Damn. I'm sorry, I should have told you. He didn't want me to tell you and we were busy ..."

"It's okay! Please don't worry, Diana." Though Tierney was now worried for Diana. She changed tacks. "When was it?"

"Three? Maybe four months ago?" She thought for a moment, "Might even be six."

If they hadn't found the emails the night before, Tierney would have been stunned by that. Now she understood Elliot had been working his way into her world for some time, somehow managing to stay off her radar.

"Can I ask you a question?" She leaned in close, hoping no one was listening.

"Of course, hon, anything."

Tierney already had her phone out. Holding up the screen, she tapped at it to make sure the full name didn't show at the bottom. "Was it this guy?"

"No, this guy had darker hair."

"Hold on." Tierney flipped through the images she'd made. "More like this?"

"That's your guy?" Diana asked and when Tierney nodded, Diana shook her head. "That's him. I haven't seen him again, though. So that's good news?"

Tierney nodded, though she didn't think it was.

Diana was still going on. "I'm sorry, hon. But I didn't tell him where you live or anything. Maybe he gave up."

If only that were the case, Tierney thought.

She was stuck with things escalating but also not mattering.

Elliot would never give up. If not now, he would show up later. It was clear he'd found her and was keeping tabs.

Just then the doors to the back hallway crashed open and Ronan came barging through. "Are you okay? What happened?"

He stopped, leaning one hand flat against the wall as though holding himself up. He sucked in a deep breath. "I lost you. Don't do that again."

Oh, shit. She hadn't even thought about Ronan not knowing where she was. Diana had asked her, and she'd simply walked back here. "I'm sorry."

Was she going to be constantly in this man's sight? Under his thumb just so she wasn't under someone else's?

Tierney would have to think about it. She turned back to the restaurant owner, who'd taken time out of the busiest night of the year to give her information, even if it wasn't as cut and dried as Tierney would have hoped. "Thank you, Diana."

"Anytime. I'm just sorry, it wasn't better news."

Ronan looked at her funny, and Tierney tried to motion with just her expression that she would explain later. Reaching out, she took his hand in hers, enjoying when his fingers laced and held on tight. She hadn't meant to worry him, but there was something that melted inside her at the thought of it. Outside the diner, she relayed what Diana had said.

Then when they were down the block, in between the diner and the bakery where they promised to meet Talia because she'd originally been Tierney's date for the crawl, Ronan turned and stopped. "I was talking to Zucker in the diner. Word has traveled and everyone knows we're looking for some old stalker of yours."

She'd already figured that out. If she hadn't, she would have been stunned by Ronan's next words.

"He said some guy came asking about you, even seemed to be offering money in exchange for information."

Elliot was *paying* for information?

That was news, though it certainly smacked of the Vander clefs. "Diana saw him, too."

Ronan tugged on her hand, stopping her and pulling her back slightly. "Diana saw *Vander clef?*"

"Yes," Tierney said.

Ronan was still shaking his head at her. "I showed Zucker all the pictures. It wasn't Elliot."

CHAPTER TWENTY-FOUR

Tierney held Ronan's hand tightly and surveyed the street, her gaze scanning back and forth. As they stepped out of the diner, she realized the place was already more crowded than when they'd stepped in. The surge of people contained fewer families, and the crowd started to feel sinister to her, as if Elliot could be around any corner.

Still, she moved forward even as everyone moved around her.

"Hey! There you are!"

Tierney didn't know where to look and she turned almost a full circle with the best smile she could muster. "Talia!"

She found her friend in the crowd, probably because it was still early enough for the group to be respectful. The sea of strangers parted as Talia and her motorized chair cut a relatively straight path through. Her hair was pinned up with beads and flowers, her makeup flawless, her coat belted tight against the cold. Why did this town have to have the Crawl before the weather fully thawed?

Tierney didn't know but, leaning down, she hugged the

woman who'd become her best friend since moving to town several years ago.

"Hey, Talia!" Ronan greeting her, waving his free hand as he clutched Tierney's hand into his other one more time.

Talia raised one eyebrow at the clear signal. "I see you're not my single buddy anymore."

It hadn't occurred to Tierney that Ronan was really doing anything other than just protecting her. All feelings seemed to be on her side alone ... the same as they'd always been. But Talia had seen them together before, and only now was she commenting.

Was it true?

Tierney felt her back stiffen. She didn't quite know how to answer so she laughed awkwardly and tried to shrug it off. "He's my hired muscle."

Beside her, she felt an instant reaction in Ronan. At her palm, she felt a change in his grip. What did that mean? Surely, he'd felt her confusion when Talia had asked her ridiculous question.

Had she said the right thing? Wasn't he just her protection? Was there more actually going on than just her high school crush, flaring back up after a decade? If so, had she just dumped on him?

Tierney didn't have any answers and she wasn't going to get any soon. Right now, she needed to be vigilant. Because apparently, Elliot had been here probably off and on for months. He'd been in her email account, logging in as her and occasionally reading everything that came in with her none the wiser.

She suppressed an obvious shudder, though she still felt it down her spine. That meant he knew where she ordered her lingerie and which team Sean still played little league with. More than any of that, it meant he knew about Sean. He knew her son's birthday and had almost certainly figured it out. Sean had even been born two weeks early. It didn't change his parentage but made it even more obvious.

Taking a deep breath, Tierney was relieved she'd sent Sean with Raven.

Once again, she scanned the growing crowd. Not only had Elliot been here, but so had someone else who'd come asking about her. *Someone she wouldn't recognize.* Involuntarily, she clenched Ronan's hand tighter and once again wondered what signals she was sending.

Would everyone think they were together? As far as everyone knew, this was her late sister's husband. Did it look like she was making a move? Could she afford to care what it looked like?

"Yeah," Ronan said, laughing in a tone that echoed her own awkwardness. "I'm the fake boyfriend. So that anyone who sees her knows she's safe."

Tierney's heart stopped. She unlaced her fingers and shook her hand violently free.

She ignored the heartbreak that roared through her, too fierce for an attachment that didn't exist. One she'd told herself repeatedly wasn't real. That part she would just have to deal with. The rest was more pressing. She'd known she couldn't do this, but she'd kept slipping, kept thinking it was okay. If Ronan was staring down every guy who passed and showing the world that he was keeping her safe ...?

"No!" She turned and stared at him.

"What?" Both Talia and Ronan looked at her like she was crazy.

Tierney's gaze jumped back and forth between the two of them. "Just, no. If I look like I'm with you, it will definitely make you a target. More than just being seen with me."

Much more.

She couldn't handle that. They all thought they could handle

Elliot. Dad Doyle did. Ronan did ... everyone who heard puffed up their chest and acted like her savior. Acted like she was just scared. But she was *right*. They had no clue what they were up against.

Ronan shook his head as though she were being crazy. Exactly as she thought. When he tried to grab her hand again, she shook him off.

"One—I know Elliot and you don't." She was getting mad that he didn't believe her. She turned to Ronan, staring him down as if he should know better. "Come on. This is stalker one-oh-one. He's possessive. We might only be safe *because* I've been single."

"Tierney, I'm not going to let anything happen to you," Ronan said. "Which is why I should be right beside you."

Though she understood that, Tierney also knew Elliot. She appreciated Ronan's desire but felt the tension growing at the edges of her face, down her back, through her toes.

Was his desire to be brave and heroic enough to stop Elliot? She didn't think so, because Elliot was pathological about getting what he wanted.

This time, when Ronan's fingers lace through hers, they were less tense. He'd decided she was crazy. That she was over-inflating the situation. She'd let him have it later, now was not the time for a fight.

He tugged her and Talia away, the whir of the machinery of Talia's chair grounding Tierney's thoughts. The thing was heavy, Tierney thought, and Talia was a master with it. She navigated well, and Tierney had learned to watch for curbs and move to driveways and accessible ramps.

"Come on." Talia took the front and tugged her along. "We're going to blend in and look normal ... as normal as three people at a small town, singles-pub-crawl-turned-community event possibly can."

They were already moving, Ronan trailing along behind.

Tierney tried to get herself together to ask reasonable questions of her friend. "Did you get the bakery covered?"

"You know I wouldn't be out here if I didn't. Feels a little wrong to abandon my staff on a big night, but I worked the early shift."

"You've worked almost all the shifts without much time off. You've earned it," Tierney added with a smile that wasn't forced but was a bit tamped by her paranoia and vigilance.

"The tips are going to be really good tonight. That should be a bonus to everyone who's on shift. I told them as long as there was enough food for a crowd, they could eat what they wanted."

"Damn," Tierney grinned for real this time. "I have been working at the wrong place."

Talia just shrugged and grinned as if to say *maybe you have.*

They made it another block, the going slow even without Talia's chair. The crowds grew noticeably thicker, with officers and volunteers alike attempting to control traffic and directing people to park well off the main road. Participating businesses were lit up and festooned with color coded streamers. Ivy Dean and the town staff running the Crawl had carefully curated the decor, making it obvious which businesses were participating and creating a clear path down Main street.

The stores in between were mostly dark, either out of respect or because they simply hadn't stayed open. For most, this was beyond their normal hours. A few intrepid souls stayed open in the middle of all the rush even without actively participating.

Tierney, Ronan, and Talia made it to the next stop and as they opened the door, the bell jingled.

The hair on the back of Tierney's neck suddenly stood on end.

CHAPTER TWENTY-FIVE

"What is it?" Ronan asked, his panic picking up along with Tierney's.

"He's here," she whispered the words.

Her soft tone didn't lower his heart-rate or unclench his fist. He'd only seen the man in photos and Ronan was already beating himself up for letting Vander clef get past him. "You saw him? Where?"

She looked as frustrated as he felt. Her fingers were still interlaced with Talia's on the other side, but Tierney shrugged and waved her hands as best she could. "I didn't! I just feel it."

"Could you just be paranoid?" *Lord knew he was.* He understood. Sometimes he went into a burning building and just had a bad feeling. Sometimes, whatever it was didn't happen. Firefighters liked to believe that their bad feelings were born of gut knowledge and subconscious clues. They also liked to believe that if the bad thing didn't happen, it had been through their own successful efforts to stop it. But Ronan had no proof for that.

The problem here was that Tierney knew Elliot Vander clef intimately—or at least she *had*. Ronan had never seen the man in person and had been left to study old photos and the mock-ups Tierney had made. He wasn't entirely confident that he would recognize the man at a glance.

"I'm *not* paranoid." The edge in her voice cut him. She was mad. He shouldn't have said it and his chest caved in with a shamed sigh.

It wasn't paranoia if someone really was after her. He'd seen more than enough evidence with his own eyes that suggesting she was paranoid would be way out in left field. "I'm sorry."

"Thank you." But the words were low and she didn't look at him.

Still, he turned and scanned the crowd, doing his best to locate Vander clef. A sting ricocheted through his arm and he knew it was Tierney slapping him.

"Don't!"

He held back a yelped "ow."

"We don't want him to know that we know he's here. I'm pretty confident that he is."

Ronan almost shook his head. Was she confident or not? But she knew the man and he didn't. Who was he to say what a proper reaction was? Maybe he did need to brush up on his Stalker 101.

Still, a sweet feeling melted through him as Tierney reached out and laced her fingers through his one more time. She motioned Talia in front of them, oblivious to the revelations in his head.

He was falling for her.

No. He wasn't.

He'd already fallen.

She'd snuck under his skin when he wasn't looking, when he believed his defenses were locked down. She'd slipped past without his even knowing until it was far too late. She'd probably been there for some time, and he'd been too stupid to see it for what it was until he was threatened with losing her. The new things he'd learned about Tierney—Emily Gallagher—only made him admire and want her more. Involuntarily, his fingers twitched in hers, and he wondered how much longer he could hide this.

But she was talking, and he turned to watch her lips move even as he tried desperately to pay attention to what she was saying.

"We head in. We hang out. We act normal. Try to use this chance to turn around inside and sweep the area. Of course, try not to look like you're doing it."

"Talia?" Ronan asked her, but she quickly replied.

"I know who I'm looking for ... at least as well as I can at this point."

Just a few weeks ago, he'd had no idea that all wasn't exactly as it seemed. All of a sudden, when the shit hit the fan, the Doyles had lept into action. They'd secreted Sean away somewhere that they believed was as safe as it could be. They rallied around Tierney and educated the troops, stunning everyone. Honestly, even Ronan had a hard time believing that Ewan and Aileen Doyle had pulled off a secret of this magnitude for so long. If anyone had asked, he would have said neither of them was even capable of a lie.

He didn't begrudge them any of it, though. The good deed they'd done taking in Tierney at sixteen when she'd been in danger, and possibly even a threat to them and their family, was above and beyond. So far, no one that he'd talked to had faulted them for this either.

Squeezing Tierney's hand tighter—his head swimming with the need to stay vigilant and buzzing from the feelings he was just admitting—he pushed his way into the bustling floral shop. Individual flowers were being handed out along with candy and coupons for future purchases. They each accepted a free flower as Ronan grinned. It was hard to be mad about that, but maybe they should have brought bags for all the goodies. Talia at least had her ever-present backpack.

Turning away under the guise of looking at the arrangements on display, Ronan scanned the people in the store. No one looked like any version of Vander clef to him. Unable to stop himself, he reached out, grabbing a small bouquet of purple and white, thinking to give it to Tierney. It fit with his self-designated role as her protector. For a moment he thought about sliding it back into the holder as he recalled her admonishing him and suggesting that would bring Elliot down on him harder.

Ronan wasn't as concerned about his ability to fend off Elliot as much as he was about his ability to keep Tierney safe. He also didn't want to risk her wrath, if only because she had enough on her plate right now.

She eyed the bouquet in his hand oddly. In a moment of quick thinking, he reached out and found a gorgeous orange and yellow bouquet of the same size. Leaning in close, he whispered in her ear, "Look around."

It was stupid—as if she didn't know to do that, as if she wasn't constantly vigilant. The feel of her skin, so close to his mouth, and the scent of her wafting over him for a moment, made him close his eyes and linger. Forcibly, he shook himself out of it.

Was he going to do this? Was he really head over heels for Tierney? Just moments ago, he'd believed he was already underwater on that, but now he thought maybe it was just the stress of the situation. Was he bored because he'd been out of work for weeks? Was he lonely? He wished he had better answers to all of it.

He wished this shit with Elliot Vander clef was already over. But he promised himself it would be soon as he headed to the counter to pay for the bouquets. He came back and handed the purple to Tierney and the one that looked like a sunset to Talia.

After brushing off thank-yous, he pushed his way out the door, trying to make a wide enough path for Talia, as the two women followed in his wake. The street had once again become more crowded and noisier in the time they'd been inside.

He looked around and again didn't see anything alarming.

As he let out a sigh of relief, his head snapped up. A deep male voice called out, "Emily! Emily!"

CHAPTER TWENTY-SIX

Tierney was exhausted. Maybe it was from the Crawl itself, but she suspected it was from walking on eggshells. She'd heard shouts for "Emily" on three different occasions but never could locate Elliot. She would have fallen asleep in the passenger seat of Ronan's sports car if it hadn't been so awkward.

They'd first looped back to the Bakery—no easy feat—to get Talia to her car. There had been no way to get Talia and her chair back to the shop except to walk it. Luckily, Ronan's car was nearby. Tierney had climbed in gratefully, ready to be home and thinking she might just really sleep for the first time tonight. She was suddenly that tired.

But the seat wasn't cushy, and she leaned her head against the window watching the lights, but they weren't passing very fast. The post-crawl traffic was slow enough that Tierney figured they might have been able to walk faster.

"Are you okay?" His hand snaked out and twined with hers.

"I'm good. Just tired ... and I miss Sean." She shouldn't hold his hand.

A shout went up next to her side of the car and she straightened even as Ronan ducked his head to look out.

"Asshole," he commented at the man strutting down the street, too drunk to be upright.

Tierney felt her eyes widen. Wayne Davies.

She hadn't known him at the time, but later when she'd seen him again, she'd learned his name. She turned to Ronan. "You know him?"

"Sure, enough to know he's an ass."

But not enough to know that this man had fucked his wife at her parents' home just after they'd been married? Nothing in his expression gave away any pain, nothing personal. Tierney clenched her teeth.

Siorse should have honored some level of honeymoon phase, but clearly she hadn't. So Tierney, underwater with her own problems had kept the secret to this day.

"Why?" Ronan asked her. "I assume everyone knows he's just an ass."

"You have no idea," she answered through a nearly locked jaw.

"Did he do something to you?" The response was swift and harsh. Not *at* her, but *for* her.

Shaking her head, Tierney bit back the words, *No, but he did something to* you. *You just don't know it.*

They approached the intersection at a crawl as the officer waved them through and Wayne Davies and his just-as-obnoxious friends turned right and headed away from the car. On the other side, traffic picked up a little speed and by the time they were through the next light, the crowds were almost gone.

Tierney would have nodded off, but for the odd structure of the seat and her residual anger at Wayne Davies. And at Siorse.

She hadn't actively caught her sister with other men, but she'd caught her in more than one lie over the years. There was no reason to think Siorse had changed. She'd seen her sister in

Lincoln with a blond-haired man, but it wasn't anyone she knew, and no one who'd come into the bar ever. Tierney's heart sank with a thought that she'd not had in a long time ... had Paddy even been Ronan's child?

She'd had her doubts at the time. The child's blond hair and the timing made her wonder, but she'd held her tongue as she always had when it came to Siorse. Trying to shake her morbid thoughts, Tierney looked out the window. "You missed my turn!"

"Nope. We are going to my place."

"Mr. Kittens is there alone." It was the only excuse she could come up with as her chest tightened and her blood bloomed warm through her whole body.

"We'll check on her and the kittens in the morning."

Tierney swallowed and nodded but kept looking out the window. Before she'd had time to think about it, they were idling in the drive waiting for the garage door. Then she was in the relatively warm cocoon of the garage, the cold of the night finally wearing off. She didn't even have a bag on her, all her cash and her ID had been stuffed into pockets to be relatively carefree. There was a stash of cookies in her pockets, a bouquet in the backseat that she couldn't leave. And she was full of pie and cupcakes and shots from Snafu.

Maybe she'd had too many of those shots—more than the average crawler had gotten because she was the manager. Was she tired? Or maybe a little tipsy?

She stood up a little too quickly and covered her bad balance by grabbing the things from the backseat. Trying to stay perfectly upright, she followed Ronan inside through the small mudroom. In the kitchen that she knew almost as well as her own, she reached up for a vase and felt the warm press of Ronan against her as he seemed to realize she couldn't reach it. Slowly, he put the glass vase into her grip and she grabbed it with two hands—like a toddler ... or a woman who realized she was far too attracted to the man handing her the vase.

She was cutting the stems, so hyper-focused on the task at hand—on keeping her mind from what she wanted to do with her hands—that she was startled when he touched her. His fingers caressed her shoulders, then her neck and she had a fleeting thought that he was going to seduce her.

"Let me get this."

But he was only taking her coat.

She turned, her face surely as flushed as it felt and she was too stupid to do anything but stare at him for a moment. His own coat was gone. Her eyes flicked to the side, and saw it hanging on the stand near the door. She watched him turn and hook hers next to his ... as though it belonged there. As though this was her house and he was hers.

Tierney turned back to the flowers, chopping too hard with the knife, and setting each one into the water. As she got down to the last two, she realized he hadn't moved. Ronan was still standing behind her.

Why was he there?

She breathed heavier. She'd definitely had too many shots. She was not thinking clearly.

But her thoughts were clearer than they ever had been. She knew what she wanted. Though she reminded herself that this man had once belonged to her sister, her other half replied that her sister had never belonged to him. Even if he didn't know that, even if he never learned it, he'd not deserved what Siorse had done. For some reason, that gave Tierney an excuse to do what she knew she shouldn't.

She put the last stem into the vase, telling herself that he would move. That if she turned and he walked away, she wouldn't pursue him.

Without taking a moment to check the arrangement, she sucked in a breath. She was buzzing with anticipation.

"Tee?"

His voice was too close. Too seductive. She told herself it didn't mean what she wanted it to mean. But she wanted it too.

Turning slowly, she found that he wasn't just too close, he was so close that she brushed against him as she lined herself up. Her breath caught, her eyes flared. The scent of him in her space invaded her.

She froze.

CHAPTER TWENTY-SEVEN

Tierney stood, immobilized, pressed against Ronan and probably not quite sober enough to make the decision she was making.

Ronan didn't move either.

It would have been awkward if she had been breathing. But after a moment, she had to.

Her eyes glanced away, her heart pounded, and her fingers and toes curled. *She wanted this.* She wanted her made up past to be her real one. She wanted her name to actually be Tierney Doyle, and she wanted Ronan Kelly to love her. None of that was real, but this moment could be.

When Ronan tipped his head to catch her gaze, he likely caught more than he bargained for.

Surging upward onto her toes, Tierney wrapped her arms around his neck. She didn't mean to trap him, but the impulse was too strong and she clung to him the way she'd wanted to for so long. She pressed her mouth to his, not knowing what would happen, just giving it a try.

His breath sucked in and his hands settled at her hips and for a petrifying moment she was certain he was going to push her away. But he didn't.

Unexpected heat flared in his eyes as he leaned in closer and took what she was offering.

Digging harshly into her hips, his fingers pulled her closer. His mouth devoured hers as he leaned into a kiss she'd never expected to happen anywhere other than her dreams. Pressing forward, Tierney laced her fingers into his hair, daring him to take everything. And she was offering everything.

She was tired of waiting, tired of wondering if her past would show up to surprise her or haunt her. It was doing both, and she might not survive it, but she could have this. One night.

The counter pressed against her lower back and she used it to leverage herself into him. Surely, he would call off this craziness at any moment. But she wouldn't. As she lifted onto her toes, she felt the friction of the two of them sliding against each other, and another burst of flames shot through her. Her brain fogged and reality slipped away. Nothing mattered but now, so she clung to it with everything she had.

Her fingers found the hem of his shirt and slid underneath to smooth skin and thick muscle. Her breath escaped as his mouth moved to her ear, her jaw, and down her neck. Her fingers slid upward, just a little, enjoying the feel of him and the way his stomach sucked in at her touch. She quickly ran into the fresh scar from his accident. He was healed, but it was still new. Her fingers curled back, not wanting to hurt him.

Ronan abruptly stepped backward.

The space between them was small but cold and empty.

What had she done? Was it over? If that was all she ever got of this man it would have to be enough.

He was looking at her, examining something, and Tierney was certain she'd failed whatever test he was giving her.

Taking another step back, he widened the distance just

enough to put her out of arm's reach. It was over. Short and sweet, but done.

His hands reached up and over his head. Grabbing the back of his shirt by the neck he pulled it off, taking the t-shirt underneath with it in one smooth motion.

This stupid town had to have their annual Crawl in the cold. As though it were some show of bravado to suffer the weather like real Nebraskans. He was bare chested in front of her now, and she still had on two shirts of her own.

Tierney stepped forward, her hands on his hips, holding him to her as she leaned in and took a breath. He smelled like ice cream and whiskey. Like a night on the town. Like the man of her dreams for so long. She kissed along his collarbone while he stood still and let her worship him for a moment. Making her way down his chest, she kissed across his side, and her knees bent. She lowered her mouth down to the scar where she gently revered it with small kisses. It meant he was alive and for that she was more grateful than she could express.

His breathing was ragged beneath the soft touch of her lips. She could feel the spike in his pulse, watch his fingers clench and uncurl, clench and uncurl as she caressed him. There was no better feeling than the power of making this man want her. He sucked in another deep gulp of air as she trailed her mouth across his stomach, but then his fingers dug into her shoulders and he pushed her away.

This time, she looked up at him. Stood up and met his eyes.

This time, she saw the flames there, blue and gold and white hot.

He pulled her toward him, kissing her greedily, and grabbing for the hem of her shirts. Tierney helped, and in seconds they were off, tossed and forgotten onto the floor beside his. Ronan stared reverently at the lacy bra she wore as Tierney thanked every god she could think of that she'd decided it was comfortable enough to wear all day. But she wasn't wearing it much longer.

In seconds, he'd slid the straps off her shoulders, baring her to his view. She could have been embarrassed or shy, but the reverence in his gaze burned all of that away and he leaned in to kiss her mouth, pressing them together, skin to skin, as the jolt of it shot through her system, tightening between her legs and making her slide against him again.

There was only a short wall defining the edge of the kitchen, but Ronan backed her against it. He used the pressure to hold her in place as his mouth searched her flesh, causing her to gasp and moan. Her eyes rolled back. When had it felt like this?

She realized her hands were grasping at his waist and she didn't want to pull at the freshly healed wound. There was still a small nagging voice at the back of her head for that one ... but she quelled it, or he did, with his mouth. With his fingers making short work of the button on her jeans.

Returning the favor, Tierney tugged at the zipper on his and sighed as his warm hands slid down between the denim and her skin.

Ronan Kelly was touching her. It seemed straight out of her dreams. The dreams she'd always told herself were okay because they were only dreams. Because they'd never become real. But here she was, pressed firm against the wall, Ronan Kelly anchoring her there, the thick ridge of his erection jutting between them.

He reached back into his pocket as the jeans got lower, before he couldn't reach. He pulled out a receipt and tossed it onto the counter that was pushing at her hip. He yanked a list and tossed it, too, his eyes still holding hers. Then he pulled his wallet and set it gingerly down, so his fingers could search by touch. In a moment, he pulled back. His breath was heavy between them and tucked between his first two fingers was a condom.

A little beaten up, it made her happy. She was glad it wasn't shiny new. He hadn't put it there today ... This wasn't taking fresh advantage of that, nor had he used the last one so recently he'd had to replace it. Neither option should matter to her, but it did.

Tierney was more than willing to let this man take advantage of her. His last conquest should be of no consequence when she would only ever have this one night. But she was going to enjoy it. She plucked the foil from his fingers to say "yes."

His hand was in hers, his jeans still riding low as he stepped away. Ronan tugged her around the corner, stepping in front of the fireplace and hitting a switch that roared the flames to life. She would have laughed, it might not be the sexiest building of a fire, but a fire was a fire, and she hadn't had to sit back and wait while he assembled little piles of kindling.

She almost told him so but, before her mouth could open, he was skimming his jeans down his body. Despite the weeks off work, he was still glorious. Tierney told herself that she shouldn't already know this, but she did.

He was fully naked and fully at attention in front of her and, while she'd known she wouldn't turn back, she hadn't been sure he wouldn't until now. Making short work of her own jeans and socks she stepped out of the messy pile of clothing and reached for the sides of her underwear. Somehow, he'd plucked the condom from her grasp and he was now sliding down her body, taking her underwear with him. Taking her with him.

She was on the thick, fluffy white rug in front of the fireplace, Ronan's arms around her before she realized what was happening.

Though he tried to slow down, there were no brakes on this system and Tierney was wrapping herself around him, needing him in a way that didn't allow for time. Her hips moved, her back arched, her fingers dug in, holding him close as he quickly rolled the condom on and held himself steady as she pushed her hips forward.

He hadn't quite been ready to make the move, but she made it for him. His groan of satisfaction only encouraged her. Tierney rolled her hips again and took him in slightly further.

That was it. Any strength he'd had to hold back, to go slow, disappeared. With a thrust that strung her tight like a bow, and his arms tightening around her, Ronan joined them together fully.

The flames licked at her side, but the heat of him moving inside her shut out all other sensation. There was only her and him and this one moment. Only her own body telling her to get closer, to make him moan again, to tie him to her and let him know without words how she really felt. Because this would be all there was. This might even be too much, but it was too late to go back.

His hands found her hair and tilted her face up to his.

It was too much, the stark need in his gaze. The feel of him in her, moving, taking her higher, as he saw exactly who she was.

Arching up, she kissed him, and moved faster. She felt the heady rush of pushing him closer to the edge as she felt the electric surge of her own orgasm getting so close. He moved harder and faster and she met him at each push. Until at last she felt the dam burst and she cried out as wave after wave hit her.

With a deep, needful breath, he stared at her again as he came, but she closed her eyes against the new lies she was telling him.

CHAPTER TWENTY-EIGHT

Ronan came slowly awake to the feel of soft heat in his arms. He almost jolted as the sense of Tierney pressed warm and naked against him revived a stunning string of memories.

Had they even spoken? Had she kissed him first? Or had he made the first move?

He remembered but still couldn't quite tell.

She shuffled a little in her sleep and his senses blazed to life. The covers were pulled up to their shoulders so he navigated by touch, cupping a warm heavy breast, tracing the indentation of her waist and following the soft skin of her hip. She moaned and rolled closer.

If he hadn't woken up at full attention, he would be now.

In an effort to slow himself down, he slid his hand across her stomach and pulled her back close. She had to feel what she was doing to him. Her head tilted. Had she meant to turn to face him, or had she turned just so he could whisper to her?

"Tierney ..." He wanted her. He needed this. His hips rolled of their own accord and her responding movement caused enough friction to say yes.

He wanted to say that he didn't know where this had come from, that it had sprung up on him ... But he hadn't been drunk last night. He'd been sober enough to drive and sober enough to want her of his own true volition. She hadn't been drunk either. Her eyes weren't clear, but the three shots had been long gone before they arrived here and she took out whatever frustrations she'd had on that poor bouquet. Had he only been trying to calm her?

Whatever bullshit he tried to sell himself, he recognized as bullshit.

He wanted her. Plain and simple.

She impressed the hell out of him and there was something about being wanted by a woman who'd faked a new identity at sixteen and only gotten more badass over the years. He'd wondered about her lack of ambition, why she hadn't gone any further than the family bar. He told himself she was the only remaining daughter and she was staying close to home. He told himself she just didn't want anything bigger in life and that all the talk of med school had only been talk.

But now that he knew her secrets he understood. There was nothing about her that was only talk.

Her leg moved up and over his and he felt the groan rising from somewhere in his core at her clear invitation. His hand wandered, down her thigh and back up. To her breast, where she arched her back, pressing into his touch, and molding her ass into his hips.

He breathed like he'd climbed a mountain. Maybe he had. His hand slipped down, finally touching her in the way she'd asked for, eliciting a cry and a startled undulation up her whole body as he found exactly the right spot. He nibbled at her ear, riding the waves with her as he played her like a finely tuned instrument. His own need built with each stroke of her body against his. Each time he touched her, she rubbed against him and he was rock hard and far too ready before he'd planned.

"Tierney," he whispered again, and then moved in closer. He touched her harder and wondered if she heard him when he breathed the name "Emily" into her skin. She was both and neither and something in between as she came apart with just his touch.

With one hand wrapped around her, he leaned back, reaching for another condom. He almost fumbled it in his haste. He needed this, now.

So when she rubbed back against him one more time, he moved his hips. But she eluded him, rolling up onto her knees and inviting him up behind her. His brain short circuited as he scrambled to his own knees and plunged in. His fingers clenched her hips, holding her to him as he moved recklessly, driven only by a wild need he'd not really known he could possess.

She bucked back against him, her own pleasure not yet finished. His thoughts fried as he moved with her and against her, as the white hot sensation built until he came with a roar that burst out of him without permission, with no holds barred.

For long minutes he rocked against her, coming in waves before eventually landing back on earth.

When he finally pulled away and rolled to his side, he reached out to touch her.

He didn't quite know what switch had flipped last night but he was glad. Tierney was safer here with him. He knew that had been an excuse to keep her close. He simply wanted her here.

His eyes rolled up to the ceiling. How would he tell Mom and Dad Doyle? Would they be happy for him or think he was a monster?

But he could figure that out later. His chest was full with the strange and heavy joy that came with finding the right woman, with having her want to be with him, too. Reaching out, he pulled her back close to him again but was startled by the heaviness of her.

"Tierney?" He moved forward. If she couldn't come back to him ...

She rolled forward, too. Onto her knees, where she scooted away and toward the edge of the bed.

"Tee? Come back?"

She was walking away, looking over her shoulder. "I need to go home."

What?

"I'll take you home. Just come back for a minute." He wasn't whining, but the heat that had filled him started to falter. "Tee?"

"I need to go home." It wasn't mean, just firm. She was out the door before he could even get his brain to function.

Standing, he felt the welcome tug of muscles long unused. He hadn't been celibate since Siorse had died, but ... close.

The carpet was soft and familiar beneath his feet as he stopped in the doorway and saw her there, stepping into yesterday's lacy panties that in no way matched the bra that had to still be on his kitchen floor. "Tee?"

"I need you to drive me home. I don't want to call a ride at eight a.m. on a Sunday wearing yesterday's clothes."

"Of course not!" He would drive her. But he stood there, naked, until she gave him a nod that told him to go put his own clothing on.

He was dressed and heading out to his car, the garage door rising and letting in sharp winds that had thankfully stayed away last night. Her hair picked up, auburn curls dancing around her head as she shuffled herself into the passenger side of his car. As he slid into the seat and started the engine, he turned toward her. "Tierney?"

She shook her head at him.

What did that mean? Did it just mean she hadn't had her coffee yet or was she completely denying that last night had happened?

"Are you okay?" He had to know that much at least.

"Yes." It was an odd answer, too formal.

Ronan put his hands on the steering wheel to steady them and resigned himself to not knowing what was in her head for a while. He made it partway down the block before she started talking.

"Last night was—"

"Amazing." He interrupted her on purpose. As if he could stop her from feeling what she felt or saying what she wanted to say.

"Yes, it was."

He breathed out a sigh of relief and took a right hand turn onto the main road. He was opening his mouth to tell her ... what? He didn't know if he could define how he felt, but he had to let her know he didn't want to forget about it. She beat him to it.

"Last night was wonderful. I always thought—"

He waited but she didn't finish.

Eventually she said something else. "Last night has to stay last night."

"What does that mean?" He'd almost hit the brakes and sent the tires squealing. This was not a conversation he wanted to have on the road, but he kept his eyes on traffic, no matter how slim it was. Hadn't he just learned that lesson the hard way?

"It means we can't be together, and that you and I really need to be physically far apart for a while—"

"Tierney, no. You have a stalker after you."

"Yes, I do!" Why she was so mad about a fact like that, he didn't know. "Ronan! You don't believe me how dangerous this man is."

"He's—"

"A *murderer!*"

CHAPTER TWENTY-NINE

He'd almost slammed the brakes at the last thing Tierney had said, but this made it even harder to hold onto his focus.

That she was calling Elliot Vander clef a murderer was news. Ronan clarified, "He *threatened* to murder you?"

Tierney shook her head. She was looking out the window, but he could tell she was irritated at him. Not that he knew why. Her jaw clenched. "It was more than that."

"What, Tierney? What did he do?" She'd told him a lot about Vander clef, but Ronan would have remembered if there was murder in the listings.

"One of the guys I dated ... I can't prove it, but I found a few things."

"I don't understand. How is that murder?"

She sucked in a breath. "I went on one date with this guy and that night, after he dropped me off, he got mugged. Stabbed. He died from his injuries in the hospital."

"It could be a coincidence."

"It's not *a coincidence*, Ronan!" Her words were sharp, her anger aimed right at him. "And this is exactly the problem!"

He wanted to make her not angry at him. Why was she mad at *him*? He wanted to yell, *What, exactly, is the problem?* Because it seemed to him that her stalker was the problem, not Ronan trying to help. But he didn't have to ask.

"The problem is that you don't believe me. You think you're some superhero-firefighter-god who can handle anything that comes at you! But you can't!"

"Ouch." The word fell out. The hit was more than damaging to his ego. It was bad enough that she thought he was so arrogant. He knew better than most that people weren't as immortal as they liked to believe. But it also hurt that she clearly thought he couldn't take on this Elliot Vander clef dude. He almost said, "No offense, Tee. But I think I can handle a little posh fancy boy like that." Nevermind that Vander clef was over six feet tall. At least Ronan was, too.

None of what he wanted to say mattered. Tierney's anger was rolling off her in waves. "You don't believe me. You think I'm overreacting, but you weren't there."

The last part at least was true. He had no doubts that whatever Vander clef had done, he'd frightened her. Ronan didn't think she was overselling that. Taking a deep breath, he tried to navigate the choppy waters of her anger. "I don't think you're overreacting." It wasn't really a lie. "But I do think your perspective might be different. You were sixteen the last time you were around him. He must have seemed larger than life."

She let out an ugly sigh. *Still angry?* "Yes. I was only sixteen, but I still remember his words. I remember how he came in and threatened my parents—"

"I don't hold up to threats—"

"Yes, you do, Ronan!" She yelled it at him, her anger bouncing around the small car and hitting him from all sides. "Yes, you do! You will when he's threatening your parents and your brothers. Or he's threatening your fire station. When he tells you that your family will die and you know he's willing to kill them, there's nothing you can do but give in and you know it."

Ronan frowned, thinking through those possibilities. His parents would be okay. His dad was a tough old bird and his mother was too stubborn to let anyone take advantage of her. His brothers were also firefighters and he had faith that they could take care of themselves. So as much as Tierney might be threatened by those things, he wasn't. He didn't even have a child that Vander clef could use against him anymore. The one thing that might begin to sway him was if this asshole got his hands on Tierney.

He made the last turn onto her street.

Her arms were crossed, and she shook her head, still angry at him. "Just drop me off."

Whatever Vander clef might be, he was just a man. Did she not understand that the firefighters had been trained to go in and defuse domestic violence situations? Maybe now wasn't the time to say that, but damn, if not now, was she going to walk away from him? Could she really pretend that last night had never happened?

He had to consciously slow his speed. Kids lived on this street. People might be leaving for church despite the Crawl last night. They passed the first few houses as she started to talk again. At least she was talking.

"I don't know if he saw us last night, or if he saw us leaving together, but the more I think about it, us being there as a date was a bad call. It's waving a red flag at a psychopathic bull."

Even so, Ronan thought, *she was safer with him than without him.* "Tee?"

He was pulling up closer to her home, the whole time keeping his eyes in front of him, hoping that he could think of something to say to make her change her mind. There was an odd shadow across the front doorstep and he tried to focus, but she was still talking.

"Look Ronan, I know that you don't think that I'm right about this, but it doesn't matter what you think."

This time, his head swiveled to look at her. The daggers she was slinging today were incredibly sharp.

"I'm asking you to drop me off and leave me alone. It's safer for everyone."

"What are you going to do if and when he confronts you and you're by yourself?"

All she said was, "I've got it covered."

Ronan didn't know what that meant. "Tierney—"

He cut his own words short. His eyes had been scanning the road and the shadow on the front doorstep had grown larger.

"Don't argue with me about this."

"Tee?" He tried again to cut her off as he slowly turned toward her driveway, not liking what he was seeing.

The shadow was orange and unmoving. One small paw stuck up into the air.

"Look Ronan, you don't get to make my decisions for me. I'm sorry that I led you on last night, but—"

"Led me on?" His attention torn between Tierney lighting into him and his growing concern about what he was seeing.

Pulling into the driveway, he leaned a little forward, hoping he was blocking her view. Maybe he was doing it on purpose. "I don't think you led me on. I don't think that's really a thing. I just knew what I wanted and I acted on it."

"That's good. I don't regret it," she said, and what had to be coming next wasn't good. He could feel it in the air. "I just—"

He cut her off again and held his hand out as if to hold her into the seat. "Tee!"

His hand laid flat against her chest where he could feel the heat of her and the subtle pulse of her heartbeat beneath his palm. He shouldn't have touched her that way. He shouldn't have made last night's memories flare. "Tee, stay in the car."

"What?"

But he couldn't answer. He couldn't handle both things coming at the same time. So he pulled the handle, opened the door, and unfolded his legs out the side. He was heading up the walk, his heart pounding and a knot forming in the center of his chest as he saw for certain the orange cat gutted and draped across the front doorstep as if waiting for Tierney to come out and step on it.

The car door popped behind him as Tierney absolutely did not follow his instructions. Why had he even expected her to?

Turning around, he said, "Tee, don't look!"

But the expression of horror that crossed her face told him he was already too late.

She gulped hard, swallowing down whatever painful emotions were assaulting her at the sight. Tierney whispered, "Mr. Kittens!" Then she sucked in a breath as if to cry. "What will I tell Sean?"

CHAPTER THIRTY

Tierney stood on her own front walk staring down at the lifeless body. She fought the overwhelming urge to vomit and cry. It was a struggle just to breathe. She should never have fed the cat. Just being near her had put the sweet creature in danger. She wanted to fall to her knees and sob, but the neighbors were likely watching.

They might not have noticed the dead rats before, but this? Her thoughts pinged from the mundane—how would she clean this up?—to the painful—she hoped the cat hadn't suffered.

But the suffering was the point with Elliot. He was sweet and charming until he decided that he liked it better when he was hurting you. Tierney tried to focus on the present. She would kill Elliot for this.

Just like the rats, Mr. Kittens entrails had been pulled out and draped over the steps. Only Mr. Kittens was much larger, and it was much more personal of a hit. She wanted to yell at Ronan that someone who does this to an animal—any animal, let alone a beloved pet—is someone none of us wants to be dealing with! But it wasn't worth her breath. Ronan thought he was better than Elliot and that he'd easily best the man if it came down to it. So Tierney consoled herself by hoping she might be able to narrow Elliot's focus to herself. She had nothing left to lose.

Well, she had a *lot* to lose, but she knew that when her back was against the wall she would have to accept that everything else was already lost. She would fight like it.

She couldn't say any of that, though. The words wouldn't form. A knot, cold and heavy clogged her throat.

"Please don't look," Ronan begged her, as if she could turn away. As if that would be enough to scrub the horrible image from her mind. "I need to go check around the house."

He stepped up onto the porch, reaching for the front knob and clearly finding it locked. "Please," he said, taking her hand and leading her back to the car.

She let him move her. There was nothing she could do for Mr. Kittens now. As Ronan walked around the side of the house, Tierney watched him disappear through the gate and head to the back. There was probably a window smashed out somewhere, maybe a lock picked. Hell, knowing Elliot, he already had a key to her home, and maybe he'd simply gone in the front door like he lived there. He would love that.

But, as she leaned back against the car, the metal still warm from the drive over, she realized her mistake. *The kittens! Where were the kittens?*

She yelled out that she was going inside, just as Ronan called out to her, "I don't see any sign of entry back here."

Tierney had already bolted to the porch, fumbling in her pockets for her keys, hoping they were still where she had stuffed them for the crawl. Last night seemed a thousand miles away, now, but she had to get inside.

The kittens were far too young to go without a mother and Tierney was in no shape to bottle feed them. How long had they been alone? What would happen to them? She couldn't check in every few hours and watch out for Elliot all the time. Then again, this might be Elliot's only move for the next three or four months. A horrifying thought occurred to her: would Sean even recognize her when she finally made her way back to him?

Her hands were shaking as she jabbed the key at the lock three times before finally sliding it into place. She twisted the knob like a fool and tugged on the door. Luckily, it didn't give. She fumbled again, now looking for a second key. What if she ever needed to get *inside* the house quickly? Maybe two separate keys hadn't been her best decision. It had simply seemed the most secure at the time.

Unlocking the top bolt in a rush of success, she almost threw the door wide, slamming it into the dead body across her doorstep. Instead, she stopped at the last moment and squeezed her way through. Stepping into the living room she called out, "Snack babies!"

It was the stupidest thing. Ronan was stepping up behind her as she neared the large cardboard box where she'd made Mr. Kittens a bed to deliver in. She'd tucked in old towels and a few puppy pads she'd splurged on.

"What?" he asked clearly confused by what she'd called out.

She was frustrated. This was hardly the time. Per Zadie's instructions, she'd found a box with high enough sides that the kittens couldn't escape. So she couldn't see if they were still there, but the box was silent. She called out again, "Snack babies?"

Then again, maybe a mundane task like explaining was exactly what her brain needed now. "I named them after snacks. There's Cheeto and Dorito and Tostito and Frito and Pringle—"

He started laughing. It *was* funny, and she'd done it because she'd thought Sean would like it. Would he get back in time to see the kittens at all?

Tierney inched closer and looked down into the box, the tiny mews finally reaching through the fog of her brain and catching her attention.

Were the babies already hungry? She reached in and picked one up, wondering if it was cold. She hadn't given it a heating pad or anything, thinking their mother would keep them warm. Thinking she hadn't wanted to spend the extra money and she didn't have that much to spare anyway. She'd spent the last ten years saving every bit she could for an escape she might need to make one day. Now, she regretted her decision. Saving up to run again had not been her best thought.

Soft tears rolled down her face as she held the tiny squalling pale kitten she'd named Pringle up to her chest. She whispered onto his tiny head, "I'm so sorry, baby."

"Tee?" Ronan was tapping at her with the back of his hand, "Tee. Look."

Look at what? But a hefty meow grabbed her attention. Stunned, she watched as Mr. Kittens strolled her way out of the laundry room, where Tierney had set up a placemat with food and water and a litter box. *"What?"*

"What was on the porch?" Ronan said, speaking as he figured it out for himself. "Apparently, that wasn't Mr. Kittens."

Tierney sucked in a deep sigh of relief. "I didn't look at the face. I just ..."

"Saw exactly what you were supposed to see," Ronan told her.

So Elliot had figured out that not only did she have a cat that she loved, he knew what it looked like. Despite the fact that Mr. Kittens had not been outside in well over a week now, he'd known what her cat looked like.

Another meow from Mr. Kittens as she jumped into the box, let Tierney know she was being talked to. The cat turned and looked expectantly, making Tierney realize she was still hugging the poor cat's kitten, maybe a little too tightly. "Here you go, baby. I'm sorry. I took Pringle."

"I like their names," Ronan said with a small grin. "At least it wasn't actually Mr. Kittens."

She was nodding, her emotions had been pulled back, tense, then shot from a slingshot and bounced off the wall.

"I know where the shovel is," he volunteered. "If you grab me a trash bag, I'll clean the front porch for you."

She wanted to tell him no. That she would take care of it herself but, for once, she thought she would step back. Reaching down, she stroked Mr. Kittens' soft head. Then she didn't answer but headed into the kitchen, where she pulled out a dark trash bag. A smaller bag would be the better size but she did not want to look into the can later and see the shadow of the dead animal through the thin plastic. This one was far too big for the job, but she simply handed it to Ronan and let him head out to the front porch.

Sitting on the floor next to the box, she enjoyed the simple pleasure of the tiny kittens stretching their little twig legs. They were starting to walk, though mostly they still rolled around. She touched each tiny head, repeating the little names, grateful that they were all here. She was thinking even as she sat and relaxed the best she could, that she shouldn't have let Ronan clean the porch for her. She should have done it herself.

What would the neighbors think? What would they tell Elliot when he charmed information out of them?

She heard the noises of the shovel scraping on cement. Tierney figured he was dumping dirt onto the blood like she'd done before, so he could scrape it off and mask the stains. She heard the trash can bump against the fence as he lifted the lid and dropped the dead body of some poor orange tabby cat. This poor cat was getting garbage can treatment simply because he hadn't been Mr. Kittens.

As Ronan came back in through the front door, announcing

that he was finished, Tierney looked up from her spot on the floor. Her hands still lingered in the soft fur of the kittens, as if that would give her strength.

"Ronan," she told him, "Thank you for cleaning that up for me. But you need to leave and please don't come back."

CHAPTER THIRTY-ONE

Ronan had little to do given that it was Sunday and he didn't even have any errands to run. He'd woken up, thinking he might spend the day with Tierney. Even just the thought of it had made him happy but, instead, he'd cleaned entrails off her porch and was summarily dismissed.

She might think she didn't need him around, but he was going to make himself useful one way or another. He didn't question why he felt this core need, he only knew that he needed to do this. So he headed toward the police station, but stopped in at the Firehouse to see B-shift and say his hellos.

It still felt odd to be here in civilian clothing. The firefighters did sometimes stop by when they were off duty, so maybe it was that he didn't have a date or time to show up again, maybe it was that he was still twisting in the wind, that made this feel so odd.

"Good to see you, but when are you coming back?" It was a question that didn't really need to be answered, but Ronan did anyway.

"One more week. One more week." He repeated the phrase

as if saying it like a mantra would make it come true. But a few moments later he saw that the day was sliding by, the guys were watching TV and clocking time until afternoon training or the alarm rang. There was nothing for him here, so he told them goodbye and headed out the front door into the wind. A few short steps later, he was at the local police department.

The fire station and PD shared a building. The town was small enough that it made sense. Pulling the door open, he stepped into the warmth of a building again.

"Hey, Ronan, Honey. How are you doing?" Marlene Davies waved at him as he came in.

He barely stopped at the desk. "Hey Marlene. How are you? Can I see Gomez?"

She didn't even flinch at his stacked questions. "Sure, Hon. He's in the back."

The PD usually had an officer at the front desk, but on nights and most Sundays they had Marlene. She was more like a receptionist than an officer of any kind. Her hold on the front line was slim at best and her ability to intimidate anyone was nonexistent. So she smiled at him and hit the buzzer as she was wanting to do for most anybody. The door to the back swung open on her command, giving him free access to the station.

He waved her a polite goodbye as he headed into the back. At least, he consoled himself, he wasn't here to do any harm.

He passed by various officers that he knew, so he waved and said a quick hello, but he quickly found Gomez, who looked up. "Hey, Kelly, how are you doing?"

"Much better. Fingers crossed, I'm getting cleared next week and can go back to work." He told people this a thousand times a day it seemed. He needed to get back on shift just so he could stop talking about it. Ronan hadn't even admitted to himself that he'd felt a stitch in his side last night. He wouldn't admit it to anyone else either, because no one needed to know what he'd been doing last night. And no one needed to know that he felt a little different.

He told himself the difference was normal. He'd been cut apart and put back together. He might feel a hitch when he moved that way for the rest of his life, but it didn't necessarily mean he wasn't healed.

"The look on your face says you've got something for me," Gomez sat back down in the old office chair that creaked under his slight frame.

"Don't I ever." Ronan pulled out his phone and explained the situation. He'd taken pictures of the cat. He held up the phone. "It looks like her cat."

"Oh man. I hate that for her, but I don't think there's any legal category for *it looks like her pet*. Do you think it could be coincidental?" Gomez had taken the phone and was checking the images.

Ronan shook his head. Animals gutted and left on her front step weren't coincidental. That someone had gone out of the way to find an orange tabby simply couldn't be anything other than purposeful.

"When did you find it?" Gomez handed the phone back.

Ronan gave all the details he had before asking, "Do you need the body? It's in the trash can. Her trash doesn't get picked up till Tuesday."

Gomez didn't ask why Ronan knew that. Ronan didn't know why he knew that. He just did.

"No, we don't want the body any more than you do." Then he asked Ronan to copy him on all the pictures, which he loaded into the current file on Tierney's stalker. Then he had Ronan sign off on another official report.

Tierney might not be reporting what was happening to her, but Ronan was. When this blew up—when Elliot did something they could pin on him—there would be clear evidence of a persistent campaign against her. Though Ronan wasn't sure yet what that slip-up might be, he was going to be ready. So he would file a report each time. There was nothing else to do, given that there were no fingerprints and nothing they could use to tie the crimes to Elliot Vander clef.

"Is there any way we can get a restraining order?" he was asking as the two of them looked up at a commotion.

An odd noise came from the front, and in the distance Ronan heard the faint sound that he knew was the fire alarm.

Something was wrong. He knew the usual order of events the way people know how to ride a bike. First, the phone rang in the Chief's office, then the fire alarm went off, followed by the slamming of doors as they all headed out to the trucks, then the slamming of lockers as they stepped into their gear and climbed into the truck.

This wasn't that. Something was *off*. There were too many voices, too much alarm. Firefighters had been on far too many runs to do anything other than do their best to stay calm.

Ronan and Officer Gomez looked to each other, and Ronan saw his confusion and concern mirrored back. They both understood that whatever was happening next door was unusual. Without a word, they were on their feet, slamming out of the small bullpen and past Marlene who asked them what was going on. Neither had time to answer.

The front door swung wide as Ronan barreled into it and aimed next door. Even though he couldn't quite see in, it was obvious there was a commotion in the bay. With two more steps forward, he spotted the smoke begin to billow out the large garage doors. It poured gray and thick and quickly turned to black in a single column that poured backwards into the sky. Had it flooded the ceiling of the bay?

He stepped in, seeing only the backs of his fellow firefighters and handheld fire extinguishers in their hands. That alone meant the fire was small and he wasn't that worried about the station. Most of the bay was as fireproof as it could get: concrete floors, metal lockers, and even their gear that sat ready was mostly fire resistant. Aside from exploding one of the engines of the trucks, there wasn't much that could ignite. It was quickly clear that all those gathered around were looking down. A few had their SCBA on so they could get in close without breathing the smoke.

Whatever it was was on the floor.

Not dressed for any occasion with fire, Ronan tried to hang back. Soon it was clear they'd quickly dispensed with whatever flames were there. With the smoke no longer being produced, the last of it rolled away. Rex headed to the wall and flipped on the fan, only then seeing that Ronan was there. "Dude, you need to come see this."

Another quick burst of fire retardant from the canister blew out the last of the smoke and Ronan looked down. A burned effigy lay on the floor. It was wearing poorly stitched clothes, but they were made to look like fire gear. On the back of the fake turnout coat was the name "KELLY."

"It could mean me," Aidan offered, stepping back away from the detritus that still floated in the air.

"It was meant to make smoke. It burned like a mother," Rex offered.

Ronan stepped forward, putting his hand on his brother's shoulder. "It wasn't you. It's me."

With a dead serious expression on his face that Aidan wasn't known for, his brother asked, "Is this about Tierney?"

"It has to be," Ronan answered.

Rex looked up, seeming to understand the dire situation. "I thought I saw the two of you leaving together last night."

"You did." There was no point in denying it now. What Tierney had suspected was true: People had seen them together and seen them leaving together. If Elliot had been there, maybe this was his response.

But throwing fire into the fire station didn't scare Ronan. This was an irritation, a red flag, but not a real danger.

Just then the door slammed open and the chief came out of the station house, billows of smoke following him. "Get your asses in here. We need suppression."

CHAPTER THIRTY-TWO

Tierney was wiping down the counter at the bar when her phone dinged again. Even before she looked at it, she could see that it was Ronan, once again asking her to meet up.

She'd already told him this wasn't a good idea. Tierney was about to message him back to stop bothering her when the couple at the back corner table said something loud that grabbed her attention. Wayne Davies voice always grated on her nerves.

They didn't need her, but they'd pulled her attention away from the phone and she decided it was maybe better to just not answer. Maybe then Ronan would understand that she wasn't going to put a target on him, even if he didn't believe her.

The seemingly mundane activities of taking care of the bar were crawling under her skin. Sean wasn't home. He was living an alternate life with her friend—with people he'd never met before a week ago. How long was he going to be there? And she was constantly checking everywhere for signs of Elliot.

This was exactly what he wanted. He just needed to show up often enough, hurt her often enough, to let her know he could get to her any time, anywhere. She was constantly on edge even if he wasn't thinking about her at all. It worked, too well.

The hair on the back of her neck prickled as she undid the lock this morning. She'd debated between looking around and seeing the asshole who was watching her, or not giving him the satisfaction of knowing that she knew.

Instead, she'd come inside and had a perfectly normal day, except for the part where she was waiting for the other shoe to drop.

The lunch crowd had come and gone and she'd seen nothing unusual. Had Elliot been here for the Crawl and then gone home to New York? Should she follow him in the news and on social media, so that she might know those times when he wasn't here? Maybe she could breathe a little easier then.

The bell over the door rang as someone came through, but she was still eyeing Wayne and Jessica Winters at the back table. There was only one other table occupied now by two brothers who had lunch here every Sunday. But Tierney had her suspicion that the duo in the far corner were having an affair. She knew for a fact that they were both officially with other people, and she knew Wayne had a penchant for pretty, but married, women.

"I'll be right with you," she called out toward the door even though she didn't look.

As her patron finally came into view, she saw that it was Ronan. In an attempt to act normal, she waited until he was sitting on a barstool in front of her before she told him, "You shouldn't be here. You're supposed to stay away."

"I had to tell you something, and you weren't responding to my texts."

Of course, she wasn't responding to his texts. Just then the bell rang from the kitchen behind her. Carter had the burgers ready for the back table. She raised an eyebrow at Ronan as if to say he'd better be gone when she got back. Reaching up into the window, she grabbed the two hot plates with a towel and headed out to deliver the food.

It took two more runs to get everything the couple had forgotten to order the first time, which again, made her think they were having an affair. Or that Wayne knew she hated him. She'd never seen two people less familiar with their own burger orders.

When finally she was back behind the bar, she turned to Ronan, still sitting in the same place. In need of something to do, and normalcy, or at least the appearance of it, Tierney admitted he wasn't leaving. She reached into the fridge under the bar, pulled out his favorite beer and popped the top before setting it in front of him. If she smacked it down with just a little too much force that wasn't on her. At least it hadn't frothed over.

He eyed it for a moment as if understanding what she'd done. Then he picked it up, took a sip, and pulled a folded, printed page from his pocket. He slid it across the bar to her as if he were on some clandestine case. But the case he was on was hers and, with all the people around town who knew about it, *clandestine* was hardly the word she could apply to it.

Trying to hide her irritation, she unfolded the picture and examined it. "A traffic cam photo?"

The image was too grainy to actually recognize either the face or the car.

He nodded as he drank more of the beer, maybe searching for his own normalcy. There was none.

She looked at the date stamp. It was several weeks old. "It's not Elliot."

Tierney shoved the page back but he slid it toward her one more time rejecting her attempt to return it. "Look again. Do you know this person?"

"He looks a little like one of the guys who worked for Elliot.

But I don't even know what that means. I can't tell for certain and I haven't seen Barker in over a decade."

"You told me, one of the guys you dated had been in a car accident."

With those words, Tierney caught on. If she didn't like where this was going, at least she was prepared. It wasn't a new thought. She'd let herself believe that the police department would have alerted her if there had been anything strange about Ronan's accident. When no one had said anything, she'd sat back, thinking it was merely a horrible coincidence.

"This is from your accident?" she asked, though she didn't need to. She recognized the date and she'd heard about the white paint on the side of his truck from the SUV that had hit him. Somehow it completely T boned him and then managed to leave the scene of the accident.

She paused for a moment, her fingers rubbing along the paper for some tactile sensation to ground her thoughts. "There aren't cameras at that intersection."

He shook his head no, agreeing with her. "But I know which direction he came from. So I had Gomez look it up. This is him. This is the only white car on record that night and the timing fits. He was two blocks away from the accident and speeding up. Thank God, they got this shot."

She'd wondered about it all before but it just seemed like phenomenal bad luck or a curse. Ronan had gotten hit almost to the date from when Siorse and Paddy had been killed.

But Ronan wasn't done with her.

"Also, you should know that someone just threw an effigy into the fire station. It was on fire."

"In the bay?" She was so confused. "Someone just burned an effigy in the fire station?"

He set the beer down, twisting the bottle in his fingers. The nervous gesture telling her there was more to this than he was saying.

"What, Ronan?"

"It wasn't a big deal. The guys put it right out."

"But?" she pressed.

"It was dressed in handmade clothing made to look like turnout gear. And it said *Kelly* across the back."

It took her a moment to absorb the hit. Of course, it said that. It was supposed to let them all know that Ronan could burn. That meant Elliot was here today.

"When was this?" she asked.

"Right before I came here. I wanted to tell you before you heard from anyone else."

She nodded slowly. This sucked, but maybe he would understand the real level of threat. Elliot was here now, or at least someone working for him was. Someone willing to commit crimes for him.

That was when Ronan told her about the chief coming out the door with smoke behind him.

"Wait, so the effigy in the bay was just a distraction?"

Ronan nodded. "They burned the bunk room."

The place where the firefighters slept. But if the person—Elliot? —had gotten inside the room to light it, then they'd known no one was in there asleep. Right? She had to ask. "Was anyone hurt?"

He shook his head. "It's embarrassing to have your own fire station catch on fire."

Yes, that was it.

"And you were there?" she pushed. This was Elliot.

"I was next door." He looked down, twisting the beer bottle again. "I went to report the cat from this morning."

She nodded. Unable to hold back, she told him, "Thank you. I should have done that."

But she wasn't finished. Elliot, or whoever it was, had thrown the effigy into the bay *on fire*. It seemed the fire was less the point of the whole thing and more to get the firefighters out of the back. She needed more information. "How did he get in?"

Ronan shrugged, took another sip of the beer and set it, now finished, back on the counter as he stood up. "That's just it. We can't figure it out."

When she didn't say anything else, he nodded at her and tried to pay for the beer. But she rejected that as sternly as she rejected him. He only nodded and said, "I thought you should know," before he headed out the door.

She watched him leave, her heart breaking all over again. She loved him. But being near her was clearly making him a target.

The events of today sounded exactly like Elliot. He loved to make it clear that he could get to anyone she loved and he wouldn't hesitate to do so.

CHAPTER THIRTY-THREE

Tierney had lied. She told Dad Doyle that she was fine and everything was good when she left the bar in his hands for the evening.

It was a good lie, things *looked* normal. Dad Doyle had showed up in the middle of the afternoon. As per their usual routine, they traded everything out. Tierney took her cash tray and counted it. She told him what they were low on and which deliveries had arrived and which hadn't. All the mundane things of her everyday life.

This life wasn't the one she had aspired to, but it was the one she was more than happy to have. Today had been less than stellar though and it was pissing her off.

She'd seen a high-end sports car go blazing down the street just before dad had come in. No one in Redemption owned a car like that, everyone would have known about it. The very presence of it on her street had raised prickles of alarm. Then, when she'd let herself out the back door, she'd walked across the small employee lot and felt *that sensation* again.

On the drive home, she saw the sports car again.

It crept up slowly, coming closer and closer behind her. She told herself it was just a driver not paying attention as it snuck up near and then drifted back several cars. Then it would come closer again. She should ignore it.

Then the car had gotten close enough that Tierney could see the driver. Elliot grinned at her from behind the wheel and waved.

Suddenly frantic to get away, she pressed her foot more forcefully on the gas pedal than she intended making her car leap forward.

Rookie mistake.

Don't let Elliot see panic.

He laughed, she could see it in her mirror. The move had been too stupid to not be noticeable. He managed to stay almost bumper to bumper behind her on the small town roads as her heart raced. He was here. He was right behind her. He *had* been watching as she left the bar.

The light changed and she was forced to stop. Her breathing seemed to stop with the car, her eyes almost squeezing shut. But she couldn't afford to not look. If he got out of the car and came after her—if he tried to kill her now—she needed to be alert. It might be her only chance to get away.

She willed herself to be calm, not that it worked. But she wasn't going to get murdered or have a car chase in the middle of her hometown.

"You can do this, Tee," she told herself, using the nickname that Ronan had bestowed upon her.

With a determined breath she headed straight through the light, though normally she would have turned. Not that anything so mundane would deter Elliot. He'd already left enough dead things on her porch.

Only as she headed the long way around did it occur to her than it was painfully obvious he already knew where she lived. Still, he had taken the turn, heading right back into her neighborhood with a faster route than she was now taking. *Fuck*.

She was finally alone on the street—or at least without Elliot. But now he was heading straight to her house and she wasn't. Should she just drive around aimlessly? Take her chances that he could get inside and actually get to Mr. Kittens and the babies this time?

It was an easy decision and Tierney cranked the wheel, trying not to peel out as she did. She had to beat him there. As she squealed around the last corner, she slammed on her brakes then managed to just slow the car enough to not act like a complete maniac. Though her reasons were good, no one else would know that and acting crazy would only support Elliot's claims when he told everyone she was the problem. *She'd been here before ...*

She moved slower, hating that she had to be safe when she knew he was anything but. This was *her* neighborhood. There were kids here and she breathed a little easier as she scanned the street and didn't see the sports car. If he'd come through, he'd already gone.

Or maybe he'd ditched the car and was walking to her house. She couldn't help imagining the worst. Looking around nervously, Tierney did the thing she promised herself she wouldn't do. She let herself be afraid. There was no way to fight this spike of adrenaline from knowing that he was near.

Slamming into her own driveway and blazing out of the car, she barely got the door slammed behind her as she jammed her key into the front door lock. Undoing the first bolt, she then went for the second. Tierney barely made it inside before vomiting up her lunch in the closest trashcan. Finally standing upright, alone in her own home—or at least she thought she was alone—she took a deep breath hoping to clear her system out.

Then her stomach rolled again. The fear heaved up, as she

doubled over and lost even more of what she'd eaten. Acid burned the back of her mouth and fear stung her eyes.

When at last her stomach was empty, she headed into the bathroom and used the shower to clean out the trash can. Leaving it wet in the empty tub, she shuffled to the sink, her limbs shaking as she pulled out the toothpaste and brushed her teeth. Eyes darting everywhere she tried to focus on the mundane task. But she was petrified that she would lean over to spit and, when she stood up, she would see him in the mirror over her shoulder.

She turned and put her back to the sink, but now was afraid he could appear in the frosted glass window above the vanity. The house was so small, even the laundry room had a window. Was there anywhere she could escape him?

She desperately wanted to call Ronan, to have him come and be a welcoming second warm body ... and be Ronan. But that was absolutely the worst thing she could do. She had no doubt that Elliot was tracing her calls. Hell, he might even have someone in the police department working on his side. She couldn't call anyone without having to assume that Elliot knew what she was doing before they even answered.

She needed a burner phone. She needed to buy it in cash in case he was tracing her purchases, too.

With her mouth finally tasting of mint, and her shakes at least mostly under control, she moved her way around the house. She grabbed the bat and checked first on Mr. Kittens and the snack babies. The babies didn't react in the slightest, and the big orange tabby only looked at her as if she were a little out of her mind. After patting their heads, which calmed her more than she expected, she resumed her check.

She double-checked the knives in the block. After finding every weapon she'd hidden, she touched the gun that still rested at her hip. Without thinking twice, she moved the safety strap aside which she should have done first. Then, she checked the house again, this time looking in every closet, under every bed, and behind every curtain. She was in the laundry room at the back of the house, leaning over the washer and peering through the sheer curtain, trying to determine if anything had happened in the backyard, when the knock came.

For a moment just the sound froze her solid, every muscle stiffening and reacting. Then she reminded herself it could be anyone.

Dad was at the bar, but it could be Mom Doyle. Hell, it could even be Ronan, even though she'd told him to stay away. It could be Talia. It could even be the new vet, Zadie, wanting to check on the kittens. Telling herself it was any of these non-lethal options, Tierney made herself move to the front door.

As she passed the living room window—with the sheers still closed from when she had left that morning—a quick glance revealed the shiny sleek sports car in her driveway. It sat right behind her own car, blocking her in and making a safe escape impossible.

It was Elliot and he was here.

Reaching down, she flipped the safety on the gun. Tierney knew she was more likely to shoot her own toes off but, frankly, she didn't care—as long as she also shot Elliot. Still, she couldn't just open the door and fire at him. What if she hit a kid across the street? What if Elliot died? The Vander clefs would make sure she rotted in the worst of prisons, and that she never saw Sean again. They would claim custody of their grandson—one of Tierney's worst fears.

So she lifted the hem of her shirt, just enough to make the gun easier to access but not quite enough to fully reveal it, *she hoped*. Then she took a fortifying breath and stepped to the door, knowing that Elliot Vander clef stood on the other side of the heavy wood. Reminding herself he didn't want to kill *her*, she lifted the bolt, grabbed the knob, and opened the door.

There he stood, his hair as blonde as she remembered. His

blue eyes bright, his smile wide and white and perfect. Now, all the charm had given way to the evil she could see underneath. His grin was genuine as he saw her, and that was maybe even more terrifying.

His eyes sparkled as he greeted her. "Hello, Emmie Baby."

CHAPTER THIRTY-FOUR

Ronan had driven around town almost aimlessly. He told himself he was looking for Elliot Vander clef in every face on the sidewalk, in every strange person in every shop on Main Street. He knew the residents of this town better than most. He'd been in far too many of their homes over the years. He told himself he was the perfect man for the job.

He didn't see anything helpful, but he did pull over to field a call from his doctor's office. Unfortunately, they were rescheduling his appointment to get cleared to go back to work. Ronan reluctantly agreed to push it back one day. He was so close that each extra day seemed an eternity but there was nothing he could do. Even more irritated than he'd been when he started this drive, he hung up the phone and resumed driving around.

He saw nothing out of the ordinary. Of the people he didn't recognize, several were women and two were men who were old enough and frail enough that they couldn't possibly be Vander clef. Ronan got the feeling that Tierney knew something she hadn't told him. Since he had no idea what that might be, and no proof that she was actually holding back, he couldn't pressure her to tell him. It wasn't as if she was talking to him anyway.

When all of this was over, would she go back to being Emily Gallagher? Would she move back to New York? Introduce her parents to Sean—the grandchild they had never even met. Maybe they didn't know her child's name, or even that he was a boy.

Ronan hoped that wasn't the case. From what she'd told him before, however, it seemed the most likely. She'd cut off all contact so that Vander clef couldn't track her. But he had anyway.

Ronan still felt a scorching need to protect her, no matter what her choices were.

His phone rang again and he dreaded answering it. Though it was probably bad news, he wasn't going to let it go to voicemail. Pulling over as he put the phone to his ear, he said, "Hello?" with no idea who was on the other end of the line.

"Hey man! I got something to let you in on."

It took a moment to figure out the voice belonged to officer Gomez. "A new development in the case?"

"Yeah. We've got your guy down here and we're questioning him right now."

"You have Vander clef?" Ronan was startled, and glad he wasn't driving. Looking around, he headed down the block to park at the gas station there.

"Sorry, no," Gomez told him. "Harris was following up on the rats."

"That's been a while," Ronan said, then immediately regretted that it sounded accusatory. They were just now checking that out? And who did they even have if not Vander clef?

"I know." The tone was an apology. "Manpower and all that."

Ronan understood, but he stayed quiet and let the officer continue.

"You said that the rats looked clean and pale, not like wild rats. So we followed up with the pet store but it took a while. They had to pull a ton of receipts and so on ... anyway, we have sales to Wayne Davies for one rat each time. He bought the rats approximately twelve to fifteen hours prior to them appearing on Tierney's doorstep."

"Davies?" Ronan asked. That didn't make any sense. Though the man had never struck Ronan as anything other than a grade A asshole, why would he do that Tierney? What was happening at her house was positively psychopathic.

"It's him. He admitted he bought them. But, he says somebody *paid him* for information on Tierney. He told them he had an in with the family—"

"Hold on." Ronan felt a twist in his gut. "He said he had an 'in' with the family?"

"Said he knew your wife, knew the Doyle girls, or something like that."

None of this was processing. Ronan knew Tierney disliked Wayne Davies, but she'd never said why. Maybe this was it. Maybe they had some kind of history. At least that piece stitched together, even if he didn't understand the details just yet. But he still couldn't quite place Wayne getting the rats ... *And what about the cat?*

"Davies said he didn't know what the animals were for," Gomez continued. "He claims he bought them and handed them off."

But to who? Ronan didn't get to ask, he needed to be listening. For whatever reason, this seemed important.

"The pet store clerk noticed him buying these feeder rats, so she asked him about his snake. He'd said it was a viper, which she thought was odd. No one keeps Vipers, unless they know what they are doing. So she thought maybe he just had pet rats and didn't want to say. Regardless, it was weird."

It was that, Ronan thought. Had Gomez stitched enough of the pieces together? Ronan thought there were still too many gaping holes. "He gave them to Vander clef?"

"That's just it," Gomez said. "From what he just told me, he's never even seen Vander clef. He gave the rats to some other guy."

Silence fell between them as the information ran out. Both were trying to think of an option that would make the pieces click.

"What about the cat?" Ronan asked finally. "Was that from the pet store too?" Just the thought made his stomach turn.

"Davies says he doesn't know about the cat." He paused a moment. "I'm not questioning him, but I've been watching. His reaction seemed genuine."

Ronan thought for another minute. "Did you show him the picture from the traffic cam? The guy who hit me?"

"No! We haven't. I'll get that picture into the room and worked into questioning. They're almost done with him."

And they would let him go ... Ronan hated that. This man had been part of a clear threat to Tierney, but he'd be put back out onto the street.

Davies had taken money to provide information on her ... That made his blood boil.

"I'll call you back if we get anything more," Gomez promised.

Hanging up with more questions than answers, Ronan ran his thumb over the face of the phone. He hadn't meant to pull up all of his messages to Tierney, but there they were. Bold reminders of his failure.

The first message he'd sent was answered with *please don't contact me.* All the others simply lined up on his side of the screen with no response. She wanted him to leave her alone. She seemed to have some idea that Vander clef was a threat to

Ronan and, while he might be, Ronan considered himself a good fighter. He was almost entirely healed now from his accident that maybe wasn't an accident.

Hell, he couldn't be sure. It was impressive how paranoid he could become so quickly. He reminded himself to cut Tierney a little slack.

He had to be in peak condition to get sent back to his job. One angry ex-boyfriend shouldn't be a problem. Once Elliot was taken care of, he could do whatever he needed to convince Tierney they belonged together, even though he was still trying to convince himself they didn't. She didn't want him, and he didn't want all the red tape from dating his late-wife's sister. But he wanted *her*.

The engine still running, he threw the gear into reverse and backed out of the space. As he started to turn onto the main road, he suddenly slammed his brakes to avoid a slick sports car going far too fast. Had Ronan been an officer, he would have flipped the sirens and run after the guy. But none of the local PD seem to be in sight and the car sped down the street into the distance. As though the owner needed to let everyone know what a big cock he thought he had.

Ronan was done with this day. He was just going to try to not get hit again. He'd go home and play video games or figure something out. He would avoid thinking anything paranoid.

One block from home the phone rang again. This time he had the phone up on the dash. His eyes glanced over as he decided to just hit the button. He kept his eyes on the road.

"Hi Gomez, something new?" Ronan asked.

"Good call. Davies says that was him."

It took a moment for Ronan to absorb what that meant. He was just trying to keep his tires on the road as his world rolled over several times.

What was he supposed to do with this information? Could

he prove that the other man had hit him on purpose? The police still had no idea who it even was. Or did they?

The white SUV that had T-d Ronan had been a rental and the Police hadn't been able to chase down who was driving. Maybe this would give them more impetus. He asked Gomez, "Do you have a name for him? Could you look into him being tied to my car accident?"

"You'll press charges?"

"You know I will. Every charge in the book," Ronan told him before he hung up.

This could be great news. It might even shut Vander clef down. Ronan was smiling as he slowed enough to turn into his driveway. Hitting the garage door button, he waited while the door slowly cranked its way up.

Siorse had wanted the prettier model rather than the faster one he'd preferred. The house did look better with these, not that she was here anymore to see it. Had she even really enjoyed it when she was alive? He was learning to let go of unanswered questions where his late wife was concerned. It was past time to change things.

He parked the car but exited out the front of the garage, sending the door down behind him. Along the front porch, he checked on the little garden of shrubs. It was barely eaking its way through the harsh Nebraska winter. The plants should start bouncing back soon, as long as they didn't get another freeze.

Climbing the front steps, Ronan told himself he hadn't been looking for odd footprints or evidence of anyone casing the house. But he hadn't seen anything. With his key, he flipped the bolt that was still securely locked and let himself into the front room. The white shaggy carpet still lay in front of the fireplace —the one he hadn't wanted to buy, but Siorse had insisted on.

She'd left, but it had stayed. Another thing to remember her by. Then he'd screwed her sister on the same carpet they'd fought over. He hadn't wanted white and now he didn't want to get rid of it for more than one reason.

Trying to shake off his morbid feelings about both the Doyle women, he headed through the kitchen. He needed to get his keys into the little dish at the edge of the mudroom before he lost them. He needed to hang up his coat. His thoughts were swirling, but he still couldn't miss the dead white rat gutted and smeared across his kitchen counter.

CHAPTER THIRTY-FIVE

Tierney didn't respond to Elliot's taunt. She didn't answer to *Emmie Baby* anymore, or even to *Emily*.

"So how is the future Mrs. Vander clef?" He grinned again. Leaning on one hand propped on her doorframe, his body tilted in a cocky pose. One that said he knew she wasn't going to do anything.

"I don't know who that is," Tierney replied, proud of herself for the rapid comeback.

She almost crossed her arms, but realized she needed her hands free for quick action. Crossing her arms might mask that she was shaking. Putting her hands in her pockets would be good too, but it created the same problem. Her heart was pounding, and she was afraid he could see it.

Elliot just laughed at her response. "I just wanted to know how you were doing."

"I suspect you already know exactly how I'm doing ..." she paused. "And I've already reported you to the police."

A dark cloud swept across his features before he could hide it. She wondered if anyone else would have seen it had they been here. He was so fast to cover it up.

"Honey, you don't report your husband to the police."

She tried to stay calm. "You're not my husband. You never were."

"I will be." He said it with such certainty that it was clearly a threat. To Elliot a wife would be owned. Hell, he thought he owned her when she was just his girlfriend.

"No." Tierney issued the one word like a command, as though she were pushing that idea out into the universe. "You never will be."

He raised one eyebrow, challenging her in a way that she couldn't rebut.

She hated him having the last word. *Hated it.* Her insides were churning, her anger rising. At least that was better than the fear. "You need to get off my property."

He let out a small chuckle. "It's not your property. You rent it."

Did he know everything? She would have to assume he did, but still stay on her toes so as not to hand him anything he hadn't found out for himself.

"As the tenant, I'm still in charge. Only the owner can challenge me." She saw her mistake the moment the idea passed across his features.

Fuck. He was going to own this property as fast as he could. He would make her little old landlord an offer he couldn't refuse.

Tierney tried not to let it show on her face and she wondered if she had the same kind of rapid micro expressions that Elliot did. Did it matter anyway? He seemed to be able to read her in an almost psychic manner. "You need to get off of my property."

Even though it hurt to do it, she stepped toward him. She was in the legal right here. She should have looked up what kind of laws there were for shooting someone on her own doorstep. His refusal to leave probably wouldn't count as provocation enough if it went to court. It didn't matter anyway. Elliot always managed to stay just under the wire when he committed a crime. When he went too far, he made sure there were no witnesses.

This time he nodded and stepped back as if acknowledging her power in the situation. Tierney knew that was a false flag.

"Sure thing, Emmie." He turned and took the first step down even as her gut churned again at the old term of endearment. It had once made her swoon. Then it struck fear into her bones. It still held far too much power.

She should have known he hadn't really given in. He glanced, too casually, over his shoulder. "How's that boy of mine?"

"I don't know what you're talking about." How many times could she repeat the one phrase? She kept her expression as blank as possible and prayed that she gave nothing away.

"You know." Reaching the walkway, he turned back to face her. Looking up left her towering over him, once again in a position of power that she knew was completely false.

Diagonally, she saw one of the neighbors come out the front door. Anyone looking would see only a friendly check-in. Oh, Elliot would have made sure everything appeared copacetic. Anything Tierney complained about was just her imagining things. He was always the good guy.

"He's a Vander clef, Emmie. And he's going to be a Vander clef."

This time she didn't answer. *What could she say?* That Elliot would never find him? That was a challenge. She'd learned a long time ago not to issue them. Should she just deny him and say *no, he never will be?*

Instead, she said nothing. Tierney simply stood on her threshold, defending the unspoken threat as best she could. If her sheer force of will could move him, he would have blown backwards off his feet. But still he stood there, smiling up at her as if he had a secret.

To her right, a series of clicks and a squeak signified that her neighbor was coming out onto the front porch.

Elliot waved to the woman, his sense of familiarity making Tierney's blood run cold. He glanced up to her, catching her gaze and winking before he turned to the neighbor. "Hey Mrs. Wentworth! Good to see you again. I just came by to say hello to *Tierney* here."

There was something in the way he emphasized her name that showed he was making a point. *She wasn't who she said she was and he might just let the whole town know.*

For once, Tierney found she didn't care. Her time was up. Elliot had found her and the only thing she could do was protect Sean.

"Oh hello, Elliot!" Mrs. Wentworth said, "I'm so glad you found her."

Tierney was done playing by the rules, done being nice. She turned to her neighbor. "Mrs. Wentworth? I'm sorry to do this to you. And I'm sure he's been absolutely charming, but Elliot Vander clef is not welcome on my property." She turned to face him. "Please, leave *now.*"

He simply grinned, unaffected by her threat or her statement to Mrs. Wentworth. He waved at both women as her elderly neighbor frowned, finally realizing all was not as it seemed. He climbed into the sports car with all the cares of a man who'd been visiting friends, not one who'd just been told he had to leave.

As he pulled out of the driveway, Tierney considered her options for future interactions. He *would* confront her again, maybe at the bar where she would technically be in a public space. Maybe on the street. Maybe in her own bedroom in the dead of night.

She considered calling the police. The question was, *were any of them in Elliot's pockets?* And if they weren't on the Vander clef's payroll now, would they be in a little while?

She was glad she hadn't threatened to call them. For as many missteps as she'd made, she had to be proud of herself. He used to manipulate her into giving him all the information he wanted. Elliot was so good at forcing the results he wanted.

Now, Tierney turned to her neighbor as her driveway cleared out. "I'm sorry to put you in that position, Mrs. Wentworth. But I'm sure you've heard the whole town talking about the fact that I had a stalker years ago."

"Oh, my dear. I did. I didn't even put it together." The woman had her frail hand, knuckles thick with arthritis, pressed to her chest. Her house coat billowed a little in the cold wind. She shouldn't be out here. So Tierney tried to make it quick.

"That was him."

"Oh my. He came by here before and asked me about you. He was so charming!"

"He's good at that," Tierney told the woman. She didn't like making her elderly neighbor a target, but there wasn't much she could do about it now. She reminded herself that none of this was her fault. Maybe it was a good thing the rumors had spread. It got her in front of Elliot. "He uses his charm to get in places where he shouldn't be, and you have to stand up to him. I learned that the hard way. Go back inside though."

"Okay, Honey. Well, I'll let you know if I see him again!"

Tierney realized her busy body neighbor might be used to her advantage. "I appreciate that!"

She watched as the old woman grabbed her printed newspaper off her front porch and headed back inside as Tierney closed and double bolted her front door. Still Elliot's threat lingered. He intended to get custody of Sean and he had the money and the legal team to make it happen.

There was only one way Tierney knew to stop him.

CHAPTER THIRTY-SIX

R onan opened his front door to Detective Gomez, letting him in the house.

"You haven't touched anything?"

Ronan took a moment to trace his path for the man. "For some reason I decided to check on the front garden." *Because it was another thing that Siorse had left for him.* "I walked through here," he pointed, "And I saw it and stopped and backed up."

He'd put his keys in his coat pocket and draped the coat over a chair in the living room, wanting to be sure he didn't disturb any of the evidence.

Gomez examined the bloody scene for himself. Ronan would have followed but another car pulled up, parking at the front of his house.

This time it wasn't the police, but Tierney. He was already opening the door as she came up the walk. The look on her face accused him of manufacturing a way to make her talk to him. But he shook his head and waved her inside.

Gomez didn't seem thrilled that Ronan had invited someone else to this little shindig, but Ronan wasn't going to apologize. Tierney needed to see what was happening.

At least, Gomez decided to share. He waved her closer and, without a word, she stepped into Ronan's kitchen to look at the rat.

"Do you see anything you recognize?" Gomez asked and she responded with, "That's his liver, and there's his spleen."

She pointed to various pieces that Ronan would have simply called guts.

"Ha ha." Gomez was not amused.

"It looks the same as the ones on my porch. Though maybe a little more smeared around," she conceded.

Ronan watched as her head turned and she caught his gaze as if to apologize, almost as if she were the one who had done this.

"You left the bar when?" Gomez turned away from the scene and began questioning Ronan.

There was nothing to do but answer honestly, even if that meant Tierney heard everything.

"You got home when?"

Even Tierney raised an eyebrow at the time Ronan gave.

"I drove around town."

"For?" Gomez wasn't one for prompting answers and Ronan was forced to admit that he'd been looking for Vander clef.

"You weren't going to find him driving around town," Tierney said with all the confidence in the world.

When he turned and looked at her as if to question this confidence, he didn't like the answer.

"Because he followed me down the street and then showed up at my doorstep."

"*What?*" Ronan almost yelled it. His breath stuttered. He'd been taking a step backward and he almost tripped on air. There was no doubt that Elliot Vander clef was here if he'd shown up on Tierney's doorstep.

"When was this?" Gomez asked, furiously scribbling his

chicken scratch into a tiny, spiral bound notebook he kept in his pocket.

"Ronan called me just after I bolted the door ... Here." She pulled her phone out and held it up, showing Gomez the call time.

"How long was he there?"

This time she shrugged to the officer. It was clear to Ronan that the interaction had taken more out of her than she was willing to say. She was petrified of Vander clef even though Ronan figured she could take him. She had the gun. Though, despite everything she'd said—how she believed she would have no trouble killing her ex—people often found they weren't willing to pull the trigger when the time came.

"Give me a minute." Gomez shooed the two of them out of the kitchen as he began taking pictures.

Ronan turned and left, following instructions, hearing or maybe sensing Tierney right behind him. He couldn't help it. He stopped in front of the fireplace, staring at the white fluffy throw rug. The last time he and Tierney had been here, they'd been peeling their clothing.

When he turned to look at her, her arms were crossed, and she was defiantly avoiding looking at the fireplace.

He wanted to say he missed her, as silly as that seemed. It hadn't even been a day.

But this morning she'd turned him away. She seemed to be upset that, despite telling him to leave, she'd had to encounter him twice more.

A moment later, Gomez was going out the front door and making calls. "I'm bringing all of this in. Full scale."

Tierney obviously wanted to ask a question, but he was gone before she could. So she turned to Ronan. "Nobody wanted any of the evidence when it was at *my* house."

Ronan shrugged. "Maybe this is just the number that was high enough to get them to keep it."

He could see she didn't believe him. Maybe she'd dealt with the Vander clefs and stalking laws in the past and knew that they were never going to be enough. He tried again. "Maybe it's because this one was *inside* the house and yours were on the front step. Also, you cleaned them up before you reported them ... Or I did."

Maybe that had been a mistake. The problem with stalking laws was that people failed to report until it was too late. Ronan knew this. Yet, for all he felt he'd been getting ahead of it, he'd still been too late with Tierney.

His thoughts tumbled and swirled as he once again tried to stitch all the pieces together.

Tierney caught his gaze. "I'm going to go."

She was already turning away as he reached out and lightly grabbed her arm. "Please don't. Vander clef was at your house. You said he followed you down the road."

She nodded. "He seemed to be playing bumper tag with me. He got close enough that I could see his face in my rearview mirror. He wanted me to know it was him."

"He followed you right to your front door?"

She shook her head no. "That's just it. I took an odd turn, went the long way so he *wouldn't* follow me. When I got home, everything was fine. Five minutes later, there he was at my front door."

She stared at Ronan as if to challenge him. To be sure he knew she didn't lead Vander clef to her.

Not that it mattered anyway, Ronan thought. The number of dead rats, and even the orange cat that looked so much like Mr. Kittens, had made it very clear that Vander clef knew more than enough.

"I don't think you're safe by yourself," he pleaded.

Tierney offered a bitter laugh in return as she pulled her arm from his hold. "*You're* not safe by *yourself*, Ronan."

The comment made Ronan's head snap back.

But she wasn't done. "I don't know that he's gotten into *my* house." She tapped her own chest in anger to make the point. "But we all know he's gotten into *yours*."

The finger jabbed out at him, making the accusation harsher. And pointing out a reality Ronan hadn't quite grasped yet.

But she was still going. "This was *inside*. This dead rat was on your kitchen counter. You told Gomez all the doors were locked!"

Shit, Ronan thought. Whether it was Vander clef or someone working for him, whoever it was had come in, done the damage, and left without a trace.

As he was still trying to sort that, Gomez came back inside. "I hate to do this to you, but I'm going to get a tech out here. They'll lift some prints. So you can't go in your kitchen at all until we're done."

After Ronan nodded his agreement, Gomez started again. "I'm going to check all your locks and windows. Give me a minute." He was back on the phone then, even as he walked around the house and took pictures. He checked every bolt and doorway, every window or point someone could have come in. He looked inside and out, before he announced. "I didn't find anything. All the screens on the windows look intact."

Tierney crossed her arms and raised one eyebrow at him as if to point out that Elliot proved he could get inside Ronan's house. He'd already proven he could get inside the fire station.

The unease settled deep in Ronan's gut as what he believed about himself began to crumble.

CHAPTER THIRTY-SEVEN

Three Days, Ronan thought.

It had been three days and he was about to explode from sheer frustration, impatience, and boredom—a combination he hoped never to face again. He was still four days out from his doctor's appointment to clear him. Even if he sailed through that checkpoint, it would be the next day at the earliest before the chief managed to get him back into the rotation. Likely not even that fast.

For three days, he had not spoken to Tierney at all, though he'd seen her.

He'd driven around town, looking out for Elliot and spotting Tierney where he could. He'd not driven aimlessly, so he watched her as she clocked into the bar or out. He was probably obvious, driving up and down a side road that he had no reason to be on, just to make sure that he saw her car in the back lot.

He went to the park and ate a sandwich on an icy cold picnic table and crunched his shoes into the small inch of snow at his feet. He'd examined his footprints in detail. Then he fed the remainder of the sandwich to the ducks who, for whatever reason, didn't have the minimal intelligence to fly south for the winter and headed home. . . still alone.

He was almost grateful for the effort the first evening alone had provided him. The crime scene tech had come in after Tierney left. She'd made as much mess as she'd cleared. In her Tyvek suit, she bagged up the rat, then swabbed the blood and dusted everything for prints. She'd even taken Ronan aside and used a digital capture to get all ten of his fingerprints and then his palm.

He'd gone along but asked, "Why do you need these?"

"For comparison." She'd grinned through her clear face shield. "Unless you cleaned the counter with bleach right before the rat was laid there, some of your prints are probably in the mix too. We don't want to get them confused."

"But my prints are on file with the city. All firefighters are."

"I could use those. But these right here—" She held up the small scanner. "—are ready to go. Plus, I can see you right now. Unless you're a twin—"

"I'm not," he assured her.

"Then I am my own best evidence." It took a long time but eventually she cleared out, taking the rat but leaving black dust.

At least scrubbing everything down had been something to do. Siorse would have been proud of him for the job he did keeping the house so neat. Though honestly, maybe it was simply because he didn't have anything better to do.

It was easy to keep the lonely house clean. No one got the toys out in Paddy's small room to make a mess. No one threw parties and had friends over. No one made dinner for a whole family and had to slide the highchair back into the corner. When he was finished eating there weren't multiple plates and glasses and bowls. Hell, there were rarely even pots and pans that needed scrubbing. He ate take out too much of the time and watched too much TV.

Deciding he was done with staring at stupid programming

he wasn't even really watching, Ronan threw his empty soda can into the recycling bin and passed through the kitchen. He tried not to look at the counter that now gave him the willies. Grabbing his keys from the dish, he shrugged into his coat and headed over to Tierney's.

It didn't matter if she didn't want a relationship with him. They were friends. They were at least family, and that couldn't quite be shaken despite the loss of their tie. Maybe she was right and Vander clef was now after both of them. Then the least she could do was talk to him about it.

The drive didn't take as long as he needed to get his head ready, and he found himself on her doorstep with no plan. Knocking, he waited and was almost ready to knock again, when the sheers at the front window jostled ever so slightly.

She opened the door and greeted him with, "It's not really safe for you to be here."

"It's not safe for me to be anywhere apparently. You pointed out it's not safe for me to be in my own house." He almost added *aren't we safer together?* but he didn't continue. He just stared at her as if to say he didn't want to have this conversation on the front porch.

Stepping back, she waved him inside before closing the door and turning both the bolts. The sound of metal sliding into place for a moment overrode the mews of tiny kittens.

He headed over and looked at them. It seemed an easy thing to do. Their round little bellies and spindly little legs somehow noticeably bigger than the last time he'd seen them. Leaning down, he scratched each tiny head and asked her their names again.

Patiently, Tierney provided each one and it made sense. The orange ones were Dorito and Cheeto. The paler one Pringle. Still, she was staring at him as if to ask, *why are you here?*

Finally, he stood up and faced the truth. "I just needed to check on you."

"Well, you've done it. Every moment you're here, every interaction you have with me, is another chance for Elliot to think something is going on." She said it so calmly, arms crossed as if daring him to disagree that he just exploded.

"Something *is* going on!" He yelled it, surprised at the force of his own words. "We laid waste to the shag carpet in front of my fireplace. You do remember that, right?"

Her gaze darted away, her head turning as if the blow glanced off her. But she didn't reply.

"It was amazing." The words made him feel as if he was taking a knife to his own chest and pulling his heart out for her to watch it beat. "Don't deny that."

The last statement was a dare, but she still didn't look at him. The only satisfaction that he got was that she didn't say he was wrong.

"And then you just walked out."

He didn't say the rest, but the words flared in his thoughts. The way things had gone when he'd woken up ... She'd been almost animalistic toward him. Turning him on in ways that he either hadn't felt in so long he'd forgotten them, or maybe never felt before at all.

Was he in love with her? Or was he just so mad that his emotions were pinging too wildly for him to read? Maybe he'd known her for so long, and he knew her so well, that it seemed impossible he could suddenly feel whatever crazy lust this was without it being something deeper. But did it matter? Tierney had tilted his world on its axis and then walked away.

Had she known she was going to leave while she was screaming his name?

"You need to leave." She said it with no intonation. Maybe that was worse than if she'd yelled it.

He didn't get to ask what she'd felt that morning.

"You need to leave, Ronan."

"We're stronger together," he countered, falling back on the argument *against Elliot* rather than the one *for them.*

She shook her head. "The longer you're here, the more you're a target."

"I can handle Vander clef!" He knew as soon as the words were out of his mouth that he'd made a blazing, stunning mistake.

All of her calm facade disintegrated in a blink and she exploded at him. "No. You can't! You *think* you can. You think that because you haven't seen him in action. Your car accident was caused by him. He intended to kill you over a month ago, before anything happened between us!"

Was that true? Ronan wondered. Was it really before anything had happened between them? Or had Elliot set his sights on Ronan because he could see even then—even before Ronan had known himself—that Ronan was a threat.

"Ignore all of that," Ronan told her, thinking he could just put his feelings on hold until she was safe. "We have a connection. It goes way back."

"We do," she agreed, raising his hopes. But then she dashed them just as quickly. "You were married to my sister once."

"Not that."

"Yes, exactly that," Tierney argued. Then added again, "I need you to leave. And if you don't leave, I will make you."

He shook his head at her. The threat only made him plant his feet and cross his arms. *As if she were big enough to push him out of the way!* What was she going to do? Call the police?

He shouldn't be so stubborn. He shouldn't go against her wishes, but they needed to have this conversation.

"You don't want this, Ronan." Her tone was laced with warning.

Was she going to pull the gun on him?

"You're just some guy who was married to my sister. Some guy I fucked one night."

He stayed stoic, pretending her words didn't hurt. He hoped his blank facial expression called her a liar.

"Fine, if that's how you want it." She waited another beat, giving him another chance to leave but he refused to take it. "Do you know why I hate Wayne Davies?"

Ronan frowned, cracking his own facade. *What was this?*

"I hate him, because more than once, when I came home early with Sean, I found him and Siorse fucking at my parents' house."

The hit was a lightning bolt to the center of his chest. He calculated the math, thinking she had to be wrong. But if Sean was born, then he and Siorse had been engaged or married. He should feel more than he did, but the very thought was too overwhelming to do anything other than numb him. It was worse than a bullet. "You what?"

But Tierney was true to her word. She was going to make him leave. Apparently, she didn't need a gun or any physical force to do it. "Paddy was blonde," she said, pulling out yet another verbal dagger and slashing him to ribbons. "I'm not even sure he was yours."

CHAPTER THIRTY-EIGHT

Tierney almost vomited again. The only thing good was that Ronan had left, that it had worked. He likely didn't realize that it hurt her almost as much as it hurt him.

When she first said it, he looked so stunned. He hadn't known at all. Then he had looked at her as if to accuse her of lying. But she wasn't. Unfortunately.

She'd hoped to never tell him. She'd certainly thought that if it ever did come out, it would be some kind of midnight confession, and that it would happen because he suspected it anyway. She'd not thought to use it like a dagger to wound him. Because there was almost no way he could learn that and have it not wound him.

Hopefully it would make him stay away.

She could face Elliot on her own. Where before she'd been afraid the Vander clefs would put her in prison and she'd never see Sean again, she was willing to take the hit now. Sean could stay with Raven and Raven would surely read about the case. Her son would have the best life he could.

Though the elder Vander clefs weren't anywhere near as bad as Elliot, they'd certainly allowed him to be what he was. They backed him when he told his lies, whether they were about Tierney or anything else. Though they cajoled her with bribery rather than threats, they still seemed to think they could insist she marry their son. They told her that she loved him, despite her own refusal.

Barely managing to keep her breakfast down this time, Tierney plopped down onto her couch, her head sinking into her hands. Then she cried. She heaved great sobs for Sean, who might be scared without her. For Ronan, who she'd had to wound, because she couldn't face Elliot with Ronan nearby.

She only allowed herself the respite for a short while. It suddenly occurred to her that Elliot could maybe see her. She hadn't found any cameras in her home, but who knew what he could do?

Sitting up, she wiped her tears, headed into the bathroom, and washed her face. If Elliot had seen her cry, the damage was done. He would know that pushing Ronan away had hurt her and he would know that going after Ronan would damage her further. What if he threatened the man she loved? Would that be enough to override her concern for Sean? Or would she simply have to let Elliot do his worst and hope Ronan could defend himself? As he so ardently believed that he could. Maybe she'd shown him what it would be like. He sure hadn't believed her when she told him that Elliot's worst wouldn't come with bullets or even fists.

With a deep breath, she plopped back onto her couch, sinking low, so a well-placed bullet couldn't crack her front window and go right through the back of her skull. She turned on the TV and flipped channels for longer than she should have until her phone buzzed.

Pulling it from her back pocket and expecting the worst, she still thought maybe a distraction was welcome. As she looked at the screen, she felt her face pull into a frown. The text message read "911" from Dad. Her dad wasn't much for texting, and *911?*

Scrambling and ignoring the stupid show she'd left the station on, she tapped at her screen to call her dad, frantic until it started to ring.

But her father didn't pick up. Why would he text her and then not answer? Was he not able to answer?

She looked up at the wall clock. She'd been in earlier to open the bar but hadn't even stayed for the lunch rush today. The time told her that her dad would likely be starting the evening shift.

Scrambling out the front door so fast she almost forgot to bolt both the locks behind her, Tierney wondered if it would keep Elliot out. He'd certainly gotten into Ronan's home.

She checked her phone again as she ran the short distance to the car, and reminded herself to be cognizant of the snow and maybe ice on the roads. As she looked and found that she hadn't heard anything from Ronan or her Dad, she climbed into the driver's seat and hit the gas. She'd been topping the tank up every time that she could, not wanting to be caught unable to run far and away if she needed to, now she was glad.

In a few moments, she was squealing her way into the last employee spot and slamming through the back door. She skidded past the office, but the door was open to show it was empty. The front of the house was starting to grow noisy as people came in for beers and early dinners often after they left an early work shift.

"Dad? *Dad!*" she called as she scrambled into the front of the restaurant to see he stood behind the bar talking to Axel, one of his oldest friends who often came in when the crowds were low. The two men were just chatting and her father turned, both of them looking surprised by her presence.

"Hey, Tierney." Her dad said, an odd look on his face. "What's going on?"

"You messaged me!" she told him. Then as things became more confusing, she added, "You messaged me *911.*"

He looked at her oddly and her heart started to sink. *He hadn't messaged her.*

"I'm sorry. I didn't mean to scare you." But she was starting to shake and trying to hide it. Holding out her hand, she asked as politely as she could. "Can I see your phone?"

Though he was still looking at her askance, he readily pulled it from his back pocket. That gesture alone making her think the information had been false. If it was in his pocket, how would Elliot have gotten it to message her with it?

She scrolled through and, sure enough, her dad's last text to her was different, one she remembered from a few weeks ago. He didn't show the incoming call though. But it had rung on her end. *Who had she called?*

Fuck. She almost let the word slip out. Her father would have chastised her. She might be behind the bar, but she was in front of paying customers. She held her phone up to him as way of explanation. It was better that they all knew what was going on, even if she hated that it had happened.

Her incoming message said "Dad" at the top and the little icon was the picture she'd taken of him years ago. She constantly used her phone. What she hadn't noticed before was that there were no previous messages in this thread.

"What does this mean?" her dad asked as he paused his usually busy hands. That alone told her he was worried.

"I don't know. I don't know if he got his hands on my phone physically and set this up. Or if he just managed to hack into it. Either way, he made me think you were having an emergency, then not answering your phone."

"That's not good." Her dad stated the obvious.

"No. It's not. And it shows us that he's willing to send us messages as each other. If you get a message from me that seems odd, you may need to double-check it first."

Her father nodded, catching on. "Call your mom and tell her what happened, too."

Tierney agreed as, across the bar, Axel tipped his beer at her. "This the guy that's been bothering you?"

Such a mild way to put it, as though she were dealing with a bully in the school hallway. She nodded.

"I'll keep my eye out," he volunteered, and she appreciated the gesture, as though anyone keeping their eye out for Elliot would solve any of the problem.

Heading into the back office, she was already dialing her mother and took a few minutes to explain not only what had happened, but what her mother should be on the lookout for. She considered calling Ronan and warning him but contact between them would still be harsh. Clearly, Elliot had a way into her phone. Maybe he'd installed a hidden tracking app, too.

Getting a burner phone was looking smarter and maybe even necessary. Climbing into her car again, an impending sense of dread settled over her. This was just what Elliot wanted. Another reminder to let her know he could get to her anywhere, anytime.

Still, she stopped at the gas station, paid cash and bought herself a cheap phone. Maybe he wouldn't know about this.

Tierney tried to figure out how to message Ronan. But if she messaged him from the burner phone, and Ronan's phone was also being traced or watched, then the number coming in and the message would be a clear line right back to the burner phone, making all of this completely useless. At least her stop at the gas station would appear normal.

She was just leaving when her old phone buzzed again. She wondered if it was Elliot mocking her once more. Again, the message said it was from her father. But this time, she knew better. It was on the new chain, the one that clearly wasn't her dad.

The new message made it clear that he knew that she'd caught on. It said only, "hahaha."

She was shaking her head, her anger flaring, both at him and at herself for falling for it. *How had she been so stupid?*

She'd been so adamant that Ronan wasn't prepared for what Elliot would throw at him, that she'd missed a softball herself. Stuffing the phone into her back pocket, she climbed furiously back into her car to go home. As she did, she heard the sirens and saw the fire truck whizzing by.

CHAPTER THIRTY-NINE

The noise of the trucks should have gotten quieter, not louder, as Tierney made her way home. As she followed their call, the dread that settled over her changed from nebulous to solid.

The lights were turning down her street. The chief's little red pickup was strategically parked to stop her from even turning onto her block.

Shit.

Smoke billowed upward as Tierney was forced to drive past her turn. Slamming the brakes, she squealed the car to a stop on the side of the road that was perpendicular to hers. She jumped out so fast that she forgot her purse, then slammed the door behind her and bolted forward. In a moment of clarity, she remembered to turn around and aim her key fob back to lock the car ... as if any ordinary lock would keep anything safe.

She desperately wanted it to not be her house. *But what would that mean?* Would it be Mrs. Wentworth's house on fire? Would the woman already be dead from smoke inhalation?

The smoke wasn't a tiny spire of gray headed into the sky, but a column of black, rising up wide and ugly. She heard the shouts of the firefighters and even recognized some of the voices. She knew these guys. They'd been in the bar more times than she could count. Chief Taggert was always friendly to her, often buying a round for the guys when she tried to insist that it was on the house. Now all she could do was be grateful they were here and helping.

She ran down the street, where she could see that no, it was not Mrs. Wentworth's little bungalow that was on fire, but her own home.

Rex stood at the perimeter, holding up a hand to stop her. He was clearly watching for civilians, but she wasn't a civilian here, was she? She was the one whose home was burning.

"Tierney? No, you can't," he said when his hand out didn't stop her.

Turning, he laced one arm around her waist, pulling her back against him in a way only the most familiar could do. For a moment, she forgot who and what she was. She kicked and screamed.

"Is Sean in there?" he asked calmly.

She knew the technique: demanding a yes or no answer about something important enough to get her attention.

"No," she said.

Shouldn't he have known that? Didn't they all know Sean was gone? That he was somewhere they couldn't find him.

This couldn't be a coincidence. Tierney was simultaneously grateful that Sean wasn't here to see this and petrified that she'd never see her own son again.

"No," she said again. "Sean's not home."

But something so important to Sean was.

"Mr. Kittens!" she called out and Rex shook his head. She tried again. "I have a large orange tabby cat!"

Even as she got smart enough to quit struggling, Tierney realized that she wasn't being smart enough to tell him pertinent information. "It's a mama cat. There are five baby kittens, just a week old. It's a box in the corner of the dining area! Right front corner of the house."

She was trying so hard to be useful.

"I got it," he told her as though she were making sense. "I'll get the guys."

Still holding her tightly with one hand—as if he knew she would run if given a chance—he restrained her even though she'd quit struggling.

Tierney wasn't sure if she'd actually decided to trust the firefighters or if her quiet was going to be a decoy so she could bolt later. Rex was having none of it anyway.

She listened to the comms as he relayed all of the information. She heard the responses as the guys said they were on it. But were they? Could they be? Was Mr. Kittens even still alive?

Behind her another voice came up. "You can go join the crew. I've got her. I'll watch the street."

Tierney turned around, almost saying his name. But what was even the point? Of course, Ronan was here. No matter what she did, he wouldn't stay away. He refused to make her life easier.

Rex looked at him for a moment. "You're not on shift."

"Humor me, dude. I've been listening to the scanner. I've got nothing better to do. At least let me be useful."

He didn't try to go closer to the fire. Even Tierney knew that he shouldn't without the proper gear. And being off duty would create a legal nightmare should anything go wrong.

But this was just the end of the street, and Ronan was one of their own. So Rex nodded.

Tierney watched as Ronan took over for his shift-mate, placing himself between her and her own home. Rex returned to the group in front of her house. They'd hooked up a large hose, and she couldn't see if anyone had rescued her cats.

Ronan's gaze scanned down the street, as though anyone else

might go running and yelling and try to get past him. She stood there, breathing heavily, not realizing until she felt the wetness on her shirt that she was crying.

Everything was in that house. Everything she hadn't been able to pack in one duffel bag for Sean. His baby clothes, the book of photos from his whole life, the ultrasound from her first visit to the doctor here in Redemption. She remembered Mom Doyle clutching her hand and, instead of berating Tierney for being a stupid, pregnant sixteen-year-old who was still hardly answering to her new name, the woman had been excited about her new grandchild. Tierney's own parents—she thought of them so often as Emily's parents—hadn't cared as much for the child as for the fact that Emily had managed to tie them to a family as wealthy as the Vander clefs.

She sniffed as she thought of all of it burning. Thank God Mom and Dad had their own pictures.

Ronan stood, not making contact with her, not treating her the way he had just a few moments before. She deserved his silence. She knew she'd skewered him with what she'd said.

Now he pulled his phone out of his pocket, tapping on an app and listening to the scanner. She could easily hear police chatter about the fire that was consuming her home as she watched. At least the water was turned on now. It must have happened right after she bolted to go see her dad.

She heard Taggart saying he suspected arson. Ronan didn't need to relay the information to her. Her life shattering around her could be heard clearly enough.

Her tongue filled her mouth, her jaw clenched, and she fought back the second onslaught of tears as she waited for word of the kittens. Having no idea how long she'd stood there, she pulled her own phone out and noted the time. At least she would have an actual account of her personal tragedy as everything about her internal radar was completely off.

Her thoughts slowly righted themselves, and she

straightened her back. Elliot would want her distraught and cowed. She couldn't show any weakness, even if it coursed through her veins, overriding the furious heat that threatened underneath. Wiping her face clean, Tierney slowly rotated until she'd scanned the entire neighborhood.

Elliot had texted her *hahaha*. She thought he meant he'd fooled her, that he'd made her think something was wrong. But what it really meant was that he was laughing about something he knew that she didn't. Something he hoped would break her.

More chatter grabbed her attention from the scanner. In the distance, she watched chief Taggart pulling up his own comm even as Ronan frowned at what was coming through. It was another house fire being reported. *What was the likelihood of two, simultaneous house fires in a town this size?*

The voice rattled off the address, and she didn't put it together until Taggert and Ronan turned to each other. They made eye contact across the distance. Stark looks mirrored on their faces before Taggert bolted for his truck. Ronan abandoned his position as he ran, probably aiming down the street for his own car.

It was his house.

Oh shit, she thought. *Elliot was just getting started.*

CHAPTER FORTY

R onan stood beside Tierney, neither of them speaking, both with their arms crossed as they watched the firefighters put out the last of the blaze at his house. The fire had mostly damaged one room—Paddy's.

Tierney hadn't commented on that and neither had the chief. Certainly, something in that particular room could have short circuited and started a blaze, but the initial assessment by the investigators was that a candle had been knocked over and caught the fluffy, baby-room curtains on fire.

Ronan didn't for one second believe that he'd left a candle burning in a room he didn't go into. He also didn't light candles, because he was a damned firefighter. Not only had his house been set on fire—at least it hadn't burned to the ground—but they'd gone after his most sentimental room. And made it look like it was his fault. This wasn't random, he knew. This was Elliot Vander clef.

Finally, as the chief turned and looked at the two of them, Tierney whispered, "I'm sorry."

As if any of this were her fault. He didn't blame her, and she'd certainly taken the worst of it. At least his house was salvageable. Hers wasn't going to be. She'd be lucky if she could even save a few items.

"Can I go inside?" he asked the chief but wasn't surprised when he was told no.

"You know the rules. Later you can have a guided tour. In this case, you're a civilian and can't touch the evidence and all that."

Chief Taggart then looked to Tierney, as if she might not know the rules. "You can't go inside your place at all. I'm afraid it's a total loss. It's not even about evidence, it's about safety."

She nodded, having already figured that out.

"You'll both need to find somewhere else to stay tonight."

The chief turned as if to return to the work, but then looked back at them. "My dad has a cabin out of town by the lake. It's nothing special, but one or both of you can use it. It's free." He paused. "Who would even think to look for you there?"

"That's ... generous," Ronan replied, not quite sure how to respond. At least the chief understood they were both likely in shock and he made it easy.

"The key is under the stone frog at the corner of the porch. I'll text you the address."

Ronan was nodding, but Tierney jumped in and said, "No. Please write it on paper? We don't know that he's not monitoring our texts."

It took a minute to find paper and pen, but then Ronan was holding the note and had nothing else to do. He still couldn't quite find the urge to move. He just stared at the gray smoke swirling upward into the sky as if his memories and hard work were being carried away with it.

Tierney had driven him here. They'd both jumped in her car because it was closer. The firefighters had come out just then and thrust the box of kittens at her. As of yet, Mr. Kittens was nowhere to be seen but the babies—despite having little sooty marks on their fur—seemed to be fine.

So Ronan held them on his lap as they raced over here to assess whatever other damage Vander clef had caused. The two of them for whatever reason, were suddenly operating like a well-oiled machine rather than two people who seemed to have completely opposing feelings for each other.

Ronan surveyed the wet home, knowing the power and water had been cut and the place was going to have a gaping hole in the side for a while. More than that, he was waiting for the next hit to come. Tierney's home, then his, had been a nice one-two punch.

It was Tierney who moved first. He should have figured that she was far more resilient than he'd given her credit for. Though he'd seen things, and even lost his wife and child in a horrific tragedy, he'd always been given his time to grieve. He'd not needed to be as resilient as Tierney clearly already was.

"I need to get the kittens to the vet."

He nodded and turned to follow her, still not ready to produce words.

It was only after they were both back in her car, driving away from the police officers lining his yard and front door with crime scene tape, that she asked, "Do you want me to drop you at your car?"

All he could do was shake his head *no* and look out the window. Clearly, he didn't know what he wanted. He'd become completely untethered. No more home, no more illusion of safety. Ronan found himself needing Tierney as his anchor. Taking his non-comment as a chance to make her own decision, she had taken the shorter route and gone directly to the vet.

She'd knocked on the door despite the sign. A young woman had come to answer. "I'm so sorry. We're actually not open for three more days."

"I know," Tierney agreed. "Can you tell Zadie that it's Tierney and the kittens? We were just in a house fire."

"Oh, my God!" The young woman looked them up and

down, swinging the door wide now to let them in. Within moments they were in one of the brand new exam rooms, possibly the first patients. Maybe not, Zadie had been running a small animal shelter next door that she'd managed to open in time for the crawl.

Five quick exams later, Zadie pronounced all the kittens in good health. She offered a trap on loan, which Ronan readily accepted, so they could hopefully capture Mr. Kittens. At least there was absolutely no sign she'd stayed in the house. Then Zadie loaded them up with treats for bait and kitten milk in case they couldn't find mom.

A handful of instructions later, there was a bill that clearly made Tierney wince and had Ronan digging in his pocket. Between his accident, his car insurance, and his weeks at partial pay for medical leave, he didn't quite have the balance either. But Tierney had just lost *everything*. He didn't have it in him to make her pay for it.

Zadie eyed the two of them as they looked at the paper. "*Shit.* Hold on. How about you cover just the costs? We're not really open yet. You didn't get the full treatment and you shouldn't have to pay for it ... I'm guessing you guys just lost a lot with the fire."

Tierney nodded, clearly relieved as Ronan paid the reduced bill as Zadie tried to figure out how to work the machine and take money. Clearly, it was something the front staff was going to do.

"If you need me to cover more, I can," he told her.

Zadie waved him away with a look that told him more than she said. "I've been there."

Whatever had happened in her past, she understood what it was to lose everything.

Reaching out, she hugged Tierney. "You're doing a really good thing." She nodded toward the kittens. "Especially given everything else on your plate and you saved them from the house fire—"

"The firefighters did that," Tierney corrected her, but Ronan shook his head.

"I heard you. The kittens were the only thing you told them to save."

Tierney offered a reluctant grin, thanked him for covering the bill, and thanked Zadie for reducing it. Something in the vet's eyes told Ronan she was far more worried for Tierney than for the too-young kittens.

But all he could do was follow her out the door with a box of mewling babies. In the car again, he figured Tierney would drop him off and head her separate way. But he couldn't bear that.

Somehow, she managed to get a word in first. "Are you going to stay with your parents?"

"No. You?"

She gave a very solid *no* answer. She was not going to bring this to their doorstep, and he felt the same about his own family. But how could he protect them? He wasn't sure how many layers out the circle went. Obviously, his being separate from Tierney didn't keep him from being a target.

They could stay together. They could *be* together.

But did she really hate him and want him gone? Or had she just lashed out to make him leave?

Though the truth about Siorse still pierced him, he could separate it from Tierney. "We can find a place together."

She nodded, acquiescing easily, though it clearly wasn't what she wanted to do. Maybe it was simply because she needed to save the money.

He figured she could drop him at his car. But he wasn't quite willing to let go that easily. What if she drove away? What if she changed her mind while they were in separate vehicles? So he copied the information the chief had given him onto a separate paper and he asked, "Should we take Taggart up on his offer?"

Tierney acquiesced. It wasn't like either of them had money

for a hotel. Certainly not when they were facing whatever extra charges would come from fixing their homes and replacing their damaged things. Elliot was leaving a wide swath in his wake.

They made a plan and he handed over the copied address as he climbed out of her car and watched her drive away. He couldn't help the sinking feeling that everything was going to go even more sideways than it already had. *Would she even show up?*

CHAPTER FORTY-ONE

Tierney read the message that Ronan had already settled in to the cabin. He had said earlier that he was picking up dinner. There had been something in the wording that suggested he didn't think she would show up.

She could admit she'd almost turned around several times. It was easy to talk herself out of getting her own hotel room—too expensive, too easy for Elliot to find her. It was harder to talk herself out of taking her nearly full tank of gas and just driving away. She could grab Sean ... if she even knew where he was. But that was the point, even if Elliot tortured her, she *wouldn't* be able to tell him where to find her son. In the end, she'd headed to the cabin simply because it was the only reasonable option.

First though, she had gone back to the house and worked with the officers on scene. It took three of them and the whole bag of treats to find Mr. Kittens. The big lug was cowering under a bush. Probably a smart move, she was near to where she'd last seen her babies, but safe from most of the damage. Mr. Kittens was a mess, but one of the officers provided Tierney with an old towel and she had the cat wrapped up and brushed off quickly. Within a few more minutes, the panicked mama was back in the cardboard box, reunited with her babies. She licked each one of them, checking them over and making Tierney glad the vet had cleaned the soot off.

Maybe the mama cat hadn't abandoned them after all. Maybe she'd simply been petrified, just like Tierney. Maybe running was the only thing the cat could think to do.

"Same, sister. Same," Tierney told the cat as she buckled the box into the passenger seat.

She was exhausted and not ready to face Ronan again. But there were no distractions left. Also, she needed to get the kittens into a house and out of the car. She told herself Ronan would have food waiting, and she knew she needed it.

By the time she walked in the door of the small cabin, she was ready to fall over.

He must have found the frog by the porch, because he had the lights and the heat on. The one-bedroom bungalow somehow managed to be even smaller than her place was ... *had been.*

The neighborhood was worn down just like the outside of this place. Repair patches littered the walls. It seemed as though someone was attempting to remodel it, but at none too quick a speed. Tierney couldn't complain.

"You made it," Ronan greeted her, making it sound again as though he had doubted she would show up.

Did he not realize she had no other option?

She set the box of kittens onto the table, but even before she let go, she realized that was not safe. So she moved it to the corner behind the couch. Tierney couldn't help but wonder if this house, too, would burn and if it would burn with them inside.

One task down, she headed back to the table where Ronan had set out the food. It was nothing brilliant, just Philly cheesesteaks and fries, but it was hot and she desperately needed it. But she didn't quite make it to the table. She needed something else more.

Ronan was standing in the kitchen, leaning against the counter, in the same place he'd been when she walked in the door. He stayed motionless as if afraid to spook her, as if waiting for her to make a decision. So she made one and she walked right into his arms.

For a moment, he didn't seem to believe her. Or he didn't want her there.

For the moment, she didn't care. She just needed to feel him there, solid and steady. Upright when she was about to fall over. She could hold onto him, even if he wouldn't put his arms around her.

Tierney knew she didn't deserve his touch, not after what she'd put him through, not when it was so complicated even before any of that.

Her breath let out and her shoulders dropped. She felt safe here, even if it was just an illusion. She didn't know how long she'd plastered herself to him before his arms lifted and held on loosely. He seemed to understand she just needed a rock to rest against for a moment.

When she finally felt like she could breathe again, she lifted her head to say, "Thank you." But the words didn't come out.

His mouth crushed down over hers, the heat flaring immediately. Ronan's arms tightened, no longer comforting her, but holding her in place so he could ravage her.

She'd been so tired, but every cell flared to life. She needed this, needed him inside her, needed to escape for a moment and pretend she could have him, that she could love him. His hands were already unbuttoning the front of her shirt, finding her breasts, peeling back her bra and making her arch her back. She pressed toward his touch then his mouth, her fingers lacing through his hair, holding him in place.

But only for a minute. Then she was scrambling to unhook

her bra and toss it aside. She yanked at his shirt ungracefully, tugging and twisting until he helped. He was still pinned between her and the counter, but she wasn't going to give him space to get away. They kissed like hungry lovers as they tried to unzip and shed each other's jeans. It would have been comical had Tierney been able to feel anything but the flames that consumed her. She wanted this man.

Everything was going to go to hell. She knew it.

If she could have this one moment, this one more time with him, she told herself she would be okay.

She wasn't sure she was even going to survive the next several days, and somehow that made this free-for-all a ride with only pleasure and no consequences.

They stood naked and needy, hands reaching, clothes balled and dropped on the floor. She stroked him, enjoying the way his head dropped back, the way he was held mesmerized by her touch. But then he returned the favor and she cried out as his fingers found her wet and ready.

The world tipped and tilted, and she could have been falling but she was safe in his arms. It took a second to realize he'd lifted her and was carrying her the short distance to the table. Instead of sweeping aside the food and drinks, movie style, he pulled out a chair. Setting her on her feet, he sat down, grabbed her hips and pulled her onto him.

The hot pressure of him sliding inside sent her head back as his fingers gripped into her hips, moving the two of them together.

They pushed against each other, each reaching for a peak. It was one Tierney knew she'd only find with him. Whatever she was to Ronan, he'd always been her dream. And here she was, getting one tiny slice of it. As usual, they didn't talk, but moved together like they were one.

Her name was reverent on his lips as he came. Tierney, not Emily. She didn't want to go back to being that naive, stupid girl. She liked who Tierney was, even if she wouldn't be Tierney for much longer.

When her own waves of brain-melting pleasure had finally left her human again, she leaned her head down onto his shoulder.

"Tee?"

She didn't answer. She liked that name, too. It made her not just Tierney Doyle, but *his*.

The world came back into focus. She was naked, straddling a man with a scar on his side, in a kitchen that had seen better days.

"Tee?"

She shook her head again. She could feel the world crowding in around her, stealing the joy she'd found.

CHAPTER FORTY-TWO

I t had been two days and they should have been blissful. But somehow the happiness couldn't creep in around the corners. Tierney remained walking on eggshells that Elliot Vander clef had scattered in every direction.

He knew that by laying low he was keeping them guessing, making sure they never really rested. It was working.

She'd been waking at all hours. Though she slept well when she slept next to Ronan, she still wasn't making it for more than a few hours at a time. Often, she would get up and check all the locks before coming back to bed. She'd lost the knives and the baseball bat in the fire. The gun had been on her, but she liked knowing there were other options. She'd been pulled from the safety of the familiar, and it was another layer of stress.

Elliot was good at that.

This time, however, before she could roll out and put her bare feet onto the hardwood floor, Ronan had draped his arm across her waist, his naked body pressing into hers. Despite the fact that she'd had more sex in the past two days than she'd had in the past 10 years, she could tell that wasn't what he was going for.

With a soul deep sigh, feeling something big coming, she rolled over to face him. She tried to keep his arm across her, wanting or needing that contact. "What is it?"

With a deep breath of his own, he shook his head. His expression was pained, and she hated that he'd woken up that way. She was afraid she knew what he wanted. The thing they hadn't yet addressed.

He didn't look away from her, but he wasn't quite making eye contact either. "What you said about Wayne Davies ...?"

Though she'd seen it coming, Tierney still felt it pierce deep in her heart. Her whole throat clamped down and she waited, unable to speak.

"It was true, wasn't it?"

Fuck. Why this, why now? But she'd thrown it at him, hard. She had to expect it to bounce back sooner or later. "It was true."

"Tell me." It was soft, but a command she couldn't deny.

So she barely raised her voice above a whisper, unable to speak the words loudly, unable to wound him any more than she already had. She told him about Sean getting sick and needing to go home early. "They had been together upstairs."

"No question?" he asked.

Somehow, she understood: He wanted to be sure that she wasn't misreading the situation. She almost said, *they weren't fucking making crafts, Ronan,* but she held it back. This time, she said as little as possible. So, she simply nodded. She was certain.

"I'm assuming it wasn't the only time?"

This was harder to answer. She looked away, though she didn't mean to, and hoped he didn't think she was lying. She was just uncertain how to tell this man that his wife, her sister, had not been the faithful woman he'd believed she was. "I saw them together other times over the years."

"You said you thought Paddy wasn't mine."

Shit. She'd had to throw that back at him. "I don't know, Ronan. I really don't."

227

"It's okay." He held his hand up. But it wasn't to stop her from talking, just from apologizing.

She was grateful he felt that way. The whole mess wasn't her fault, but she had certainly had her own role to play.

When he'd been quiet for a while, it was clear he was waiting on her, and Tierney could not deny this man anything.

When she started talking, it all came gushing out. "I saw her with other men over the years. I ran into her in Lincoln with some blonde guy later. That might be Paddy's father ..." But she didn't finish the sentence. *Father* wasn't the right term, sperm donor was correct. Ronan had been Paddy's father. She skipped beyond that. "The day that I caught them, it wasn't the only time I saw her with Wayne. And it was clear it wasn't ..."

She didn't know how to say this next part.

"A one-time incident?" Ronan asked, sarcasm dripping as he saved her from having to tell him.

They stayed silent for a few moments, Tierney absorbing what she'd just done. Had she pulled out the knife she'd stabbed into him earlier? Or had she simply twisted and plunged it deeper? She didn't know yet.

Ronan seemed to be trying to make sense of it all. His next question was one she was wholly unprepared for. "Why did you keep it a secret? I thought we were friends. Wouldn't you tell your friend something like that?"

It had been hard enough hurting him but the twist of shame at her betrayal might be worse. She deserved to be held accountable for the part she had played. She was in large part responsible for this hell. She'd wondered sometimes if Siorse and Paddy might still be alive if Tierney had told Ronan what she knew. They might have gotten divorced, and her sister wouldn't have been in that place at that time. But Siorse would never have forgiven her.

"I love my sister," she started. "I know we were only actually sisters for a handful of years. And I know she didn't make the decision to take me in, her parents did. But she hugged me and welcomed me and told me she'd always wanted a little sister. She never called me stupid for the mistakes I'd made with Elliot, even though I called myself that over and over again. She was the one who told me that anyone would have fallen for him and that he chose me because I was young and beautiful. Siorse is the one who built me back up when I needed it the most."

The tears were flowing freely now. It was complex. "Siorse at eighteen kept a monumental secret for me. So when I caught her with Wayne ... I don't know. I don't know what it was. Clearly, she wasn't as sweet and angelic as everyone seemed to think." Tierney had always known her big sis had done ecstasy on school field trips, called her younger sister in the middle of the night to come drive her home when she'd been stumbling drunk, and maybe high as a kite. But now was not the time to tell Ronan that. Siorse was every direction at once, and this was the time for simple. "Maybe she panicked, but she threatened me. She told me she'd keep my secret as long as I kept hers."

Tierney wanted to explain more, to tell him she hadn't been able to break that. Siorse had put Sean's safety on the table, and there was nothing Tierney would put in front of her child. But now, all of it seemed like excuses that she didn't want to make.

There were no more words between them as he nodded. Maybe he'd suspected all along, because he absorbed it but didn't seem devastated. A moment later, his arm tightened around her waist. His mouth found hers and she felt forgiven, even if she knew they still weren't safe.

CHAPTER FORTY-THREE

Tierney wiped down the bar as though it were another normal day. Nothing was normal. Her world was tilted.

Elliot might not have meant it, but his games had pushed her and Ronan together, giving her even more to lose.

Then, this *nothing* had set in, forcing her to pretend that life was as it always was. Though her father had managed to keep her out of the job for three days, suggesting it was better if she laid low after the house fire, she'd had to do something.

Unable to simply sit on someone else's couch and watch their three channels of TV while drinking soda and eating carry out pizza, she'd gone stir crazy very quickly. Sooner or later, Elliot would find them in their little cabin haven—if he hadn't already.

The world kept turning. She was getting updates on her house. Everything was either burned to a crisp, smoke damaged, or waterlogged. There were just a handful of items that could be saved. Oddly enough, strange random things made it through. Sean's baby book had a burned corner. But once she'd washed it off, it mostly survived. She'd handed it to Mom Doyle for safekeeping. The woman had cried grateful tears and hugged her tight.

A package of bacon had somehow been flung from the fridge into the side yard, perfectly intact. Two of the pillows from her bed seemed like they would be usable again. And the wall to her bedroom and the bath remained standing, most of the cleaners and bath items under the sink had made it just fine. Not that any of this was the kind of foundation she could rebuild her life on. She would simply have to start from the bottom up and it was going to be a harsh blow when she saw Sean again and had to tell him. *If* she got to see Sean again.

At least Ronan had his job again. She was happy for him, he'd gone as stir crazy as she had, and he'd been waffling back and forth on the border of batshit bored for weeks. But his return to work was another layer of "normal" that hid the stark fear that was now the base of her everyday life.

The front door opened wide, and Talia came through, her chair whirring. She showed up often once the lunch crowd was gone, when she could leave the crew at the bakery and head here. It was the right time for the bar, too, when Tierney would have time to chat and not just throw food at her and yell it was nice to see her as she whizzed by. She rolled her way down the street and the door opening wide to let the chair through always made Tierney feel better.

Tierney smiled at her best friend but didn't push her to move faster as she made her way to the bar. This was the best time for the chair not to have to fight general bar traffic, too. But Tierney did order up a grilled roast beef and cheddar on rye before Talia even made it to her barstool.

Tierney topped off a lemonade as Talia carefully handed over two tall cakes—one peach and one chocolate.

"Oh yes!" Tierney traded the drink for the cakes as she sniffed at the air. Technically this was a business delivery, but she loved Talia's style. It was great that her friend came into the bar all the time even though she didn't drink. For a short while, Tierney's day actually felt normal, like easy times when she didn't have a constant cloud over her head.

Talia chatted her way through her sandwich and then stood up, aiming back toward her chair. "I've got to get back to the shop. No one wants cupcakes anymore in the cold. It's all hot pies, and they're more time consuming."

As per their usual song and dance, Tierney spoke up. "Can I pay you for the cakes?"

Snafu was going to sell them by the piece.

"Nope! I just got a free meal. And it's advertising," Talia grinned.

The sandwich Tierney had handed over wasn't worth anywhere near as much as the two cakes. They'd be gone before the dinner rush was halfway through. Tierney would send those who missed out down the street to get their own at Baby Cakes.

"No worries!" Talia called back as she whirred her way toward the door. It opened before she got there, Elliot Vander clef walking through.

He smiled at Tierney and waved to her as though he were an old loyal customer.

"Oh!" Talia's chair stopped and her head snapped around, darting to Tierney. The smile she plastered in place wouldn't pass even the simplest test. There was no mistake that Talia recognized this man.

With his false coating of charm firmly in place, he grinned as he held the door for Talia. Tierney watched as her friend thanked him with the most saccharine smile she'd ever seen and rolled her heavy tread tire and her battery-laden chair right over his foot.

Jolting back he yelled into the room, "*Fuck!*"

Everybody's eyes snapped up at the sound, many of the small town faces offended by the word. Tierney didn't mind that Elliot had garnered negative public attention for once. Talia was gone out the door, not looking back, but Tierney was grateful for the point her friend had scored.

His contorted face snapped back to a friendly smile. "Don't worry about it," he called after Talia.

Talia clearly wasn't worried in the slightest, but now Tierney was. *Shit*, had her friend just put herself on his target list? Her only hope was that he would be too busy hunting Tierney down to remember. What was he here for now anyway?

He looked to everybody in the bar. "I'll be fine. It's not a problem."

Slowly, they turned back to their food and drinks as he let the door swing shut and headed across the bar.

Tierney once again found herself facing down a man who had an agenda. Still she looked at something else, checking the drinks behind the bar and looking at the two order tags that hung in the window. She wouldn't even give him her attention.

He took the seat next to the one Talia had just vacated. "What does a man have to do to get a little service around here?"

Something in his tone was dirty and gross, but Tierney gave him only her most straightforward and curt voice. "What can I get for you?"

"You know what I like." He almost leered. But not quite. Not Elliot.

"No," she shook her head. "I have no idea what you like." She slid a short menu across the bar at him before turning away.

She would not give him an inch.

In a moment, he ordered, still acting overly familiar and still she rebuffed him with cold replies at every turn. If anyone paid any attention to the interaction, she didn't want them thinking she was friendly with him. In the end, he paid for his food by sliding a platinum card across the counter and leaving a twenty-dollar bill as a tip, which Tierney refused to touch.

Carter saw it sitting there through the kitchen window and told her if she wouldn't take it he would.

"Have it," she waved it through the window to him. "It's as dirty as money can get."

Several hours later, by the time she was close to leaving, things seemed to have returned to normal. But Tierney knew there was no normal. Whatever Elliot had come in for today, he had an agenda. He'd been looking for something. Checking for some reaction. Maybe remotely downloading data from her cell phone. Who knew?

He had a plan and she'd probably played right into it, because, once again, she didn't know what it was.

CHAPTER FORTY-FOUR

Tierney was startled as Ronan burst into the bar not fifteen minutes later, his movements choppy and disjointed.

With the bar still relatively empty, Tierney turned her attention to his worried expression. He practically charged at her, trying to say something but she figured she already knew what it was.

Frowning at him, she waved him over to a barstool. It wasn't even worth trying to get out from behind the long bar to greet him. She filled him in on the fact that she understood. "You just missed Elliot."

That, at least, seemed to snap him out of whatever it was that had him worried. For the moment he looked confused. Maybe she hadn't been right about what Ronan wanted to say.

"What?" he asked.

"He left here maybe fifteen minutes ago." She turned around and looked up at the clock only then realizing she hadn't noted the time when he'd showed up or when he left. Probably a mistake on her part.

"Why do you keep talking to him? Just turn him away!"

Ronan seemed irritated as he pointed to the sign behind her that allowed any of the workers to refuse service to anyone anytime.

Tierney shook her head. "The best way to get information is to let him talk. I need to know what he wants."

"He wants to kill you." Ronan's irritation was justified, even if he was wrong.

"No. He wants me back," Tierney corrected him as Ronan pulled out his phone. "He doesn't love me or want me. I'm not even a person to him. I'm a prize—valuable because I got away. I'm more valuable because I managed to stay away for ten years. And I'm an insult. He needs me back on his arm in New York society to prove that he won."

Ronan's face showed that he thought it made no sense. "What does that even prove?"

"To normal people? Nothing. But to Elliot, it proves that he won. He won't kill me until it's impossible to have me."

"If he can't have you, no one will." Ronan nodded along. "But—"

"Right," Tierney said and added, "We're still in the phase of him trying to get me back."

She'd been through this before. For everything Elliot had done, he had threatened everyone *around* her. Everyone who got close to her. He peeled them away, isolating her. Though he didn't have a problem hurting her, he didn't want her dead. At least, like Ronan said, not yet.

"So if he just left, what, fifteen minutes ago, then tell me what this is?" He held up a picture on his phone screen.

Suddenly, Tierney understood why he'd come in here as agitated as he was. The image showed a long barrel of a rifle with a scope on top. It seemed the scope was sighted on Mrs. Kelly, who was working in her garden. Tierney sucked in a breath at the sight.

Ronan hit the button making it play. The only audio was

heavy breathing, but the short video made it clear she was moving around.

Ronan looked her square in the eyes. "Is this real?"

He tried to take the phone back but Tierney was re-watching the video. "It looks real."

"So he's right there with the rifle sighted on my mother, right now? And there's nothing I can do."

"I think he wants you to follow the scope and the angle and come find him."

"I can do that." He was starting to stand up and leave, his eyes again on the short video.

"Don't! Not yet. By the time you get there, he'll already have her hostage."

"Jesus," Ronan replied. "What do I do? Just wait? For what? This bastard is threatening to murder my mother. Right now."

As much as Tierney's heart was beating too fast, she knew Elliot. Elliot was an asshole. "We need a plan. We cannot leap into whatever he's doing. He lives to make you suffer."

"Well, it's working." Ronan's jaw was visibly clenched as he started to pace a small circle, clutching the phone tightly, as if crushing it would crush Elliot.

"If he kills her, he loses her as leverage," she pointed out.

"Jesus, Tierney!"

She knew it sounded cold, but it was true. Elliot was very unlikely to kill Mrs. Kelly. He was trying to get Ronan to do something. There was a plan here. "Hold on. Just think. If you go running in there, you're doing exactly what he wants and he'll be ready for it. So we can't do *that*. We have to do something else."

She wanted to be sure Ronan knew she wasn't sitting back. She wasn't going to let Mrs. Kelly pay for the shit Tierney had brought to everyone who'd been so good to her.

Ronan swallowed hard and sat down on the barstool even harder.

She had him on board. Good. "Let's check everything. Are you certain that's your mom?"

"Yes!" He was clearly irritated that they weren't operating faster.

"We have to ask the obvious questions. He would fake something like this just to torture you."

He took a deep breath and nodded. "Yes, that is my mom and that's her garden. And, you know, that's the corner of our house. Come on, Tierney. This is real."

"No. Wait." Her blood rushed through her system, she wasn't calm, but she was trying. She couldn't place her finger on it but ... "Something doesn't look right."

"Of course, it doesn't!" He snapped back. "There's a rifle aimed at her head! She doesn't even know it's there!" He paused, taking in a deep breath. "Do you think the video of my mom is one video and the rifle is overlaid over it?"

"I don't know." She didn't have those kinds of skills. But something else was bothering her. "But, wait, is this *now?*"

She hadn't been outside for hours, but she looked up and out the few small windows at the top of the walls. They lined the whole opposite side of the room. The natural light that was coming in today wasn't the brightest. "Ronan, it's relatively cloudy today."

For the first time, he truly paused. When he looked at the video again, she could see that it was with a true critical eye. He, too, turned and checked out the window. "It was a bit cloudy when I came in. What day is it?"

"Thursday."

"Right, I'm back on my first shift tomorrow ... Friday." Then he paused again. "I don't think she's supposed to be home. Hold on."

Already pulling her own phone out of her back pocket, Tierney began to check, too. Another patron came in the door, pushing it shut to keep the chill out. She waved to him to choose a table but didn't pay any more attention. She couldn't afford to.

She'd already found his mother tagged in a photo on social media. "Look! This looks like this was posted thirty minutes ago. What is it?"

"I think it's her book club?" He said, clearly not sure.

"It looks like they're eating cake and drinking wine."

"Probably. I think they just call it a book club as an excuse," Ronan agreed, finally starting to let his shoulders drop a little.

"Do you think this is an old picture?" Even as she asked, Tierney saw the tag "Thursday afternoon book club."

"It's not." She answered her own question. "Do you think she would have gone right home and gardened?"

"No." He said that with conviction. "She wouldn't drive home after drinking. Not even just a little. Dad drilled this into us even as kids. That's what happens when your dad is a firefighter."

"So, I think this video is real," Tierney said, "but it's not today. Or at least not right now."

Ronan finally nodded along, already calling his mother and letting out a long breath when she answered. He'd interrupted her book club, and her glass of red wine. Tierney only heard his half of the quick conversation, but he didn't say why he'd called.

He was much more relaxed as Tierney pointed out again, "Elliot's trying to lure you out someplace."

"What do we do?"

"We sit back." She grabbed a beer from under the bar and popped it for him. "We have a beer. And we let him know that he didn't fool us."

"Or he'll think we don't care about my mother."

"That would be good, too. It takes her out of the pool of targets," Tierney pointed out, her own cold beer now in hand. She needed it to calm the shakes she'd tried to not let show. "Either way, we score a point."

They both pocketed their phones and took another maybe-too-long swig of the beer.

Still, when Ronan set his down, he gave her a serious look. "Either way, he threatened to murder my mother. It's not a game, Tierney."

For a moment her anger flared. She understood but ... She tried to say it as calmly as she could. "Ronan, I left everyone I knew behind. I changed my name and moved in with a family I'd never met before—while I was pregnant—at the age of sixteen. You don't have to tell me it's not a game."

His expression was contrite as he took another sip of his beer. They stayed like that, silent and hanging somewhere between celebrating a victory and being scared out of their wits. Tierney wondered, how was Elliot going to slap back from this loss?

CHAPTER FORTY-FIVE

Ronan headed into his first shift back on the job. Though he'd been there for six hours, and nothing out of the ordinary had happened, he couldn't shake the uneasy feeling that rode with him.

It did feel good to be back at work. It felt good to have something useful to do. But if he wasn't out on a run, he was checking his phone, constantly worried that Tierney would tell him something horrific had happened. Or worse, Elliot would send him some other terrifying message. At least this time, he knew to be skeptical.

He'd called his mother again and explained what had happened. She'd told him she'd been in her garden two days earlier and it appeared that was when the video was shot. That matched to Tierney's comment about the weather, too. It concerned his mother as much as it concerned Ronan that she'd had a sniper rifle aimed at her head at one point.

Tierney had warned him that the game would be psychological as much as anything else. He hadn't quite believed her. He did now.

When he was home—or at the cabin—he checked the locks

and windows like he was paranoid. He did the same thing at the station, looking out windows, watching the corners, and generally trying not to look like he was doing it. When the bell rang, he did his best but it was an effort to focus on his job.

That focus was a huge part of the training. This was the job: No cell phones, nothing from your life beyond the station was allowed to come in. It was you against the fire, saving property and lives if you could. So Ronan told himself that Tierney could handle herself, and so could his family, and he let himself fall back into the pattern of stepping into his turnout gear and climbing on the engine.

The team arrived at the edge of town. It was easy to spot the plume of smoke from a mile away. When they pulled up, it was exactly as reported: last house on the street. Old and decrepit. Did it mean anything that this house was at the absolute edge of their jurisdiction? Fifteen feet further north and the volunteer station took over.

Ronan shook off the thought and listened as the Chief sized up the blaze and organized the fight. The place had been abandoned for some time. The siding was falling off and the roof had caved under a fallen tree that no one had moved for some number of years. Though Ronan knew the chief had talked to the city about it before, clearly, it had not been taken care of. Now, it was their problem.

Smoke, thick and gray, roiled up. It snuck under and around the edges of the roof. It poured from one broken window. The tree that had fallen on it had been there long enough to be dry, and it was burning as readily as the house. The crackle of the flames matched the heat he could just detect through all the turnout gear.

There was no property here to save. But there were properties next door and a wildfire that they couldn't afford to let start.

As the firefighters pulled out the hose and started to work in a coordinated effort, Ronan could hear Taggart behind him. His chief was asking, "What do you mean there's no record of the call-in number?"

Ronan wanted to turn and ask about it, but this wasn't the time and it wasn't his job. He had to trust that his chain of command would work and that he'd be notified if it concerned him. He focused on his place on the hose and the fire was quickly put out. It was a relatively short job, although the cleanup took several hours. Everything had to be inspected. There could be no stray sparks allowed to hop to a dead tree in the next yard over. There could be no studs or roofing trusses that held an ember that could flare again hours later. This was meticulous work, and maybe the most important.

Eventually, they made it to the last stages of putting the equipment back on the truck. Dirty and sweaty at the end of a run but still functioning as part of his unit, he moved as part of a team. The old synchronicity came back easily and the motion of it soothed him. Ronan had to say he was grateful to be back, grateful he hadn't felt the tug in his side as he'd held the heavy hose and fought the force of fast water. There was something about the work that was restorative ... until Taggart came and tapped him on the shoulder.

"You'll want to come look at this."

He followed his Chief back to the scene, around the back of what was left of the small house. Taggart pointed at the tree trunk, still sideways where it had been for several years. "There."

"What am I looking at?"

Taggart reached up and pointed with one gloved finger, following cuts in the tree that weren't obvious but were deep enough to remain after the burn.

The cuts looked to be made with a chainsaw, crudely forming the letters R T K.

"You know anything about this?"

"Shit," Ronan muttered.

"Your initials," Taggart said. He didn't have to ask. He had files on all his firefighters. The Chief asked a very pertinent question. "So what the hell's going on back at the station right now?"

He meant, what had Vander clef lured them out here for? What was he doing now that he had the fire house cleared out?

Ronan didn't know. He asked for permission to check his cell phone, but when he fetched it and held it up for the Chief, there was nothing. No incoming calls, no new messages.

"Do we even get signal out here?" Taggart looked up and around. He communicated through a comm system and a satellite phone. He wouldn't have been alerted to any cell gaps.

When Ronan held the phone up, sure enough, nothing was coming through.

"Fuck." The Chief looked at him, but Ronan knew it wasn't blame.

Turning to the rest of the crew, Taggart issued instructions to complete the job. Then he and Ronan climbed into the fire chief's truck and zipped back toward town. Within a few blocks, Ronan's phone lit up with messages as they flooded in, having finally linked to a tower.

He scrolled through, trying to quickly sort the important from the unnecessary. Tierney had messaged— "Elliot was here again."

So he'd been at the bar. If Elliot was watching their exchanges, that might alert him, but it didn't give him any information.

But another message came in. "Hope you're having a good afternoon."

He held the phone up and told his boss, "This is from an unknown number." Then he read the stupid little message out loud.

"You think it's him?"

"I don't see how it could be anybody else." Ronan thought for a moment. "I suppose it could be a random wrong number, but ..."

"But we don't believe in coincidences," the Chief filled in.

"It's barely been twenty-four hours since he threatened my mom," Ronan commented, as if that meant anything.

"Does he not have anything else to do?" The Chief was taking the turns a little fast, getting irritated at the lights. Ronan could see him itching to put the sirens on, but he hadn't done it yet.

"He has enough money to dick around for forever," Ronan reminded his boss. It was something else Tierney had warned him about. "If he wants it, he buys it. If he needs to do something, he has all the time and money to make it happen. And he has more than enough to hire out any job he wants done but doesn't want to get his own hands dirty."

"You think he didn't do the rats himself?"

"I don't know about that." Ronan truly didn't. A normal person would hire that one out, but he was learning that Elliot Vander clef was far from normal on many measures. He was beginning to think the man wasn't just misunderstanding what love was, he might be an honest-to-God psychopath. But he wasn't sure he needed to tell the Chief that.

They finally pulled into the back lot, where the Chief kept his small pickup out of the way of the engines. They slammed their way out of the vehicle and burst into the station. But found nothing amiss.

Thirty minutes later, the rest of the crew rolled in. They all took turns in the showers. Rex made chicken with green beans and rice for dinner. And all around him, Ronan watched the evening roll on as normally as possible.

One by one, the guys peeled off for the night, leaving him and Rex in the main room watching old game shows and trying to outscore each other. It was well after midnight when Ronan admitted that he couldn't shake the uneasy feeling. He'd thought it would dissipate as the day seemed more normal, as there were no further signs of Vander clef, but it had gone the other way.

He was still awake long after most of the guys crawled into their bunks. Ronan normally would have been with them, but tonight he simply couldn't sleep. He'd probably stay awake for the full twenty-four hours. Someone usually did, tonight it would be him. He could claim it was just because he was glad to be back.

An hour later, Jordan hollered out from the bunk room, "Holy shit!"

Ronan jumped from his recliner, almost falling on his ass in his haste. But he was out and aiming toward the short hall even as he heard other voices. "Have you got it?"

"Hold on."

"What the hell is that?"

Right behind him, Rex came barreling down the hall, too. He'd been on the couch and only a moment slower because he'd actually fallen asleep.

They saw the oddly colored smoke streaming from under the door as it flew open and most of the crew came stumbling out coughing and grabbing at their throats.

CHAPTER FORTY-SIX

The sound of his phone ringing in the most obnoxious tone he'd been able to find dragged Ronan from a deep sleep.

Reaching out, he smacked at it as though it were an alarm clock. But as his eyes opened and he took in the world around him, he realized he was in bed in the cabin. His house would be repaired enough to return soon, and he was tempted to take both himself and Tierney back to it. Hers was getting razed and the owner would rebuild. There was almost no way Tierney would ever live there again. She'd lost most everything.

Ronan had held her while she cried on his shoulder and eventually consoled herself that Sean would be at least six inches taller when he returned soon. She would have had to buy him all new clothes anyway. They still hadn't figured out how they would break the news to him. Ronan liked that they talked about it in terms of 'them.' But first they had to get Sean back, and before that they had to figure out how to make Elliot Vander clef stay away forever. That was proving difficult.

His eyes drooped and he tried to pick up the phone. He'd

stayed awake for the entire twenty-four hour shift. None of them had been able to sleep after the smoke bomb had been thrown into the bunk room. This time, the room had been occupied and the guys had been asleep. No one knew how long the device had been there before it went off. The timer on it appeared to only go to one hour. Which meant someone had planted it while the men were in the house, while some were asleep in the room it had gone off in.

Officer Harris had caught the case and Ronan had pulled her aside to suggest she confer with Gomez about Tierney's stalker. He'd been assured she would, and confident that Vander clef had cleaned up his tracks or bought off enough cops to make sure it didn't connect.

The guys had coughed themselves awake. Ronan and Rex had run in, each clutching extinguishers which didn't quite work when there was no fire. Noxious fumes had been released into the room and eventually they'd all looked at each other. Ronan hated knowing that Elliot Vander clef had once again proven that he could get to Ronan's friends.

As the memories forced him awake, and the fear of what might be happening now dragged him fully from sleep, he sat up in the bed alone. Tierney was at the bar, he remembered. She had not worked twenty-four hours the day before and had gone back today for another shift. Both of them still needed their jobs and their income, unlike Vander clef, who could afford to spend his time thinking of the best ways to torture them.

Looking at his phone and finally clearing his blurry vision, Ronan saw that it had been his mother who called. Did he need to call her back? Maybe, maybe not. Sometimes she just liked to chat. She would know he wasn't on shift today, but also likely knew that he was asleep. So if he didn't answer, she wouldn't bother him again. She couldn't have known that he'd turned the ringer up so that he *would* be bothered by every text and notification.

After staring at the phone for a long silent minute, he took a deep breath and decided that if it was important, she would have called back. Setting it onto the nightstand, he snuggled back under the covers trying to stay warm. Though he and Tierney had cranked the heat, the little cabin leaked like a sieve. Burrowed deep was the only place to really stay warm.

Just as he was falling back asleep, the phone rang again. This time he managed a better reaction, reaching over and grabbing it as he opened his eyes. It was his mother again and his heart rate kicked up. *This was important.* This was something that was worth her calling back, he realized, wondering what he might be dealing with.

Dread settled into the marrow of his bones though he told himself it would be fine. This time, he didn't fumble but hit the green button accepting the call.

"Hey, Mom," he answered, hoping the tremors didn't show in his voice. Because that was what Elliot wanted—Ronan and Tierney on edge. It didn't matter if anything was actually wrong. It only mattered if they worried that something was.

"Hello, Mr. Kelly."

That was not his mother's voice. Only then did Ronan realize he'd never heard Elliot Vander clef speak before.

He held his reply, waiting.

"I'm going to assume that you're there, Ronan?"

This time his name was spoken in the informal and with a touch of disdain. Vander clef wanted to be sure that he knew he was being spoken down to, that he was not in charge here and he was not the better man.

"Why do you have my mother's phone?" It seemed the obvious question. And, given its obvious threat of the very call, Ronan worked to hold his tone together and not simply cave. This was already different from the picture that Tierney had quickly debunked.

"I don't have your mother's phone so much as I have your

mother. She's right here. Say Hello, mom." Again, the tone was deriding, and Ronan felt the fear sinking deeper when he hadn't thought that would be possible.

"Say hello!" Elliot demanded again.

For a moment, Ronan was of two minds. Possibly his mother wasn't there and this man had simply managed to get a hold of her phone and was trying to make it appear as a way that it wasn't. That was exactly what he'd done before. Or else his mother was already fighting back.

It turned out to be the second option. His mother's voice came across the line sure and steady. "Hi Ronan. This asshole has my phone."

He had never heard his mother swear before. The very word out of her mouth made him wonder if Vander clef had already pulled her fingernails or cut her or threatened something more.

"What does he want?" Ronan tried to speak directly to his mother but wasn't surprised that it didn't work.

"Let me tell you what I want." Elliot sneered.

Ronan, inspired by his mother's resistance replied, "Fuck off, asshole. I'm talking to my mom."

He could almost see his mother's eyebrows lift. She had taken him to church every week. Though she still attended regularly and went to her book club, and drank wine with her friends, she'd always admired a snappy comeback. She and his dad had trained their boys that loyalty and strength in the face of danger were some of the best qualities that people could have. Now, she was proving it.

Her voice came over the line again, only this time she managed to sound bored. "He wants to know where Sean is. And I want to know why he's so stupid as to think I would know that."

There was an unspoken suggestion that he was after the wrong mother. Not that Ronan wanted him to go after

Tierney's mother either, but clearly, Elliot was willing to take anyone that got in his way. Use any leverage that he could find.

Vander clef's next words made the reasoning obvious, "Bring me Emily or lose your mother."

The last thing he heard as the phone went dead was his mother's terrified scream.

CHAPTER FORTY-SEVEN

The door to Snafu slammed open, as though blown by the wind. As Tierney looked up she saw that it wasn't the wind, but Ronan.

He'd already covered the distance between the door and her spot behind the bar before she even recognized what was going on. Her heart dropped and so did the glass she'd been holding. But as it bounced on the floor mat at her feet, she ignored it and dropped the hand towel, too.

This was no frantic panic, but clear focus. His stance held only determination lead by utter fear.

What had Elliot done? She had a feeling she was about to find out.

Reaching across the bar, Ronan grabbed her arm and pulled her forward. Tierney didn't fight it. She simply followed the motion, climbing up and over, yelling backward. "Carter! Take over."

Her eyes were wide, her throat closing as she let Ronan drag her right out the front door. He chucked her into the passenger seat of his car and she barely got her feet inside before he closed the door, shutting her in. It was difficult to wait even the few short seconds it took him to cross the hood of the car, open his own door, and slide in next to her. He sucked in a deep breath as if needing it for strength, but even then she wanted to throttle him and make him talk. Something was clearly very wrong.

"He has my mother." Ronan's conviction was solid, even though it hadn't been the time before.

Tierney wanted to ask if he was sure but didn't want to insult him. So she asked, "How?" But it only came out as the slightest whisper.

"I talked to her. She screamed, Tierney. She screamed, and I don't know what he did."

"You didn't ask?"

"I couldn't." He shook his head, silent tears making tracks down his otherwise stoic face. "It happened as he was hanging up on me. And no one will answer when I call back."

Her eyes fell closed. She'd hoped it was a ploy, but this time it wasn't. Her chest caved in, her breath left her body. For a moment, she thought it might be easier if she just didn't breathe in again and let it all end here. If she died right here in this car, Elliot would have nothing to come after. He could just leave the town.

Still, she knew that wouldn't work so she gulped in air. Because Elliot wouldn't do that. He would be mad at everybody she'd ever known and her death would send him into a rage. He would destroy them all in his anger at losing.

"What did he want?" She asked it quietly. Elliot always wanted something, and she suspected she knew the answer.

"You." It came out as a single long sound, his voice almost cracking as he said it.

She nodded, the dread now somehow replaced with calm. She'd always known that it would come to this. "He wants you to trade me for her?"

Ronan nodded.

"He wants to make you choose." Tierney said it into the air as a statement and Ronan nodded again. Elliot would get his prize and Ronan would get tortured in the process.

He'd done it to her parents, too. Her parents hadn't chosen her either. Tierney said softly, "Take me to him."

She knew it was the right thing to do. She had brought this here and Ronan shouldn't have to lose his mother because of Tierney's mistakes.

"No, Tierney!" he protested, this time turning sideways in his seat. Reaching out, he grabbed both her hands and held tight. "I can't do that. I can't hand you over to him."

Her lungs sucked in air, the sob breaking out of her throat. Her parents hadn't chosen her. They had handed her over willingly, and only eventually had they agreed to do their best to help her escape when they were literally held at gunpoint. But Ronan—whose mother was already in Elliot's hands, who'd already been hurt in some way—was refusing to do the same.

How could he do this to her now? How could he love her more than anybody else ever had? How could he choose her in this impossible situation?

Tears streamed down her face. Her breath came short and choppy. She knew she would never see Sean again. The dream she'd had for herself—a life with Ronan—would have to be satisfied by the last few days. He had chosen her and that was more than enough.

She squeezed his hands, breathed in a ragged gulp, and told him, "You have to trade me. Take me to Elliot."

CHAPTER FORTY-EIGHT

Ronan had driven to his parents' house, his foot heavy on the gas, but his heart torn in two directions.

He kept telling Tierney, "You don't have to do this."

She looked at him as if he were stupid, as if of course she had to do it. But he didn't want her to. He'd just found her.

But how had he found her? Was he just lonely? Or using her to be the better version of Siorse, now that he knew what Siorse had been? But when he asked those questions, he kept coming up with only one answer. *No.* He'd known Tierney for a decade and he'd loved her for a long time now.

Ronan had denied the spark of feeling, because she was his late wife's little sister. Now, finally out in the open, it was fierce and strong. Though it had barely been a few days that they'd actually admitted what they could be, it was far, far too soon to imagine a life without her. And he had no doubt that Elliot Vander clef fully intended for Ronan to live a life without Tierney, one way or another.

His ribs ratcheted down, constricting his heart. His knuckles tightened on the steering wheel. Every bone turned to steel as he pulled into his parents' driveway. He told himself that he was coming here, but he would make the decision only when he arrived. And he had.

Now, turning to Tierney as she put her hand on the door handle—ready to open it and hop out to exchange herself for his mother—he grabbed her and held on tight. "No."

"I have to, Ronan. This is my fight, not hers."

Still, he didn't let go. Even though Tierney was now standing outside the car, her hand held back in the car where he still clutched at her. This time though, she let go with her own hand, leaving him holding her by her wrist. "Ronan, you have to let me go."

Was that the hardest thing in the world to hear?

"I'm going with you," he demanded. "We go together. We get him to release my mother—"

"He doesn't want both of us," Tierney said again, shaking her hand as if she could shake him off.

Ronan only let go because he was coming out the other side. But even as he bolted out and ran for the front steps, he saw Tierney was far ahead of him, already slamming through the front door. As he fought to catch up he realized how stupid they had been.

They came with no weapons except what they had on them. They hadn't planned ahead. His mother was being tortured and he reminded himself of what firefighters always did when they faced a fire: What was gone was gone. You could only ever save what was left.

If he ran in here, and Vander clef killed his mother anyway, what would he have accomplished? Because he did not expect this man to make a fair trade.

Even as the door hit the wall and he watched Tierney racing down the short hallway, he heard his mother scream again.

It ripped his heart out, the pain in that sound. But it was followed immediately by her angry words. "You fucking son of a bitch!"

He couldn't help it, he almost laughed. His mother would not take anything from this man that she didn't have to.

"Elliot!" Tierney screamed as she came running in. "You fucking stop this moment!"

As if Tierney's words would have any effect on him. The man was truly a psychopath, pulling strings and playing everyone like a fiddle.

Ronan slammed into the room behind her, almost smacking into her. She'd stopped, her eyes wide open and Ronan did, too. Blood covered Mrs. Kelly's forearms and her legs. Ronan froze before forcing his professional self to take over.

Vander clef had stuck a knife into his mother's leg, slicing her thigh open, where it bled freely. But it didn't appear that he'd hit an artery. She was still awake, anger radiating from her face. Her forearms, too, had been slashed, but again away from the artery. The man was going for pain, but it was survivable.

Without thinking about it, Ronan pushed past Tierney. Moving forward to where his mother was tied to the chair, he ignored Elliot, probably his biggest mistake, he leaned forward and looked at her. "I've got you now."

His thoughts were torn between his mother in front of him, obviously wounded, obviously needing help, and Tierney behind him, so far, hale and healthy, but probably under a bigger threat from Vander clef.

They all wanted Tierney as a prize, but Elliot wouldn't hesitate to kill her if it didn't work out. And the things that he would do to her in the meantime, while he worked at breaking her, Ronan had always tried not to think about. Now he'd brought her here, probably placing her directly into that man's hands.

He reached for the bindings at his mother's wrists, starting to free her as Elliot's hand landed on his shoulder. This was the first time Vander clef had dared to touch him and Ronan burst like a bomb going off.

He spun around using the backside of his fist to catch the asshole upside the cheek and across his nose. "Get the fuck off me!"

His voice came out low and menacing as Vander clef stumbled backward. The surprise that flashed across his face for only a moment, let everyone know he was startled by the ferocity of Ronan's response. Ronan tried to hold on to the rage and let it guide him. Turning back to his mother once again, he loosened the bindings that she could have undone herself had she been able to get even a single hand free.

Behind him Vander clef roared and Ronan felt the impact as the man side swept him and took him to the floor. It was a clumsy tackle, and Ronan tried to roll but it didn't work. He didn't get aimed the right direction and he knew a split second before it happened.

The world went dark as his head cracked against the hardwood.

CHAPTER FORTY-NINE

Tierney had been looking for a weapon as Ronan fought back against Elliot. His refusal to yield alone would be enough to set Elliot off.

Gone was the controlled psychopath and in front of her was the raging monster she'd seen only a few times before. Elliot was a classic abuser. He didn't lose control. But when he did, all hell broke loose, and there were few survivors.

Still, she'd run, rushing forward. But the fight had happened so fast and in such quick bursts, that she hadn't even made it across the room in time to stop Ronan from cracking his head on the floor. As she watched, horrified, his entire body went limp.

Screaming, as if her voice would have any effect on Elliot, she jumped onto his back. She needed something, anything that she could do, but the gun at her hip was still in the holster. Her arms automatically wrapped around his neck. She'd trained herself to do a chokehold, imagining taking him down. Putting herself into that dream state now, she believed she was a warrior who could win.

Lacing her arm under Elliot's neck, she glanced over to

Ronan still out cold on the floor. She lifted her legs, making Elliot bear all her weight as he stood and tried to shake her off. But she ratcheted down her hold around his neck. She tried to pull one leg back and tried to knee him in his kidney. She was here to do as much damage to this man as she possibly could.

But it didn't go the way she'd always imagined. In her musings, she held on as tightly as she could, and though he tried to fight her off, she remained in place until he passed out. She knew it would take much longer than expected and she was prepared to hold on for an eternity. But he fought harder than she'd been ready for.

He roared, standing up and trying to throw her off, and it worked better than she wanted. Though she managed to hang on to him, she lost her hold and she had to tighten down again, starting over from zero at cutting off the blood to his brain.

Her knee to his kidney had worked the third try, but his response was to claw at her arms. She could only be grateful to be wearing long sleeves, but she could feel the skin ripping as he dug in, trying to pull her muscles from her bone. Screaming shrilly into his ear, she hoped that at least her pain might deafen him. But he backed up, slamming her into various pieces of furniture.

The table hit her across her lower back, sending shots of pain both up her spine and down her legs. Her toes tingled from the hit, but she tightened her arms. This might be her only chance and she held on as tight as she could.

When the hits weren't enough to loosen her, Elliot calmed. He turned around, still wearing her like an extremely heavy trench coat, but even without air he seemed to find what he wanted. Far too calm, he walked her over to a nearby wall where he burst into motion, smacking her backward, his head slamming back into hers. Her jaw took the hit, hard enough she was certain it was broken. But worse, her head slammed into a picture frame, the glass piercing the back of her head. She could feel it cutting into her skin.

Still, she didn't let go. He had to be close to losing consciousness. Leaning forward, she bit into the skin at the back of his neck and felt him jolt at the pain. At least it was some way that she could hurt him. But this time when his fingers lit into her forearms, she felt the wetness as he sank into the blood he'd released the first time, and he managed to pull her arm free from his throat.

Elliot tossed her aside like nothing, slamming her into a wall that she slid down, her head ringing and her eyes going blurry. Still she forced them open as she tried to take in the scene. She knew she wasn't thinking clearly. But she reached for the one weapon that she had.

Elliot walked toward Ronan, ignoring her as he leaned down to pick up the knife he'd dropped.

She could not let him plunge that knife into the man she loved. Tierney pulled her gun. This time, her move would be fatal.

Her arms were too shaky but, as close as he was, he made a large target. She lifted the gun, telling herself she had this as she aimed at his broad back, hoping to pierce his heart.

Her head still ringing from the hit, she didn't even register the bullet as it ripped from the chamber.

Only it didn't hit him.

She couldn't be sure if the roar she heard was from the bullet or from Elliot, turning back to her and growling like a beast as he ripped the gun from her hand. Then he laughed.

CHAPTER FIFTY

Ronan's vision was blurry as he slowly pushed his hands to the floor and himself to sitting. His head still rang but he could see the outline of his mother, the colors that made up her shirt, her hair, and the blood that marred all of her as he tried to will everything before him into focus.

He turned ever so slightly to see Vander clef coming at him with a knife.

Ronan felt as if the very air was ripped apart. Was it a bullet or a scream or a growl?

He couldn't tell. But as he watched, Vander clef's gaze was instantly pulled from Ronan to something behind Elliot. Ronan watched, not fast enough to react, as the man turned and yanked the gun from Tierney's hand and laughed at her.

"You think you can take me out that easily, Emmie Baby? You can't. Bullets don't hit me." The boast was willful.

Ronan would have liked to have laughed at the stupidity of it, except for the fact that the bullet had not hit Vander clef.

His own eyes glanced quickly to his mother, concern that maybe the bullet had hit her. But she, too, was glaring at Vander clef as if her anger alone would stop his heart from beating.

With everything he had, Ronan shook his head and cleared his thoughts. For a fight like this, he needed everything.

Quickly, he scrambled to his feet, ready to take out Vander clef bare handed. But as the man finished laughing at Tierney he turned around, the gun lifted and aimed squarely at Ronan.

The man's hand didn't shake, and the two of them locked eye to eye, each claiming the right to fight for Tierney.

"So, Emily," he called to her back over his shoulder. "Tell me, how much do you think you love this man?"

Though Ronan didn't let his gaze falter in the slightest, he could see Tierney in his peripheral vision as she pushed herself upright. Her face was covered in blood, and he wondered how badly she'd been hit. Right now, survival was the only goal and survival would mean taking Elliot Vander clef out.

He stared back at the man is if his anger alone could accomplish that.

"Turn around," Vander clef demanded of him. "Hands in the air."

There was a snide sound to it, almost laughter, but Ronan was too far away to get the gun. Still, he took the opportunity. As he turned, he stepped closer, putting the back of his head almost to the barrel.

"Look," Elliot said gleefully, though he was speaking to Tierney. "The man knows he's going to die. On your knees."

The last command was clearly for Ronan. Vander clef intended to execute him. Ronan nodded as if to acquiesce and then, once again, he burst into motion.

Spinning around, he lifted one arm using it to hook Vander clef's gun hand. He was supposed to take control of the arm and grab the gun, but it clattered to the floor. The move had not played out as smoothly as Ronan would have liked and the two were locked in close, each struggling to land the first solid hit.

Tierney scrambled forward, reaching once again for her gun. Somehow, Vander clef managed to see it coming. Keeping his cool and reminding Ronan that he had to keep his own, Vander clef's foot came out. He stomped on Tierney's hand as she got close. With a side motion, he kicked the gun closer to himself even as he still tried to control Ronan's arms.

Using Vander clef's hold against him, Ronan pulled the man forward. As he did, he aimed his knee up as hard and fast as he could. He'd never kneed another man in the nuts before, but watching Vander clef double over was beyond satisfying. Once again, the asshole roared with his own pain, as if he hadn't believed it was possible.

He came upright far too quickly, but Tierney was right behind him. Somehow Elliot managed to get a hold of the gun again. Whatever pain he was in, he'd set it aside.

Where was the knife? Ronan thought. He needed a weapon. Though he spotted it, it was too far away, clattered to the floor behind Tierney. Unless he could completely shift their positions and reach to the ground, the knife was out of play.

This time, when Vander clef held the gun toward Ronan, he said only, "I won't give you another chance."

Then he called over his shoulder, his eyes still on Ronan. "What are you going to do about this, Emmie?"

Ronan could see as Tierney closed her eyes and swallowed.

Tierney was fast, faster than he'd ever known. She bolted toward Ronan, pushing at Elliot. She was lightning fast, moving in front of Ronan before he could blink. She lifted her shoulders, because Elliot had already reacted.

His target had changed too quickly to stop the play he'd set into motion.

The sound of another bullet ripped through the air and there was nothing that Ronan could do as he felt Tierney's body slam into his. Then she collapsed onto the floor in front of him.

CHAPTER FIFTY-ONE

There was no time for Ronan to acknowledge the bloom of red on Tierney's chest, or the fact that she was in a limp puddle at his feet.

There was no time to pay attention to the fierce fire that ripped through his own side.

Had he been shot? Had he ripped his old wound open?

It didn't matter. All he had was a moment to take advantage of Vander clef's stunned expression.

The man had killed the one thing he actually wanted.

Ronan stepped over the body of the woman he loved, closing the short distance. Reaching for the gun, he simply grabbed it. He roared his anger and grief as he gripped the gun and the man's hand together and wrenched it. With his own shocked wail, Vander clef let go, but Ronan was still crushing his hand.

He was probably only able to get the gun off the man because of the shock of Tierney's death. But Ronan had to use anything he could.

With no finesse, he twisted everything he held, making Vander clef yank backwards, trying to get free. He'd probably broken the man's hand in the struggle and Ronan let him pull his hand back. But he didn't manage to catch the gun and it clattered to the floor once again. He flinched, waiting for it to go off, but it didn't.

Bending down to get it was necessary but put him in a vulnerable position. Ronan didn't care. He did it anyway. Sure enough, as his hands closed over the metal, Vander clef's foot came up, kicking him in the chest and sending him backward, stealing his breath.

Ronan managed to hold onto the gun.

Rolling onto his back, he sucked in air and aimed up. Right at Vander clef's sternum. Ronan pulled the trigger repeatedly until the slide jammed.

CHAPTER FIFTY-TWO

Ronan sat by the the hospital bed, holding his mother's hand.

He was stitched up himself, having had a bullet dug out of his side. It had gone straight through Tierney and into him. Because she was shorter than he was, it hadn't hit anything vital on him. It hadn't gone too deep into his side because it had been slowed by passing through her first.

Just the thought made his stomach clench. She had saved him.

The room filled with the beeps and whirrs of medical machines and monitors. His mother had had surgery, correcting the damage done by the knife and stitching her arms and legs back up. The plastic surgeon had come in this morning telling her that another surgery would allow him to almost entirely eliminate the scarring.

She had looked the man directly in the eyes and said, "I'm okay with these scars. I survived."

Ronan wasn't sure Tierney would.

He'd badgered the hospital employees until they put the two women into the same room.

His father sat on the other side of his mother. Aileen Doyle had set up a permanent residence in the other corner as they violated all kinds of visitor policies. His brothers and Ewan Doyle were in the waiting room, ready to be called as needed or to demand their own turns at the limited space.

A change in his mother's breathing indicated she was slowly coming awake again. Her medications made her drowsy and she often didn't orient as quickly as normal when she woke. But this time her first words were, "How is Tierney?"

Ronan only pressed his lips together and shook his head. He fought tears, finally saying, "The same. Holding on, but they don't know."

His mother nodded at him and squeezed his hand, leaving all the unanswered questions still unanswered.

No one could find Sean. They all wanted to bring him home, so he could at least stay with the Doyles—the only family he'd ever known. He needed to be here in case Tierney didn't make it. But she'd hidden him so well that none of them had been able to figure out where he was yet.

Ronan's mother asked the question she'd asked several times before, as if her memory of events was a little warped. "You got him, right? He's dead?"

She meant Vander clef.

"Yes," Ronan assured her, squeezing her hand again and repeating her words. "He's dead."

But if Tierney didn't make it, the victory would be small indeed.

With his father hovering over his mother and his brothers due to kick him out for their own turns any moment now, he turned his attention to Tierney. Her pale form lay across the bed, a tube down her throat, inflating her lungs and breathing for her. Vander clef hadn't hit her heart. He'd been just a little too low and to the side. Still, another two inches and she would have been dead instantly. As it was, he'd ripped the bullet through one of her lungs. The surgical team had removed part of it, along with her spleen. That alone should have been okay, but the damage also included shattered ribs that had needed a second reconstructive surgery, and she'd lost too much blood.

The doctors had put her back together as best they could, and they'd medicated her so she wouldn't wake up, letting her body rest and heal. Now it was just a waiting game. And Ronan hated waiting.

CHAPTER FIFTY-THREE

Ronan headed up to the bar at Snafu. Today, he needed a shot ... or several.

"Hey, son!" Ewan Doyle leaned down under the bar, going for Ronan's usual beer.

Ronan shook his head. The greeting of "son" had been there since before he'd married Siorse, but today it felt like he would need to break the man of that habit. "Something stronger."

With a nod, Doyle pulled out a lowball and poured three fingers of the best whiskey in the house, sliding it across the bar. Though Ronan gladly would have paid for it, Dad Doyle had refused his money from the moment Tierney had left town.

She'd made a grand recovery. Though, the whole time she'd been on the mend, she'd spoken no words of their future to Ronan. Every time he'd brought them up, she evaded the conversation. As soon as she was released, even though she wasn't at one-hundred percent, she'd told them that she was getting Sean back, and she wouldn't let anyone else help. She'd insisted on his location remaining secret and she'd made the drive herself.

Only, once she'd gotten Sean, she'd kept going. She'd simply sent a message to the Doyles that she was headed back to New York and the Gallaghers.

Ronan had only wanted to help. Even if she didn't want to be with him, he still loved her. He still wanted the best for her and for Sean. He hadn't even had a chance to see the kid. She'd left and she'd refused everything, including his repeated offer of a lawyer. She'd told him in the hospital, "You don't have the money to pay for it."

She needed a lawyer. The Vander clefs were coming after her, both barrels blazing. There were even rumblings that they would go after Ronan and his mother, too. As if Mrs. Kelly, tied to a chair, with a knife cutting open her arms and legs, could possibly have been at fault in any of this! But money bought them the option to be crazy and to spread the pain around.

The senior Vander clefs were livid that their precious boy was no longer with them. They were striking out in every way that they could. Tierney was their main aim, even though she hadn't been the one to pull the trigger.

Ronan gladly would have taken the hit for her. He'd offered several times to confess, as though it were a straight up murder. A local jury of his peers surely wouldn't put him away for that long. He figured he could survive prison for however long it might be. At least, that's what he told himself.

Tierney had refused all of it.

So now he sat at the bar with her father, rotating the glass in his hands, and taking sips rather than gulping it like he wanted to.

"It's been two months today," he told her dad. Two months since she'd blown town without a word to him. Two months with no word. Two months of him raising snack-named kittens and Zadie finally giving him that sad smile that said that it was past time to adopt them out. The one that said Tierney and Sean wouldn't be back to do it.

Mr. Doyle nodded, and Ronan felt his shoulders fall. He kept waiting for the man to say that he'd heard from Tierney, that there was good news. But as far as any of them could tell, she had simply returned to the arms of her New York family.

She appeared to have healed well. "Look," Ronan said, grabbing his phone and holding it up. "At least she's healthy."

The picture he'd found showed highlights in her hair. She wore it swept up with what looked like diamond-studded pins. She wore a gown that probably cost more than he made in an entire year. And she stood next to her parents at a charity gala.

She wasn't coming back.

It had been three days since he'd seen the announcement from the charity ball. Three days it took him to bring it into the bar and show it to Dad Doyle.

"She looks great." The older man offered it up with a sad smile, clearly missing his daughter. The tone in his voice told Ronan that he was just as resigned to Tierney not coming back.

Ronan couldn't blame her. Her wealthy family could give her far more than he ever could. With Elliot gone, there was no reason for her not to stay in New York.

It was time to stop waiting, Ronan told himself. So, instead of sipping, he tossed all of the whiskey back. Then he smacked the glass onto the bar, just shy of hard enough to break it, and motioned to Dad Doyle to pour him more.

There was only a slight raise of an eyebrow questioning if that was what he really wanted. But it was time to start forgetting Tierney.

For a moment, as he shot back the second glass, he thought maybe he was falling into old patterns, like he had when he'd lost Siorse and Paddy. But he quickly told himself that he didn't care if this was what it took to let go of her. He'd lost too much to hold back now.

Emptying the glass quickly, he smacked it onto the bar top again, this time a little too hard. He was surprised there were no cracks in the glass as he motioned to Dad Doyle again.

The man hesitated, but as he gave in and poured, he said the words, "You can't go on like this. I understand, but this is the last one."

"Fine." Ronan figured there were other places to get drinks. He'd sober up in time for his shift, he told himself. Still he nursed this drink a little more slowly.

As he held the phone in front of him, he looked over the picture of her yet again. He'd never seen her in a dress like that. She'd worn her hair in a ponytail or down around her shoulders. He'd not seen it in some fancy updo that had probably taken hours.

In the image, she smiled and held a crystal glass of champagne—another thing that had probably cost more than he could ever afford. He tried not to be morose as, behind him, the bar door opened. Dad Doyle greeted new customers as Ronan tried to slow his roll through the drink. Still, he hit the bottom faster than he'd intended. More people had come in while he moped.

It was late in the day. He had slept late after a rough shift and then come directly here to drink. He should probably order food, but he considered trying to get Dad Doyle to pour him just one more.

He was staring into the bottom of the empty glass when he heard the voice.

"Grandpa!"

The first thing Ronan saw was Dad Doyle's face lighting up as he yelled, "Sean!"

Ronan was already swiveling on the barstool as Dad Doyle leaped over the bar in a move worthy of a man forty years his junior. Ronan's feet hit the floor as dad Doyle's did, and he tried to stand up, but he was more than a little shaky—no food and three drinks and all that.

Behind Sean stood Tierney.

Her hair had obviously been cut by some high-class salon

the likes of which didn't exist in Redemption. He could still see the same highlights he'd spotted in the photo. They didn't look like the old Tierney, but they brought out the green in her eyes and the red in the rest of her hair.

Her hands rested on Sean's shoulders as her father reached down and swept the child up in a huge hug. He rotated a joyous full three sixty before he enveloped Tierney in his arms, too. "You came home!"

"I did," she said with a huge smile that melted Ronan's heart even though she wasn't saying it to him. "I finally got everything cleared up."

As Dad Doyle took a big breath and stepped back with Sean still in his arms, Tierney's eyes caught Ronan's.

"I didn't think you'd be back," was all he could say. He considered stepping forward, but his legs were shaky from the whiskey and she'd made it clear before that she was leaving him. "How long are you visiting for?"

She grinned. "I'm home for good."

How would he survive with her here if she didn't want him?

CHAPTER FIFTY-FOUR

Tierney stood planted where she was, letting Sean chatter on to her father, as the two of them stepped away. Her dad seemed to know that she needed a moment here.

Ronan wasn't moving toward her. So she decided that she would. If he hated her, and didn't want her back, she would step away. But it would be better to know now, rather than believing —hoping—that she might be able to salvage something.

"You left," he said again, the accusation a mild line of undertone.

Taking a deep breath, she tried to explain and did a crap job. "I couldn't let you take the rap for the murder. None of this is on you. How is your mother?"

The words all fell out in a jumble. Even though she'd had a plan for when she walked in, it had been that she would say hello to her dad and later she would find Ronan. After she'd made the initial rounds with her parents, she would explain everything to him. Instead, she had stepped into the bar only to come face to face with the man she wanted more than anything. All her thoughts had scrambled.

"My mom is doing really well. They patched her right up,

and aside from some scars—which she's refusing to have removed—she's basically back to her old self." He said it without giving Tierney any hints about how he felt about *her*.

She wished she could say she was back to her old self, too. But the last two months had been emotionally exhausting. She needed a vacation from everything for a while. Motioning him back to the barstool that he'd stepped a few feet from, she waited until he sat, then took the spot beside him. She could only hope. "Will you do me a favor and listen?"

Though he nodded, his expression stayed closed. She wasn't sure how much of it he would actually *hear*, but she had to try. With a deep breath, she attempted to follow her original plan. "None of us here has the money to fight the Vander clefs. But my parents—my original parents—do. Also, I thought Sean should meet them."

She looked away from Ronan, her eyes glancing into the corners of the bar. She was ashamed of the people she'd come from, and ashamed she'd had to go back begging. But she turned her focus to Ronan again. "I hoped maybe if Sean saw them, he would recognize what a good thing he has in the Doyles."

"They helped you out?"

She nodded her head yes, but added, "They didn't want to. They didn't want any kind of legal battles with the Vander clefs. In fact, they suggested that I come right back here and stay hidden. They'd already fabricated a story ten years ago about how I'd run off to Europe and married some kind of Baron."

She watched as Ronan's eyebrows lifted at that, and she agreed. In her old life, she wouldn't have thought anything of such subterfuge. But now, now that she'd seen how real families worked, she understood his surprise.

"So they *didn't* help?"

"They did," Tierney said. "Because I blackmailed them into it."

That put some shock across his face. She was glad to see he

was paying attention. He looked just a little drunk, but she kept going.

"I told them I would go to the media and tell my story exactly as it happened. How they pushed me toward Elliot when I was fourteen. How they sent me back to him, despite the fact that he abused me. And how, in the end, when he blackmailed them, they caved instantly." She paused. "It wouldn't be damning enough to land them in jail, but it would have killed their social standing. They would not let that happen. I held it over their heads the whole time."

She stopped, waiting for him to ask something, but his mouth and his expression remained shuttered.

She pressed on. "In return for my demands, my mother made me tell a story about divorcing the Baron and coming home with his child."

Tierney waved her hands around, trying to recount all of the back and forth she'd been through with her parents. Then she turned to Ronan, wanting to reach out and take his hands, but they weren't on the bar. They were in his pockets. His shoulders hunched in, his anger at her leaving still clear.

"It's over now," she said. "All charges are officially dropped. The Vander clefs are still angry, but they can't come after me. And I made sure they can't come after you or your family again either."

Ronan nodded, maybe it was an acknowledgment or a thank you. She didn't know.

A silence fell between them and Tierney knew it was up to her to fill it. She'd been the one who left. "I'm back here for good. I'm officially Tierney Doyle. One of the other things I blackmailed them about was ..." she paused and laughed. "They have more money than they know what to do with and I blackmailed them for everything I could possibly get!"

That made Ronan's head snap up.

She smiled. "They gave me my birth certificate and officially changed my name. They're paying for all kinds of vacations for Sean and private school for him if I want. Also all of his college. And medical school for me! I'm going to start applying to undergrad."

Ronan's face lit up at that, his happiness at her excitement letting her know that he wasn't as cold or uncaring as he appeared. "I only just now figured out that you didn't go to college because you couldn't."

She nodded, then she took another breath and added, "I made them give me enough money for a small house."

This time Ronan laughed. "It sounds like you could have blackmailed them for enough money for a large house."

"I could have." She didn't laugh. Her heart squeezed as she realized it was time to put all her cards on the table. "I don't want a big house. Just enough for a family."

She laid her hand out on the bar, palm up, waiting for his. But he didn't move. She kept trying. "For me and Sean. Another child, maybe two. Once I'm done with medical school."

He nodded at her. "It sounds like a good idea."

Was he being purposefully obtuse? Or did he just feel the need to make her say it?

"I want a house big enough for you and me. I want college and med school and I'm going to do it, but I want *us*, too. I'm finally free to be part of *us*."

This time, when he looked at her, there was hope in his face, so Tierney kept plunging forward. "I want all of it with *you*. I don't know what kind of shit we're going to get because I was born Emily Gallagher. Because of everything that Elliot rained down on this town because of me. Because I'm the little sister of your late wife. I don't know."

As she shrugged at it all, his hand came out, at last lacing his fingers through hers, squeezing tightly, as he cut her off. "None of that matters. What matters is us."

Her heart bloomed, thrilled that he thought there was an *us*.

"You and Sean could stay with me at my place until we find something new."

She nodded quickly, not wanting to turn down any offer from him. Even if it meant living in the house that her sister had decorated, that her sister had cheated on her husband in. Yet Tierney thought it was a small concession to have what she'd wanted so badly for so long.

"I missed you so much these last two months. I didn't know if it would work. I didn't know if it would take years to get out of all of the legal assaults the Vander clefs threw at us. I honestly think my mother and Mrs. Vander clef had a little heart to heart about the damage my story could do to both families—"

Her ramblings were cut off by Ronan's hands on her face, pulling her forward, his mouth covering hers in a kiss she'd only prayed for. She sank into the feeling of him, of knowing that she was finally home.

Kissing him for all she was worth, Tierney hoped it said everything she couldn't. She only vaguely heard the cheers from the bar behind her.

He whispered against her mouth, "Tierney Doyle, I will always be yours."

She smiled at him, knowing her heart was in her eyes. *If he only knew how long she'd wanted him, dreamed of a life with him. She'd always been his.*

CHAPTER FIFTY-FIVE

"No, I'm not getting on it!" Talia tried not to yell it into the phone. There were too many people around and getting into that contraption was...

Obnoxious.

Embarrassing.

Pure terror inducing.

"Can you please come down to see me?" She pretended she was baking and added a diabetes-inducing amount of sugar to her voice.

"Honey, it's too windy to go outside." The building manager was not going to come to her. *Seriously?* Stairs were likely nothing to her.

If Talia didn't hand in the check now, the rent for Baby Cakes would be late. The manager's office was on the second floor of the storefront building. It had been listed as handicapped accessible, with an elevator. It turned out, the "elevator" was actually an open-to-the-elements chair lift that rode—horror-inducing—up the outside of the building.

It was the lift or the rent. Honestly, Talia considered just not paying it. The manager would walk her two good legs right down to the counter in three days when she didn't get it—windy or not.

Looking up, she considered whether she could head to the stairs and make it up on her own two *not good* feet. She could *not*.

"Thinking about scaling the side of the building?"

Whipping her head around as her heart kicked up, Talia hoped color didn't show in her cheeks. Then she reminded herself, that was an upside: she could just claim it was a 'condition' and most people didn't know enough to know she was lying. "Hi, Rex. Hi, Hannah!"

He had his almost-four-year-old tucked up on one arm like she didn't weigh anywhere near as much as she did.

"That thing looks pretty decrepit." He seemed to zero in on the real problem pretty fast.

She liked that about him... maybe a little too much.

"Yeah, the building said handicapped accessible when I signed in. This is..."

"Terrifying."

She agreed.

"Hannah and I will ride up with you."

Talia turned to see his smile—*that damn smile*—was the one that kept making her think things. "Why in God's name would you climb on that death trap if you don't have to?"

"The company." The reply was fast and genuine and her heart flipped over. Then he added, "Also, it's inspected, and I know the guy who does it. It's terrifying but it won't actually kill you. It's quite safe."

Still holding Hannah like it was nothing, Rex skirted the contraption and on the other side and pointed to the wall. She could see him fairly well through all the open space. The device wasn't much more than scaffolding and a chain. "There's a certificate right here."

Talia didn't comment. Just sat quietly and waited.

Rex tiptoed back across the narrow ledge until he was at her side again. When he saw her sitting there in her slim-for-a-chair but still bulky wonder-machine, his eyes opened wide. "Well! That was the dumbest fuc—" he bit off the word, probably because of Hannah. "That's just stupid putting it there!"

Where no person who actually needed it could see the inspection certificate.

If Talia banged her head on the wall each time life suggested it, her head would be flat. But that was the last thing she needed, so she just nodded at him.

"I'll still ride up with you."

She couldn't help smiling and agreeing. The butterflies in her stomach made her do it. Also, the rent needed to be paid and she wanted a few minutes alone with this man. Well, him and Hannah Bean, who was an absolute doll.

He held the door—it was merely the outline of a gate—open for her, and she backed the chair in, watching for his toes. In a moment, he was crowded beside her.

The wind plucked at her hair and drifted his scent over her as the machine lurched and jolted to a start. She would have had a heart attack if he hadn't been right next to her.

"Hold her hand, Daddy! So she isn't scared!" Hannah was pointing.

Talia almost sighed in disgust at herself. She *was* gripping the arm of her chair tightly enough to break something. As Rex grinned and held out his free hand toward her, the contraption lurched again.

She grabbed him and held on and told herself it was romantic.

It was also slow as … Lord, if snails were racing them up the side of the building, they would have crossed the finish line and had time to choreograph a victory dance before Talia and crew arrived.

She took a deep breath and tried not to squeeze Rex's hand

too tight. She was trying for snark but wasn't sure she made it. "My hero."

"Gladly."

It was soft, but once again genuine. The word sent her back to the time the dishwasher broke at Baby Cakes and the kitchen flooded. Rex had saved her then. She'd been feeding him free cupcakes ever since, so he'd been there when one of the patrons slung the word "gimp" when she was out of maple bacon.

Rex had snapped, the kind of reaction that wasn't calculated or contrived. He'd bodily removed the man to a round of applause from the patrons. Then he'd returned to the counter and placed his order for Hannah's birthday cake like nothing had happened. And here he was, playing her hero again.

They were getting close to the top, and Talia was wondering if she would get to hold his hand on the way down, too, when Hannah pointed into the distance, "Look, Daddy!"

They all looked up.

The wall of thick, black cloud that rolled over the land was something she'd only read about. "Holy shit!"

She shouldn't have said it, not in front of Hannah, but even Rex was stunned by the speed with which it moved. She could see the rain pouring in the near distance, and it was headed right at them.

"We have to turn this around," Rex said, but he didn't look down at her or at the control button. He was still fixated on the storm that was too close and approaching far too fast. "Now."

Thank you for reading! I love romances with real love and believable characters, and I hope you found all that in these pages. I want to fall in love right along with the characters, and I do, while I'm writing it.

About Savannah

I started writing when I was eight--I hand wrote an 80-page novella that I believed to be (adult) romantic suspense. I'm proud to say, I've gotten a lot better since then. I've grown up to be a nerd at heart! I love neuroscience and people watching, and if you look, you'll find some of that in each Savannah Kade book. Most days you'll find me in my office, looking out my window at a handful of the neighbor's cows, or watching my dogs or my cat roam the backyard.

Follow me, find me, ask me questions! I would love to hear from you.
www.SavannahKade.com
Savannah@SavannahKade.com